SHORT CUT

OTHER TITLES BY
J. GREGORY SMITH

Thrillers

A Noble Cause (Thomas & Mercer, Kindle Bestseller U.S., UK and Germany)
The Flamekeepers (Thomas & Mercer)
Darwin's Pause (RedAcre Press)

The Reluctant Hustler Series

Quick Fix (Book 1, RedAcre Press)
Short Cut (Book 2, RedAcre Press)

The Paul Chang Mystery Series

Final Price (Book One, Thomas & Mercer)
Legacy of the Dragon (Book Two, Thomas & Mercer)
Send in the Clowns (Book Three, Thomas & Mercer)

Young Adult

The Crystal Mountain (RedAcre Press)

Short Stories

"Heroic Measures" (Amazon StoryFront)
"Blenders" (*Insidious Assassins*, Smart Rhino Publishing)
"The Pepper Tyrant" (*Uncommon Assassins*, Smart Rhino Publishing)
"Something Borrowed" (*Zippered Flesh: Tales of Body Enhancements Gone Bad*, Smart Rhino Publishing)
"Street Smarts" (*Stories from the Ink Slingers*, A Written Remains Anthology, Gryphonwood Press)
"Powder Burns" (*A Plague of Shadows*, Smart Rhino Publishing)

J. GREORY SMITH

SHORT CUT

RedAcre Press

Published by RedAcre Press

Cover design by Ebook Launch

Printed in the United States of America

First Printing, 2020

ISBN 978-1-7353889-0-8

For Julie

CHAPTER 1

"Hold that goddamn frame straight, kid! You want this to look like some hack installed these window bars?" Rollie stood behind me on the porch of this small house in the Fishtown neighborhood in Philly.

"Some hack *is* installing them," I said as the sweat crawled down my sides. My shoulders ached in protest while I tried to hold the set of steel security bars long enough for the old man to anchor it with a long bolt.

"Speak for yourself, sonny," Rollie said.

This was supposed to be the easy window, at least compared to the ladder work required to reach the ones on the second floor. Removing the old, rusted bars had been a bitch, but they had pretty much screamed "Nobody home!"

It was going to be a long day.

"I just hope these do the trick," I said.

Rollie moved behind me and I heard the cordless power drill whine as it drove a second bolt home. I was able to relax a bit since the weight of the bars now rested on the thick bottom bolts.

"Don't slack off yet. Brace the top or the whole thing will wrench free and we'll have to start over."

"Like hell we'll start over. That happens and we go to plan B: burn the sucker to the ground and be done with it."

Rollie managed to speak around the last bolt he held in his mouth. "You figure out a way to claim the insurance for yourself?"

"Not yet." I smiled back. It was a harmless joke, but it wasn't funny. Our friend Ryan Buckley's name may have been on the deed, but as of six months ago it really belonged to his estate. Rollie and I were just buttoning up the place because we knew he'd have appreciated it. It had already gone sideways in enough ways to hammer home the lesson I'd thought I'd already learned—the whole no-good-deed-going-unpunished thing—but as it would turn out, I hadn't seen anything yet. I'd thought the death of my best friend would make my life simpler.

So much for that.

The problem was that the world considered Ryan missing, but alive. Those of us who knew better—Rollie, a charter member of that club, had been with me the night he'd died—wouldn't dare say anything to the authorities. For now, we had to help pretend everything was fine to avoid drawing scrutiny from some very bad actors. Hell, even if we'd wanted to spill the beans, we couldn't have proven anything.

"I asked Beth and she told me that without evidence of foul play, the state typically waits seven years before making an official declaration."

"Jesus wept," Rollie said. "I'll be dead of old age by then and don't expect me to be patching the roof all that time."

I doubted that. For a guy in his seventies he was tougher than men twenty years younger.

"Did she say anything about coming back from Colorado? If she's moving in with you in my place, I'll have to keep your security deposit."

He knew better. "The ink's barely dry on the divorce. You're stuck with me for the time being. I could flop here, I guess." Beth and I had been on track to split up, then after getting pulled through Ryan's last adventure almost called it off. Luckily, we came to our senses and agreed to move on, she all the way to Denver to work as a paralegal.

"Crap," Rollie said. He wiped a sleeve across his forehead. He wore his dyed brown hair in a crewcut.

Rollie loved to bitch about keeping a renter in the house, but it had been his idea when my marriage was on the rocks and I was out on the street. With his own wife passed away, I think he enjoyed the conversation.

"And I might be stateside for a bit this time." Until recently I was overseas driving supply trucks in the Sand Box for Delivergistics, a military contractor and logistics firm.

Rollie secured the remaining bolt and tested the bars like an agitated prisoner in lockup. "That should keep out the riff-raff." He turned to me. "Did you hear anything new on that investigation?"

I stretched out my tired shoulders. "Local Iraqis are pissed about a shootout between our operations/security teams and insurgents. Some of our guys can be fairly energetic once the fur flies."

"Things can get full ugly in a hurry. Sometimes hitting the hardest, the fastest is the only way to come out alive," Rollie said. His dark eyes took on a hard glint and I could see the sniper he'd been in Vietnam.

"It's turned into a complete clusterfuck and Delivergistics has put a bunch of work on hold so lots of us are kicking it back here hoping the whole thing blows over."

"And if it doesn't?"

"They say it could sink the company. But it's hard to be sure from long distance. Some of those security guys saved my ass from bandits a time or two." I didn't know all of the operations guys that well, but a few were real hotheads. Who really knew?

"Get a load of this rolling freakshow," Rollie said, snapping me back to the here and now.

I followed his gaze to see an electric-blue VW Beetle, only the owner had customized the thing with the front grill from a classic Bentley, complete with the iconic chrome winged "B" hood ornament.

My heart sank as the car slowed. I was grateful for once that the narrow street was packed with parked cars. Maybe he'd go away.

"Oh shit," I said. "Now what?"

"Friend of yours?"

I couldn't see inside due to the over-tinted windows, but as it passed by the horn made a cornball "Awooga" sound like an old Model T.

The car crawled around the corner where I could see there was an open spot.

"Damn."

"What?"

"More of this weird Ryan crap." I turned to Rollie. "Remember Latimer's Fix-it-Up?"

"The repair shop? Didn't the guy die?"

I nodded. "Last year. That's his kid's car. His name is Terrance, but everyone calls him Beetle Bentley. Beet for short."

"I can't imagine why." Rollie's eyes scrunched while he searched his memory. It was a small neighborhood, but since Rollie could fix about anything himself he probably never got to know the guy well. "Wasn't his kid …"

"I don't know the clinical term or diagnosis or whatever but yeah, the kid is a little off. I think he still bags groceries, but I know he's dumped all his cash into that goofy car."

"You know him well?"

"No, but Ryan must have. Beet came to me the other day while I was over here and wanted some cash."

"Is he on drugs?"

"Illegal stuff?" I shook my head. "Not that I can tell. No, he wanted a couple thousand, like a loan. He kept asking me where Ryan was." That was a popular but awkward question on the best of days. It seemed like everyone in Fishtown knew Ryan, and wanted something from him.

"What the hell did you tell him?"

"What do you think? I'm not a bank, but it was hard to see a guy in his twenties on the verge of tears." I didn't have any better answers for Beet today and a feeling of dread grew while we waited for him to present himself.

When he rounded the corner, the first thing I noticed was that he walked with a limp he didn't have before. I pick up on things like that, having a bad knee of my own, courtesy of an IED explosion in Iraq. I'm lucky I still have a leg at all.

Somehow, I didn't think Beet was feeling too lucky. He made his way toward us with his head down. He wore dark Ray-Ban knockoffs and a blue Star Trek Federation logo ball cap to complement the faded Spock T-shirt stretched tight over his pudgy belly.

The last time I saw him he'd been wearing the exact same outfit.

"Hey, Beet. You doing okay?"

He looked up and now I got a good look at his face. Purple crescents under his eyes spread beyond the frames of his shades. His lower lip was swollen and he winced when he smiled at me. Instead of answering me, he set to probing the cut his smile had reopened with the tip of his tongue. One of his front teeth was missing.

"Jeez, Beet. What the hell happened to you?"

"It's my fault. Is Ryan here?" He looked at Rollie. "Are you Ryan's daddy?" He waved a pasty arm as if shooing an insect. "No, he said his daddy was dead. Like mine. I wish he wasn't."

Rollie's hard body language softened and he put the cordless drill down. "We were friends of Ryan's ... are friends," Rollie corrected, but Beet didn't catch the slip.

I jumped in. "You want to come inside? I think, uh, Ryan has some water or soda."

"Thanks," he said. "It hurts to stand up. Driving is okay, though."

We led him inside.

Inside, Ryan's place looked like a time capsule from our high school days. After his parents died, he'd left the house as it had been. The old furniture gathered dust and any framed pictures Rollie and I moved off the walls showed how faded the surrounding wallpaper had become.

He'd never really moved out. He'd worked with me at Delivergistics and both of us spent large chunks of time overseas, so he never got around to it. Even after his folks were gone, when I was back in town, he rarely let me inside the place. Or anyone else, it seemed.

"Will he be back soon?" Beet pressed. "The other guy gets mad real fast."

"What guy?" Rollie said.

"The money guy. He was so nice before. Until I couldn't pay."

My heart sank. "Beet, what did you do?"

He looked up at me and I resisted an urge to wipe his face for him. I never had any kids, but I imagine that's what the impulse might feel like. Except this "kid" was twenty-five or so.

"What was I supposed to do, Kyle? Ryan always helped before. He told me to go to you if he wasn't around. You said no."

The words hung in the air like an indictment. But something else had a bizarre yet familiar ring. "Wait. What, exactly, did Ryan say?" I tore off a square of paper towel and handed it to him.

I saw Rollie wince when Beet took off the shades and blew his nose. One eye looked like he was wearing a purple monocle and the other wasn't much better. At least the nose didn't look broken.

"Ryan said 'I might have to be away for a while, but you can always go to Kyle. He's going to be helping me out.'"

I met Rollie's gaze with a slight shake of my head. "Beet, Ryan did have to go away and it might be for a long time, but he never told me that."

Beet smiled and brought the paper towel to his cracked lip. "Oh! I just thought you was mad at me or something."

"Of course not. But tell me more about the guy who did this to you. You owe him money?"

Beet's shoulders sagged and he stared at the floor, nodding. "I don't have it. I'm gonna get it, but Mr. Lee at the store said they can't do advances."

I knew he couldn't be getting more than minimum wage for bagging groceries. "How much did you borrow?"

"Two thousand."

Holy crap.

"I got a new exhaust and another hood ornament. Someone stole the last one. Very fusstrating." Beet frowned. "Only, he said it was more and I had to pay to some guy named Veeg. Do you know him?"

"Veeg?" It didn't ring a bell.

Rollie was quicker on the draw: "Vig? Is that what he was saying?"

Beet scrunched up his pale, freckled face. "Maybe. He talks funny. Is that like when he calls me beeeg guy?"

The vig—loan shark-speak for interest. "Could be," I said. "Did he say how much?"

"I guess. The first week he got mad when I didn't have his money and said 'Veeg added. Next week, you pay that or else.' Only nobody named Veeg or Vig came by to collect."

Rollie shook his head and gestured toward Beet's busted-up face. "So, this was the 'next week' and the 'or else'?"

Beet nodded. "My teeth still hurt." He looked at me. "Are you sure you can't help? I think next time he might bring Veeg with him. I'm scared."

"It's okay. I'll help." I didn't have a lot of cash on me, but I thought we could get the dogs called off while we straightened it out. "Vig is the extra guys like him want for lending you money. He was asking you to at least pay that extra amount."

"I thought he wanted it all, but I didn't have any of it yet. Ryan always gave me time and he told me how much each week. Dad made sure I didn't forget or spend it."

I knew Ryan had been into a lot of shady things, but it was clear this couldn't be a huge profit center for him. More like a community service.

"We need to talk to this guy," I said. "Explain the misunderstanding." One look at Rollie's set jaw told me he was in. "Who is he?"

I saw fear trace across Beet's childlike face. "You're not gonna make him mad, are you?"

"No," I said, though the way I felt right now made that an iffy promise. "We're going to pay the vig for you and get him off your back while we figure something out for the rest."

"Son," Rollie said, "can you tell us who he is and where we can find him?"

Beet glanced at him, then back to me. "You guys would do that?"

I nodded. I'd even pinkie swear if it made him happy.

"His name is Milosh. He hangs out at a café on Girard Ave. Cream of the Cup?"

"I know it," I said.

Rollie made a stink face. "Artsy-fartsy crap. Kind of place that stares at you cross-eyed if you order a simple black coffee."

Beet smiled at that. "You, too? He sits in the back. He has black hair and round metal glasses."

"Milosh doesn't sound like an Irish name." Rollie said it matter-of-factly, but I got his point. We lived smack dab in Philly Irish Mob territory. Interlopers not wanted, as Rollie and I knew all too well.

CHAPTER 2

FISHTOWN, CREAM OF THE CUP

The moment I set foot inside the shop I knew why it was the first time. It was exactly the sort of hip-by-the-numbers place that set my teeth on edge like chewing on aluminum foil. The scent of burned sugar and almonds filled the air and a couple of white twenty-something customers with dreadlocks and assorted ink and piercings glanced up and decided we weren't worth their time.

In the back of the shop, occupying a corner booth, sat two men who didn't fit the assembly of animated clichés. One was a bookish-looking, tan-skinned man with wire-rimmed glasses and an open-collared blue button-down shirt. He had a scruffy beard and neat, short-cropped, dark hair.

Next to him was a stern-looking guy with a dark, penetrating gaze. He wore a tight gray T-shirt over black jeans. He sat facing us with his arms folded across a thick muscled chest. One arm was covered with burn scars from wrist to elbow. I had my share of similar scars so I knew he'd been through the wringer at least once in his life.

They noticed us right away and I saw the one in glasses (had to be Milosh) glance toward a door at the back of the store.

Rollie and I stopped at their booth and remained standing.

"Yes?" Milosh spoke with an accent I couldn't place right away. The bigger guy was more into non-verbal communication.

"We're looking for Milosh," I said. "We were told we might find him here."

The man sat up at the sound of his name and he looked us over. "Who told you this?"

I lowered my voice. "I am a friend of Terrance." No recognition. "Beetle?"

"Who are you?" He gestured toward Rollie. "A grandfather?"

"He's here to keep me safe," I said.

Milosh smiled at that, which I knew must have pissed off Rollie, but I'd spoken the truth and too bad for them if they learned the hard way.

Milosh spoke rapidly in what I could tell was an Eastern European language, but not one I knew offhand. The big guy laughed a bit and I figured that was at Rollie's expense. Judging by the color of my friend's face, so did he.

"If I have any business with this Beetle it is not your concern," Milosh said to me. "Unless you are the police?" His smirk told me he didn't think we were.

Familiar but unhelpful anger surged from my chest and heated my face. I forced it back down to try to avoid a head-to-head. "Look, he didn't understand. He's like a big kid."

"He's a man. He understands enough to ask for my help."

"I saw what you did." I glanced over at the big dude. "Or was it you?"

Milosh held up his hand. "I see you do know him. Please step into my office." Both men stood and I noticed the guard held the jacket draped over one hand, which I assumed held a weapon.

The office was a storage room of metal shelves and racks of food containers, coffee and deep blue mugs with cow faces grinning in half-lidded, stoned bliss.

"Why are you here? Beetle is clear on our arrangement now."

I reached into my pocket, but stopped when I saw how tense the bodyguard became. "It's just money. I want to pay the vig now, until I get you the rest. Then you leave him alone and never do business with him again."

Milosh laughed and the goon didn't. "Anything else, asshole? Can I bring my sister by for you?"

"You want money. I'll get you your money. What's the problem?"

"I don't have a problem. Beetle does. And so will both of you if you interfere."

"I'll take on the debt."

9

"Fuck you. I don't even know you," Milosh said.

I locked my gaze with the goon's, and withdrew a hundred from my pocket. "Here. That's enough for the vig for last week and this week."

"Another hundred."

"For what?"

"I don't like surprises," Milosh said. The cold stare told me he meant it.

I didn't have it on me. I should have seen the shakedown coming. "I only have another twenty."

Milosh looked bored. "Never mind, the marker is Beetle's. He will either pay or become a walking billboard to encourage others."

"Wait a minute. We'll get it to you in a week. Sooner maybe." I handed the bill to him.

"I do not do business with strangers." Milosh flicked the hundred back at me. I let it hit the floor.

Crap.

All I could see was that poor kid's confused, bashed-up face.

I pointed to the bill. "You take that and choke on it. We'll be back in a few days with the rest. If either of you touch Beet again, I'll hang you from a billboard."

Milosh placed one white leather basketball shoe over the bill on the floor. He turned to Rollie. "Grandfather?"

Rollie's jaw knotted while he produced another hundred. "Stick this one somewhere else."

I braced for a struggle, at this point part of me welcomed it, but I didn't lose sight of the goon's weapon hand. I thought a face full of stoned cow mugs might buy me the moment I needed if it came down to a fight.

But Milosh seemed content for the time being.

"One week. Twenty-two hundred or we find Beetle. We know where he lives."

"That's too high. Where are you getting that number?"

Milosh gestured for us to leave. "Processing fee."

Outside I took a deep breath.

Rollie glared at the storefront. "That went well, don't you think?"

"Where the hell did those bozos come from?" I began to think I wasn't going to be the only one interested in the answer.

"Not Ireland," Rollie said.

We walked down the block toward Rollie's car, AKA the Blue Bomber, an eighties vintage Oldsmobile Delta 88 with a tricked-out warhead of a motor.

"Speaking of the Emerald Isle, how do you think our old friends will feel when they hear about these Eastern European poachers?"

"From us?" Rollie said. "You're kidding, right?"

"I know we aren't exactly pals," I allowed.

"Interesting way of saying we just got them to stop trying to kill us."

Rollie had a point. Thanks to some fast thinking while getting out of the mess Ryan had created, we had enough dirt on the Irish Mob to become a real problem for them if we disappeared. The classic "dead man's switch." It yielded an uneasy truce, but one that had held up over the last six months.

"Yeah, but we'd only be passing along information," I said. "We're not doing anything to them."

We reached Rollie's car, and he leaned against the window frame. "Why do we want to stick our necks out for this kid again? How did it become our problem?"

I felt my collar heat up. "Did you see Beetle's face? He didn't understand the terms, and if we leave it up to him, he'll let that debt get so high they'll make him sign over his car, his house and everything his dad left him for nothing."

Rollie smiled. "I just wanted to make sure you knew why we were going back to the lion's den."

The O'Brien brothers ran the Philly Irish Mob, at least in this part of town. Their family always had, as long as I could remember. Over the years they'd tried to lower their profile after a succession of FBI agents had decided to make their careers on busting them up. They were careful, but also had a well-established mean streak that had cemented their power in this corner of Philly. And they were smart enough to know that turf wars were bad business, so enjoyed a cordial relationship with their better-known Italian counterparts.

My family never had anything to do with the Irish Mob when I was growing up. Like everyone, I knew enough to stay out of their way. Except for high school, when I dated Meg Sheehan, one of the O'Briens' cousins. Luckily for me, she handled our eventual breakup by falling right into Ryan's arms.

Small neighborhood.

CHAPTER 3

FISHTOWN, THE HEATHER BAKERY

After reaching out to Meg and convincing her that it was a good idea for us to speak to her cousins, she set up a meet at the O'Briens' place. In what had to be the worst-kept secret in Fishtown, this "bakery," offering overcooked lace and shortbread cookies, served as a front for the O'Brien brothers' main office.

I pulled my beat-up old truck into the "valet spot" right outside of the store. It was always guarded by thick-necked attendants. I didn't recognize these particular men and was glad, as some of the older crew weren't too fond of either Rollie or me.

The door opened the moment our feet hit the pavement and a scowling thug in an apron put the lie to the welcome sign in the window. Flour dusted the guy's apron and I noticed old stains that looked like they belonged in a butcher shop. He ushered us inside as though it pained him to do so.

The shop's interior was just as inviting as the last time we were here. Back then we didn't know if we were going to come out alive. Today, I was hoping just to do a little self-serving civic duty.

"The renovations are coming along nicely, I see," Rollie said. The worn wood floor felt gritty underfoot and the air reeked of cheap stogies, ginger and cinnamon. Dust coated the display cases.

"Wait here," the chef said, and disappeared through a door in back.

A moment later I saw a familiar face, though we'd never been introduced. The thin guy with the diamond earring and receding red hair was the next gatekeeper of the place.

"Out of your clothes," he said, like a cop asking for license and registration.

"Sorry?"

"Down to your boxers."

"I didn't realize it was going to be this sort of party," Rollie said.

I saw where this was going. "Getting paranoid in their old age?" I knew better than to poke the bear, but sometimes couldn't help it.

"Clock's ticking. You want to see them or not?"

We both shrugged. I kicked off my shoes, dropped trou and pulled off my shirt. The guy actually winced when he saw the twisted burn scars along one side of my torso. More parting gifts, along with my bum knee, courtesy of that Sand Box IED.

"He's the before picture and I'm after," Rollie said. "We good now?"

Red looked us over and decided we didn't have any recorders or rocket launchers on us. But he didn't touch the pile of clothes at our feet. Instead he reached under the counter and produced a pair of plush robes. I noted the logo.

"Four Seasons? They only steal from the best," I said.

"Leave your stuff and come with me."

"No slippers?" Rollie asked.

The guy just looked at him.

Rollie glanced back at me. "The service in this joint has really gone to pot."

We followed Red up a narrow set of back stairs to a non-descript hallway with a faded blue runner carpet down the center. At the end of that stood a big dude I'd seen at the same spot half a year ago. The security camera in the ceiling was the same as well.

We walked to the thick door and the guard stood aside.

"You know the drill. Wait for them inside."

We stepped from the dingy hallway into a brightly lit luxury apartment. The red-tooled leather chairs faced the brick fireplace. There were cut crystal tumblers on the wet bar opposite the fireplace. Amber whiskey filled the decanters.

"Cozy as always," Rollie said.

We heard an interior door open followed by heavy footfalls that pulsed through the hardwood floor under my bare feet.

"The return of the Hardy Boys," a voice called out. This would be the burly younger brother, Charlie.

His older brother William was shorter and had the look of a scrapper who'd traded the boxing ring for a library. Charlie looked more like a wrestler ready to fight at the drop of a hat.

When Charlie emerged from the short hallway at the end of the room, he looked like he'd bumped up another couple of weight classes since I saw him half a year ago. Fat or no, I'd learned from past dealings not to underestimate either brother and to try not to piss them off.

"We were just talking about you," William said as he followed Charlie into the room. Neither offered to shake hands.

"You were?" I crossed my arms, then realized nothing was going to make me look tough in this damned robe.

"Indeed," William said. "We were wondering what took you so long." He and Charlie turned the fireplace chairs to face us and left us standing while they made themselves comfortable. Charlie's seat cushion hissed a considerable amount of air as he sunk into it.

I glanced over at Rollie on the odd chance he knew what they meant. Nope. He stood like a soldier awaiting a dressing down. But in a big fluffy robe. I bit back an urge to laugh.

OK. I'd bite. "What do you mean 'so long'?"

Now it was the brothers' turn to look confused.

"Before we get to that ..." Charlie used both arms to hoist himself to his feet with a grunt. He picked up a metal wand from the mantle.

"We were searched already," Rollie said. "Hence the new uniform. Or are these goodwill gifts?"

"The robes stay here. You want one, go boost your own." Charlie swept the wand up and down our torsos. He nodded to his brother. I saw William relax after the electronic frisk confirmed we weren't carrying any recording devices, even in the most uncomfortable of places.

"You think we'd set you up?" I asked. "After everything?"

"Considering 'everything' includes you and the old man holding a figurative gun to our heads, we can't be too careful."

I couldn't let that go. "And you and your brother held actual guns to ours. We aren't here to upset that balance."

"I'm glad we still understand each other. Particularly if you intend to take our relationship to another level."

So much for understanding each other.

"Fuzzy robes and 'relationships'?" Rollie blurted out. "What the hell's happened to the mob, anyway?"

Even Charlie smiled at that. William pressed his lips together and returned his attention to me.

"William," I said, "the last thing on our mind was any change in our earlier arrangement. We just wanted to tell you, in person, that you have some competition in your territory."

"What kind?" Charlie said.

"I'm surprised we're the first to mention it, but there are some guys sharking. And unless you're hiring from the old Eastern bloc, they aren't yours."

I figured Charlie would at least look pissed. Instead the corners of his mouth twitched.

William spoke. "You got Meg to arrange a meet, came all the way here, all for that? What do you care?"

"The guy hangs out at—"

"We know. Answer the question," Charlie said. All hints of a smile had vanished.

"All right. A friend. Well, more a guy I know ... got himself into trouble with them. I guess you'd call him mentally slow. He didn't grasp the stakes."

"People make bad choices all the time. Sometime the best teacher is pain." Charlie cracked the knuckles on his beefy fists.

"He could have gone somewhere else for the money," William said.

"Yeah. Apparently, the kid would borrow money from Ryan sometimes."

"So much for that," Charlie said.

The O'Briens hadn't killed Ryan. But they sure knew all about it. It hadn't been their wish, but they shed no tears about his death, that was for sure.

William spoke. "Perhaps this slow 'boy' knew the old adage about one door closing and another opening."

"What does that have to do with anything?" I felt my temperature rise. "You should see this kid's face. I think those goons were happier he didn't pay, just so they could tune him up."

"It happens. Let's get to it. What do you want us to do about it?"

"I thought you'd mind that a rogue outfit was running a shylock business right under your nose."

Rollie made a groaning sound. "Jaysus, I must be getting senile."

"I see why you keep him around," William said. "Care to fill him in?" he said to Rollie.

"Kid, they know Milosh." Rollie turned to the O'Briens. "The commies in the coffee shop are paying rent. Am I getting warm?"

Charlie waggled the metal detector wand and then did an exaggerated slow-motion shrug. These guys hating talking shop outside their own circles.

William leaned forward in his chair. "We embrace the concept of diversification for risk management," he paused, I assume to let me twist in the wind like the fool I was. "That said, business, like nature, abhors a vacuum."

"And Ryan closed up shop, so to speak," Charlie said.

"He was handling small loans for you?" I asked.

William said, "Was. And any arrangement we might have had with your friend left town when he did."

"Look, I don't know what you had going with Ryan—" I began, but they laughed out loud at me. "I got dragged into that one fiasco with Ryan. Other than that, we were friends. I know he was into some gray-area stuff, but that was him, not me."

The brothers shared a look and stared back at me. "You have a weird negotiating style, I'll give you that," Charlie said.

William spoke next. "You let us know what you want to do, but when you come back, know that we're resetting the arrangements at that time. It's all on the table, clear?"

Hell no, it wasn't clear. By this point even Rollie was looking at me funny. "And my friend with the debt?"

"Pay the marker yourself if you're that worried about the retard," Charlie said.

"As for everything else, make up your mind quickly," William said. "We can't hold these things indefinitely. I get the sense Milosh is ambitious."

I wanted to ask about these "things" but all of a sudden it felt more dangerous to play ignorant. I nodded. "Okay. I'll be in touch."

CHAPTER 4

FISHTOWN

"What the fuck was that all about?" Rollie at least had the decency to wait until we'd dressed and were sitting in my truck. His place was only a few blocks away, but I suspected the ride would feel much longer.

"I'd love to say I have no idea, but the way they acted makes some of the craziness of the last couple weeks start to make sense."

"Like the old man coming by my house like you were some sort of pill pusher?"

"That's for sure. It was almost like Ryan staged some sort of epic practical joke on me in the event of his death." But it wasn't funny and that guy's tortured expression plagued my dreams.

"That old timer wasn't in on the gag," Rollie said as if he could read my mind. "He wasn't some junkie. He said his sister needed medicine. And what about the phone calls and hang-ups?"

"After what the O'Briens said I'm beginning to think Ryan had some bigger ideas for the future." I was only guessing here.

"Did you know how tight he was with the Irish?"

I shook my head. "I knew he dated Meg, of course, and after we met up with her cousin Danny Sheehan, I should have run for the hills right there, but at the time it seemed more of a beginning to his working with that branch of the Irish Mob."

"The O'Briens made it sound like a lot more than some random associations."

I had to agree, much as I didn't want to think of my old friend as a mobbed-up guy. He'd always been the life-of-the-party type who knew everybody and could put you with whoever you might need.

We crossed over East Girard Avenue and I began to look for parking spots. I grew up with the habit but as the area became more popular it got worse every year. Fortunately, it was the middle of the day and until the evening rush hour it was still possible to snag a place here and there. The neighbors knew my truck and as long as I didn't knock any plastic chairs out of the way to steal an unofficial saved spot, I'd probably avoid getting keyed.

We found one nearby and I locked up the truck. Rollie walked with me toward his place. I'd never thought of it as home, despite renting from him for nearly two years. Now that the house where I'd been married had been sold, I guess it was the only one I had. If I lost my job at Delivergistics I'd have to see about finding more permanent digs, but with all my travel, usually it was much more convenient to crash at Rollie's house.

"You got a long-lost son, kid?" Rollie's question made me follow his gaze to the small figure sitting on his front stoop.

"No, I ..." The guy noticed us approaching and when he looked up from his phone, I recognized him immediately. "He's no boy."

The guy stood up and removed all doubt. He was five foot three in combat boots and maybe weighed one-fifty soaking wet. At over six feet myself, I always dwarfed him. But mostly, I tried to avoid him.

"You're a long way from the Sand Box, Tom," I said as I closed the distance, glancing around to see if he'd brought any "friends." "And how the hell did you know where I live?"

"You ever think of answering the phone?" Tom's accent pulled my mind right back to Iraq. He sounded British but other accents crept in, reflecting his Irish mother, English education and Kurdish father, who'd dragged him to oilfields all over the Middle East.

"Why would you have my cell?" I thought for a second, confusion still washing over me at the sight of someone so very out of context here in Philly. "I never got any calls from you."

Rollie caught up with me. "Are the one who keeps hanging up on me?"

Tom gestured to the front door. "You live here?"

"Who wants to know?" Rollie squared his shoulders and spoke to me. "An overseas number calls the land line and asks for you, when I ask any questions he hangs up. I figured it was a scammer."

I stared at Tom. "It was."

Tom looked surprised at the remark and he fixed his dark eyes on me. "Do you say that to Ryan, mate?"

"I haven't seen Ryan in a while, but I might."

"Can you reach him?" Tom looked relieved.

Rollie and I shared a quick look. "Uh, sorry Tom, I don't think he's going to turn up for some time." I didn't see how Tom could know the truth about what really happened to Ryan.

"Then you of all people shouldn't be surprised to see me."

Rollie turned to me, leaving his question unspoken. I wasn't so polite. "What the hell are you talking about?"

Tom shook his head. "We need to do this in private." It was clear he intended to exclude Rollie.

"Where are my manners? Rollie, allow me to introduce Dozan Thomas Sabri, a.k.a. Tom Thumb. We're colleagues at Delivergistics and he's one of Ryan's associates."

Rollie shook Tom's hand. "I'm his landlord. You want to come inside?"

Tom shook his head. "No thank you, sir. My message is confidential. Kyle do you have somewhere—"

"I trust Rollie with my life and he can hear anything you have to say. He's safe." But I had no idea if Tom was, and I preferred to have the guy outnumbered. He was a bigger sneak than Ryan and just as smart.

"Get in here and I'll grab some beers." Rollie unlocked his front door.

Tom paused but we were already moving inside. "All right, but if you don't mind, I'd prefer tea, or water if you have it."

Rollie's modest row-home still bore most of the decorating style from his prior married life. A neat cream-colored couch with simple oak end tables and a matching coffee table dominated the front room. Old pictures of Mary, his deceased spouse, sat in new frames, courtesy of a vicious O'Brien brothers "home improvement" rampage during less cordial times.

Rollie hollered from the kitchen, "I've got some Lipton, kind of old, if that's okay."

"Brilliant," Tom called back while grimacing.

Among his other charming qualities, he was a tea snob.

He looked at me and spoke in a whisper. "This isn't for outsiders."

"The only outsider here is you. What in hell do you want?" I could hear the kettle rattle when place on the stove and began to wonder if a beer was going to improve my mood or make it worse.

"Ryan never told me about this bloke, but if you say he's part of your crew then I haven't much choice, have I?" Part of my *crew*? His expression looked like he expected me to know what he was talking about.

I let that hang in the air and made polite small talk until Rollie returned with the drinks. I took a long pull on the icy Yuengling.

"The cream is fresh," Rollie said to Tom. "I like it my coffee. Hope the tea isn't sawdust."

Rollie never took his eyes off the guy and I wondered if he'd grabbed more than drinks from the kitchen. His bulky shirt gave nothing away. For certain he didn't trust Tom, despite the good manners.

"Kyle tells me you work for him," Tom said. "Are you also with Ryan?"

"Ryan is with himself, as far as I can tell," Rollie said. "We're acquainted, can't say we're close. As for me, I don't work for anyone."

It was Tom's turn to look confused. "Then I don't think—"

"Just spill it already," I said. "It's obviously some crap you cooked up with Ryan."

"Indeed." Tom glanced at Rollie. "You're briefed in on the Mr. Beautiful project, then?"

"The what?" Rollie and I said in unison.

Tom's coffee-with-cream complexion paled to coffee with the whole pitcher. "This is no time to joke."

We weren't laughing. In fact, the beer took on a sour taste in my mouth. I swallowed hard. "How about from the top, huh, Tom?"

"Ryan is missing, yes?" he said. "Gone to ground, or however the expression goes?"

Rollie and I shared a quick look.

"He's gone dark for the foreseeable future," I said, "thanks to a caper here that went way wrong."

"Right. I wondered about that, but had little to work with from the Green Zone." Tom took a deep breath and leaned toward me. "But he's got you and whoever covering for him here?"

"Covering what? Other than picking up his mail and making sure homeless people don't take over his house, I'm not in the Ryan business."

Tom shook his head as if to clear it. "You don't have the book? The list? He said you'd be up to speed. We're running out of time."

"Slow down, Tom. Again, from the beginning. Ryan … left before he told me about any of this. You seem to think I was one of his flunkies over here. We were friends. Are, just friends. The one adventure I tried with him almost got me killed. I lost the taste after that. What did he tell you?"

Tom rubbed his face. "Bollocks. What a cockup. Ryan said you were the point person for the States' side of this plan."

"When did he say that?" I asked, thinking the little twerp had better not claim a time after Ryan had been killed.

"On and off for over a year. Mostly before the last time he returned to the States right after you'd been suspended. He said he had big plans for you. For both of us. I gather you already received your great reward." He even managed to sound envious.

I lifted my shirt and pointed to the fresh scars from a knife attack that nearly disemboweled me. "This was my big payday, champ. A million stiches, maybe. Things didn't exactly go as planned."

"Are you saying Ryan took it all? I don't believe that. And he'd never walk away from this project."

I felt oddly defensive on my friend's behalf. "Ryan didn't rip me off, if that's what you mean. He screwed up, but we all paid a price. Him most of all."

"Then why would he stay away now?"

Rollie interrupted. "Ryan made the worst kind of enemies, right here in Fishtown. He's burned all his bridges in the neighborhood and he'll never come back here. For purposes of this discussion, you need to proceed as if he's dead."

We sat for a few seconds with that punchbowl turd until Tom appeared to accept the situation, however he understood it. I couldn't tell how literally he took Rollie's comment.

"Right. Here's the situation, mate. Ryan laid a great deal of groundwork into what we call the Mr. Beautiful Project, and he said if he was unable, for any reason, to take care of things in the US, that you were his backup."

"And he forgot to tell me about this?"

Rollie cleared his throat. Right: Ryan hadn't been able to tell me anything for some time. But who was to say this yarn of Tom's was even true?

Tom was quick on his feet. Always was. "Perhaps he waited to tell you until you were ready to hear it, but he ran out of time?"

His choice of words told me Tom understood the situation with Ryan and didn't need further detail.

"Maybe," I said.

"I'll leave it to you to figure out his motivations, but here is where we are today. For the past several years Ryan and I have cultivated a prospect in Iraq."

"What kind of prospect?"

"Apparently a good-looking one," Rollie quipped. "Beautiful, even?"

"Do you mind?" Tom showed a flash of anger and Rollie held up his hands in a pacifying gesture. "The prospect is a native-born Iraqi businessman who ran afoul of the Hussein family and went into hiding along with his fortune."

"The coast should be clear now, huh?" Rollie asked.

"Not exactly," Tom said. "Once the Gulf Wars toppled Hussein, he'd planned on escaping, but the rise of the extremist factions made retrieval of the bulk of his fortune impossible."

"So, what's changed?" I asked. "Plenty of bad guys still around there."

"Yes, but he was able to convert most of his money into a tangible asset that he kept hidden. But he and his family couldn't stay near it and it remains stashed."

"Where?" I had to admit he had my attention.

"Tikrit. That was Saddam's hometown, and as you well know, not the safest of places for non-radicals, not to mention Westerners of any stripe."

"Coalition forces have liberated Tikrit," I pointed out. "I wouldn't buy a home there, but a native ought to be able to get in and out without much trouble."

Tom smiled, seemingly pleased he had an audience. "Ah, but out to where? I never said our man made his money legally, and he's decided he wants to bring his family out of Iraq."

"Hang on. I've already learned more than I want about Ryan's dealings, but human smuggling is over the top. For him, anyway."

Tom frowned. "I resent the implication. These people all want to leave. At any rate, that is beside the point. Our man already arranged the exfiltration under new identities. His problem is to get out his assets so he's not forced to wash dishes the rest of his life."

"If he can get out okay, why can't he take his stuff with him?" Rollie asked.

Tom nodded. "That is the essential question. His cover persona is from humble, even tragic origins. It wouldn't do to try to escape with luggage stuffed with valuables. The authorities are thorough and he is still a wanted man."

"Tough luck for him," Rollie said.

"But a cracking fine opportunity for the right people."

I began to get the picture. "So, he and his family go one way, meanwhile, while nobody is looking, someone else takes care of smuggling the assets out of the country to somewhere he can be reunited with his dough at a later time. All for a modest fee, of course."

Tom grinned. "Precisely. Only there is nothing modest about the fee."

CHAPTER 5

I sat in Rollie's living room and soaked in the surreal atmosphere. "Tom, it sounds like you guys have all your bases covered. I appreciate your letting me in on your situation, but as you can see, I'm obviously not your man after all."

Tom stared at me. "You don't believe a word I said, do you?"

"Some of them." I lost the fight to keep a straight face. "What's your angle, man? Where's the part where you need a small advance to get the ball rolling and that's the last I ever see you?"

"Fucking hell." Tom fidgeted like he was going to jump out of his skin. "Mate, if I could do this alone, do you think I'd be wasting my time here with you wankers?"

"Now *that* I believe. Cut to the chase. What is it you really want?"

"Ryan compartmentalized the operation. My job is to get the goods out of the country. His job was to pick them up and get them to Mr. Beautiful."

"So that's what I'm supposed to do? Newsflash, if you haven't been keeping up: I haven't the slightest idea about what those plans might be or even what this mutt looks like. I'm liable to hand off your bag of magic beans to Mr. Mediocre." I was feeling more agitated by the minute, but Rollie looked like he wished he'd made popcorn to go with the entertainment.

Tom rolled his eyes. "I *know* what to do, but you have to make the arrangements. Ryan told all the people along the way to listen to you only and specifically to shut down if I showed up alone."

"Really? Sounds like he trusted you as much as I do."

"I don't care at this point. All that matters is that you believe me and will help. You get to hold his share when it is all done, in case you were wondering."

"I wasn't. I have my own problems and no interest in getting Ryan's or yours or this Mr. Wonderful's—"

"Beautiful," Rollie said.

"Whatever. Find another sucker."

Tom paused. I could almost hear his brain whirring as he sat there staring into his half full cup of tea. "Since Ryan is off the pitch," Tom seemed to be speaking more to himself than me, coming to grips with the truth. "You're the starting team, then."

"I told you—"

"Stuff that. The spanner's in the works for sure. Right. He told me to make sure you saw the box? Does that sound familiar?"

"Nope."

I might as well have told him his house was on fire with his family trapped inside.

"We're wasting time. We need to get to Ryan's place." Tom wasn't asking and he spilled some tea when he sprung out of the chair and bumped the end table.

Rollie pointed to the spill. "Get that, Kyle. I'll pull the Blue Bomber out front."

* * *

FISHTOWN: RYAN'S HOUSE

I unlocked the door and saw with some satisfaction that the bars on the windows were secure. It felt like the last thing I'd done lately that had made any sense at all.

Inside, the house had a musty, stuffy smell from disuse.

"You should know the place got tossed when things got heavy six months ago," I told Tom. "We cleaned it up, but I don't remember any box, do you, Rollie?"

"No. Just what kind of box are we talking about, Tom?"

Tom didn't answer. He scanned the room and headed right toward the fireplace. He pulled the fireplace grate out and the iron feet left sooty black prints along the clean brick.

Tom pulled off his white-and-blue-striped rugby shirt to reveal a thin, toned, dark caramel-colored torso. I remembered seeing him scam a former Spec Ops guy in a climbing race to the top of some scaffolding. He'd gotten scarce after collecting on the bet, proving he wasn't dumb.

"You going to look for 'Santa was here' scratched in the flue?" Rollie said.

Tom didn't say but ducked his head and entered the fireplace. A moment later all we could see were his thin legs going up on tiptoes and muffled words I suspect were curses in one of the many other languages he spoke.

"We gonna have to get him off the roof?" Rollie asked.

The guy must have wriggled part of his body into the flue. Was that even possible?

Soot fell like black rain and Tom began to cough, but he let out a whoop when we heard something metallic wrenched free.

Tom fought his way back into a squat and, despite my curiosity about the blackened metal box in his hands, I couldn't help but laugh. Ryan must have never cleaned the chimney. Soot coated wide swaths of his exposed body in ebony smudges, especially on his face.

"I'd get killed in the wrong neighborhood if I made myself up like that on purpose," Rollie said. "The hot water heater is still working. Get yourself cleaned up and I can't wait to hear what is in there, assuming it isn't just ashes."

Tom took one look in a hall mirror and agreed. "I'm going to borrow a pair of Ryan's trousers, unless you think that all this was just a free-clothing scam?"

* * *

Twenty minutes later Tom returned with the box that he'd brought with him to the bathroom. He was wearing a pair of Ryan's jeans with the cuffs rolled up and had his rugby shirt back on.

We sat around the dining table.

"The moment of truth," Rollie sad.

I wasn't so sure about that, but I'd play along for now. The guy had come an awfully long way for something.

"Ryan said this was fireproof, I hope that was correct." Tom glanced up at me. "You were supposed to know all this by now."

"I'll try to catch up quick."

Tom found a catch and slid the blackened box open. Inside they all saw another box, this one a fat square one about the shape of a jewelry store ring box, only larger.

"Is this like one of those Russian dolls?" Rollie asked.

"At least it isn't locked," Tom said, and opened it to find a single folded piece of paper.

And a key.

I just shook my head.

Tom handed me the paper. I unfolded it and looked at the numbers, letters and spaces across the top third of the paper. "A code? Does it mean anything to you?"

Tom looked relieved. "It does if we can find the book."

"Care to be more specific?"

"The code is a simple book cipher. If you have the correct key book, the numbers are corresponding pages, columns and lines to give you words or letters."

"Not bad," Rollie said. "So, do you have it or what?"

"I didn't bring my copy for security."

"Ryan has a shelf of his books upstairs," I said.

* * *

Tom scoured the shelf and I watched his cool demeanor melt away with each passing minute. "Damn. We may have to hit the secondhand bookstores in the area."

"There might be more around the house or in the basement. How about you help us out? What's the book?"

"It's a dictionary."

Rollie nodded. "Simple and no trouble finding all your words for a message."

I breathed a sigh of relief. "That's easy enough. We can even splurge on a new one."

Tom glared at me. "Were you not listening? It can't be just any dictionary. It has to be the exact edition Ryan used or the keys won't match up."

Of course. I wasn't sure if I was angrier at his condescending tone or at myself for being so slow.

"There are some boxes in the basement." I was not looking forward to turning the place upside down and I already knew if Ryan wanted something hidden it usually stayed hid. I wracked my brain for any other places he might keep books. Ryan hadn't been the biggest reader.

"This was fun for a minute," Rollie said. "Time to haul up boxes?"

"Hang on. If the book is the same as the one he used for you, Tom, then it had to be his primary key."

"So?" Rollie said.

"So, more than likely he'd keep it handy. He used to sit at the kitchen table to get work done."

"Right." Tom made a beeline for the kitchen.

I was slow to keep up because my bad knee decided now was a great time to stiffen up. I had to respect the pain if I didn't want to use an ice bag as a fashion accessory for the next week.

I could hear pots and pans clang and the thump of Ryan's mom's cookbooks hitting the floor. She'd been the cook. All his recipes contained seven digits.

Rollie and I reached the kitchen and we saw Tom sitting on the floor like a toddler intent on trashing the kitchen. Mixing bowls and saucepans covered the linoleum.

And in his hands, he clutched a very old hardcover tome. Despite its obvious age it was the only book in sight not covered with dust.

"*The American College Dictionary.*" Tom searched the first pages. "Bob's your fucking uncle!" His finger jabbed at the page.

"That's what we want, right?" Rollie asked.

"I think so." I said. "Tom? We good?"

Tom was already at the table and had spread out the coded message and was flipping pages. "Better than trying to track down a forty-plus-year-old edition."

"Stay right there," Rollie said, beginning to return the cookware. "I'll get these." His own place was compulsively tidy and he never let me get away with me leaving clutter in the kitchen.

If Tom heard the sarcasm, he gave no sign. I peered over his shoulder. The guy's fingers danced through the pages and down columns with a practiced ease that told me he and Ryan must have used this code often.

Numbers translated to the paper next to the code. I could see "PNC 801 Ch ..."

Tom was beginning to sweat. "Another code?"

Rollie and I grinned. "Nope," I said. "Is the next part Christian?"

"Yes." Tom looked up from his work.

"I think we know where the key goes," I said.

"The PNC Bank over on Christian Street," Rollie finished.

CHAPTER 6

PNC BANK

The rest of the coded message after the address had read a cryptic "Kyle Only." Armed with the key, I stood outside this neighborhood bank branch. It was one block off of the famous Philadelphia Italian Market. I wore a dark blue windbreaker, as the gray skies threatened to resume spitting at any moment.

The bank sat on a street corner across from a small grocery store and a pharmacy. I opened the door not really knowing what to expect and strode up to a young lady who sat at the first desk.

Ms. Bailey, per her name tag, looked up from her computer screen. "May I help you?"

"I hope so. I guess you could say I'm here for a friend. I need to see a safe deposit box."

Her demeanor cooled and she just watched me while waiting for me to continue.

I fumbled a hand in my pocket and read the number off the tiny cardboard envelope that held the key. "It's box J29."

She typed and I could hear the sound of her long fingernails ticking on the keys. They were painted with tiny flags of different countries. I recognized Jamaica's yellow and green on her thumb.

"Are you on the list?"

"I'm not sure. I've never needed to get in, so—"

"Name?"

I shouldn't have felt like such a sneak, but all the same I hesitated before giving out my real name. I didn't see what difference it would make, as I'd never even heard of this account before.

"Name?" she repeated.

"Logan. Kyle Logan."

She scrolled down a list. "ID?"

I handed over my license.

She looked it over and stood up. "Come with me."

I followed her to a massive steel door to the safe where the boxes were stored. Ms. Bailey took out a clipboard and handed it to me.

"Sign here."

I'd never signed for anything at their branch. I didn't even bank here. But I owed it to everyone on this scavenger hunt to play it out. I scribbled my signature.

Ms. Bailey scrutinized my writing with an apparent sample, and with my driver's license.

"Thank you." She handed back the license and turned toward the vault. I didn't see her hit any hidden security buttons so I followed her inside, to a steel wall covered with numbered boxes.

She found the box, one of the big ones about the width of a shoebox and maybe twice as high. She turned the key and I took out mine and the key worked. I shouldn't have been surprised, but I was anyway. She opened the door and slid the box partway out. It was covered on top but otherwise looked like a heavy drawer.

"You can go into the room to the right of the vault for privacy. Come get me when you are done."

I thanked her and when I was alone pulled the box out.

I almost broke my foot when the thing dropped like it was loaded with concrete. If not for my work boot it would have made plenty of noise. Ryan should have mentioned something about wearing steel-toed banker shoes.

The box wasn't too much to carry. It was probably no more than twenty pounds, but the weight had caught me by surprise.

I made it to the windowless viewing room without further incident and closed the door behind me. The room contained bare walls, a single gray metal table and two folding chairs.

Okay Ryan, what's on your mind?

I lifted the lid and the first things that caught my eye were neat stacks of bills. There was a loaded stainless steel .38 revolver in a brown leather ankle holster, two boxes of ammunition. There were also several drivers' licenses from different states with Ryan's face. They were wrapped in rubber bands.

Jesus.

And an envelope with my name on it, printed in Ryan's handwriting.

My heart was thumping hard in my chest. I took a seat for the first time since entering the room and tore open the envelope. I pulled out several pages, all cursive, maybe so I'd be sure he'd written them himself. It was dated seven months ago, written just before he was killed.

> Hey Buddy:
>
> Sorry for whatever led to your reading this but here you are, so whatever happened is over and done. As I write this you probably wish you never agreed to help me out. Maybe I shouldn't have asked you but as they say, it seemed like a good idea at the time!
>
> Anyway, things have gotten hairy and if I guess right, I may have to go deep underground, probably for a while, at least until I can smooth things over with our favorite neighborhood mobsters. You should be okay, but there's a little something in here for you if you have to go dark as well.
>
> I hope not, both for your sake and for mine. I need your help. I already know you are going to be pissed, or is that more pissed? Probably the second.
>
> I'd meant to show you this stuff myself, but circumstances beyond my control seem to have intervened. You got this far, so you will know how to make sense of what is on the thumb drive. Long story short, it's all the people who I help and who help me. You should know that I have already told them they can trust you like they would me. Reach out to them if you need to and you may find some of them trying to get in touch with you. Anything you could do for them while I am away would be greatly appreciated. Feel free to use some of the money in here to keep things moving or in case of emergency.
>
> I know you may not be comfortable with a lot of this, but I didn't know where else to turn. See, part of the reason I asked you to help on the other thing was I knew you'd be great at this sort of

freelance work if you gave it a chance. Isn't that the essence of all business? Find a need and fill it. There are plenty of needs out there and I'm not talking about hard core types, just regular folk who the system can't be bothered to help. I fill in the gaps and do favors. And collect favors.

But the real thing I will forever owe you on is the Mr. Beautiful project. I gave Tom enough to get you here, and he's been covering us over in the Sand Box. If he's here now, it means things are moving. We won't get this sort of chance again, believe me.

Use what you find to make sure the package gets where it needs to go. I thought it would wait until the art project was done but hey, sometimes there's a fly in the ointment.

As for all the other hustles, you'll notice, maybe for the first time, that there are plenty of things I won't do. I'm not looking to hurt anyone and more importantly I'm not trying to piss off a certain Shamrock crew by stepping on their toes.

Since I'm writing this, obviously I did a lot more than piss them off, but I promise I will make it right. In the meantime, don't give them a reason to make an example out of you. Any loans or other stuff I get into is small time action they can't be bothered with. If it is going well, reach out and show them respect. Yes, that means giving them a taste. Think of it as PR fees. But you want to stay out of Sheehan's way. Try the O'Briens, if you need to get in touch Meg is a good starting point. You know, if she didn't still have a thing for me, I think she'd settle for you again!

You may need all of this more than you realize. I've always been a survivor and I have a bad feeling that some of the problems at Delivergistics with those shooting investigations might mushroom enough to wreck the whole company. It can't hurt to have some side hustles to fall back on, am I right? We can talk more when I get back, but there's room to expand. You might surprise yourself.

It's getting late. Use as much or as little of the cash or anything else, but please help Tom out. He knowns the plan but needs you to cross the finish line. He'll explain. This is the big one.

R.

My head reeled, trying to take in everything. All the crap Ryan had helped me into (and out of) was wrapped up in this huge idea to get me into his own little family business. Whatever it was, exactly, it was clear he had my future planned for a long time. I'd never heard of any of it, let alone agreed to it, at least until I did bite on the one project and had been sorry ever since.

Despite all the advance planning, Ryan hadn't counted on his own luck finally running dry.

At the same time, I was flattered that he showed so much trust in me. Ryan had gone to great lengths to open doors for me. Now all I had to decide was whether or not I was willing to walk through them.

It was all a bit much to take in at one sitting and there was no doubt plenty more on that thumb drive, so I pocketed that and decided to leave the rest in the box where it would all be safe from prying eyes and sticky fingers. I was still waiting to figure out Tom's real angle. Maybe he just wanted in to the box and my value to him would be over. That thought didn't scare me, as I'd never known Tom to be dangerous that way. A sneak for certain, but not a killer.

I began to close up the box and remembered something.

I lifted the lid and thumbed through a packet of cash. The paper band sagged after I had removed twenty-two of the crisp hundred-dollar bills. Suddenly I wanted some hipster coffee and a short conversation about where some Eastern European freelancers could place Beetle's debt.

CHAPTER 7

During the drive to see those assholes in the coffee shop, I kept replaying chunks of Ryan's letter in my head. So much of it confused me, but some parts made perfect sense. The random people who had begun to turn up, not just at Ryan's house but right to Rollie's door, knew where I lived, and expected my help.

Oddly, now that I had this context, I felt bad about turning some of them away. The look on one old guy's face in particular haunted me. He'd wanted medicine, he claimed, for his sick sister. At the time I assumed this was some sort of scam and he was an addict himself or he was trying to con the neighborhood out of some cash. We got those types too, though few tried that crap on Rollie twice.

This man just may have been turning to what he saw as his last resort. I still doubted I could do anything to help him. I certainly hadn't spotted a medicine cabinet in that safe deposit box.

The thumb drive might have some answers. The more I thought about that, the angrier I became at Ryan. The balls on him, to plan my life for me and not even let me in on the game. It made my blood boil. I didn't need any help screwing my life up and he'd already almost gotten me, Rollie and especially Beth killed.

I spotted a parking place near the café and angled my truck toward it only to get cut off by a Prius. Part of me relished a confrontation, but I had too much on my plate and getting busted for a beef over a parking space right now would be too stupid, even for me.

I smiled to myself, thinking that if Ryan had survived, I might have kicked his ass, especially for the danger he'd brought on Beth, despite his best intentions, but I also knew I would have forgiven the prick eventually, even if I never worked with him again. Beth had been kidnapped and held hostage for leverage on us, but Ryan died during the operation to rescue her.

After a few minutes another spot opened up. The pre-dinner crowd was leaving and I took advantage of the window. I hoped this Milosh guy was around.

I passed the Prius dorks on the way in, but they were on their phones and didn't notice me or were smart enough to make it seem like they didn't. I think I weighed as much as both of them put together.

I noticed right away another group of people seated at the back table where Rollie and I had met the Eastern Europeans before. They were oblivious millennials, not Milosh lackeys. Damn.

I had turned around to leave when I heard an accented voice call out, "Mr. Beeg Man. Hey!"

A glance over my shoulder told me the skinny kid behind the counter was speaking to me. He had a shock of dark hair that fell over his eyes like a sheepdog's, but he was looking at me all the same.

"Me?"

"Yes." He gestured for me to come closer.

"What?"

The kid lowered his voice. "He wants to see you. I will call him."

What the hell was this? "I don't have all day." The kid was already on a cell.

His accent was just like Milosh's which meant the freelance shylock might be more than a passing fad here in Fishtown. I wondered who really owned the shop and just as quickly decided to stay the hell out of it.

The kid was nodding at the phone and speaking quickly. I didn't catch the language other than it wasn't English.

"Out back," he said to me finally. "He will be waiting."

Why did this guy look like he was trying to suppress a fit of the giggles? The skin crawled on the back of my neck.

"You tell him maybe next time. I have to go."

The kid didn't even react and I stepped to the door only to find Milosh's goon filling the space. Now that he was standing, he only had an inch or two on me, but he looked like a T-90 tank, one that was at least ten years my junior.

I shuffled toward the back and he followed. The rest of the customers paid no attention. I doubted calling for help would have mattered anyway, but I noticed one guy reading an e-book had a large coffee, or grandioso or whatever the fuck they called it, sitting in front of him. The important thing was that it was full, and judging by the steam curling off the top, that it was piping hot.

Might work.

"Out back." Mr. Tank pointed, in case I missed the subtlety.

Why hadn't I waited? Beet would be all right for a few more days. Too much crap going on.

"Tomorrow, okay?"

"Now. Okay." NOT a question. The guy didn't seem concerned about witnesses here and his hands came up like he was going to push me through the back door if necessary.

A big part of me wanted to have it out right then and there, but like with the car outside, a brawl, even if I took the goon down, would flatten the place like we were a couple fleshy wrecking balls. Then the ensuing police action would surely see the thumb drive into an evidence locker. These assholes didn't know anything about it, so unless I was frisked, as far as I knew all they wanted was money and I happened to have some of that.

"Fine. I hear out back is nice this time of year."

Tank rolled on and I made my way to the rear of the place to avoid getting run over.

At the back door the hallway was so narrow both of us needed to turn our shoulders a bit to get past. The door squeaked and the low sun's orange light speared into my eyes.

A whiff of rotting garbage from a dark green dumpster hit my nostrils like a cheap-shot uppercut.

"You came back quickly. I like how fast you can move when motivated."

I recognized the voice but had to squint to see Milosh outlined in the blinding orange light. One more step back and I'd be against the dumpster.

"You have a real flair for ambience."

"If that is another word for privacy, thank you. So, you were serious about the marker?"

"I'm deadly serious about looking out for my friends. And they feel the same way."

"Yes, I know, Mr. Logan. I know all about it."

"I doubt that."

Milosh came closer and I could see his face. "If you like my office you will love my research department."

I figured that the prick would do a background check. But what would this guy be able to dig up? I was a screwed-up truck driver with a shady friend or two from the old neighborhood.

"Whatever. Yes, I have the marker." I patted my jacket. "How about you take this and leave Beetle alone?"

Milosh gave a dismissive wave of his hand. "It is done. On one condition."

"Condition?"

"Keep your cash. Instead, you'll owe me a favor."

"Huh? I got his marker. That means *I* owe you money, and if I pay up, that's that. Where did you go to loan shark school?"

"I consider it an investment. If you don't agree, then the debt is still with your precious Beetle."

Precious was an interesting description for Beet, but none of this made any sense. "You don't seem stupid. Maybe this is a language thing. If you say he has to pay you, then what stops me from just giving him the cash and he settles the debt?"

"Maybe I prefer to let him be an example after all, or perhaps I'd rather Beetle work off his debt."

"That's a nonstarter."

"Nonstarter? Does that mean you will work off his payment instead?"

I reached into my windbreaker and the Tank gripped my arm. Every instinct screamed for me to twist out of the grip and elbow the goon in the jaw. A voice in my head, sounding like a squeaky version of Rollie, chanted, "Thumb drive, thumb drive, thumb drive."

I tolerated the grip. "It's just an envelope. Why don't you take this and go run your damn coffee shop, huh?"

Milosh smiled and backed further into the alley. Tank grabbed my other arm and guided me away from the back door.

"Sometimes 'damn coffee shops' are more work than they appear. The marker is covered and your friend is safe. For now."

I shrugged off the goon's grip and held my ground. I'd never been bounced from a stinking alley and wasn't going to start today. Thumb drive or no. "And what's that mean exactly?"

"I'll be in touch. A man with your contacts and connections can be useful."

"If that touch includes Beet, I'll put you both in the ground."

I should have expected their smirks.

"Entirely up to you."

They walked back into the shop.

* * *

ROLLIE'S PLACE

I made it back to Rollie's house without additional incident though I'd kept my head on such a swivel that my neck was beginning to cramp. I couldn't shake the feeling I was about to get jacked and I wanted to get in touch with Beet just to try to explain the situation. That is, if I could get it all untangled myself. About the only thing I really understood was that whatever had just happened wasn't good, which was par for the course for my life these days.

Rollie opened the door like he was a parent waiting for a child who'd stayed out past his curfew. And it wasn't even late.

"Don't scare me like that, kid. You okay?" Rollie let me in and I glanced around the living room. Rollie guessed why. "He's gone. The little guy is a real pest. Thought I was going to have to throw him out before he made me promise to call him when you got back."

"Tom can be a little intense," I said as I plopped into a seat. "I'm fine, but it has been one strange afternoon."

"Do tell."

So I did. I told him everything, very glad Tom wasn't around.

"So where *do* you stand with that commie shylock?" Rollie's face scrunched up to mirror my own confusion. "He'll be in touch? What does that mean?"

"Clear as mud, isn't it?" I shrugged. "One disaster at a time. I have the drive. Let's see what's on it. I'm guessing we might need to decode some of the contents."

"No call first? What happened to 'trust Tom,' like Ryan said in his letter?" Rollie's eyes crinkled like he was holding back a smile.

"Yeah, well let's see what the hell is on this thing before we show our cards. You'll notice the safe deposit box wasn't in his name."

"Fire up the computer. I'll get my glasses and that stupid dictionary with the microscopic print size."

* * *

As expected, the text on the drive was awash in codes, but at least it all used the same dictionary cipher. There was a whole section specifically labeled for the Mr. Beautiful Project. I copied it onto a separate stick and made sure to exclude all the other material.

After the drudgery of transcribing the letters and numbers it didn't take long to realize that it was mostly a list of names and phone numbers or locations, just like Ryan had described in his note to me. Sometimes he added a short explanation as to what the people meant to him. We also could see Ryan's gold-standard metric. "FV" was simply short for favor. Those who owed Ryan and the few he owed. He even added a number, as if it was some sort of ledger complete with account balances. I guess that's exactly what it was and it gave a good measure of how closely Ryan had worked with someone. He also listed the sort of service or the nature of the relationship.

"Busy bastard, wasn't he?" Rollie said. "When did he find time to earn an honest buck?"

I let my eyes scan down the list. Most I'd either never heard of or had no idea Ryan dealt with them. Most, but not all. "We know this guy." I jabbed at a contact in the middle of our hastily cribbed translations.

"Crocker?" His eyes lit up in recognition. "Doc Crock? The one who stitched you and Bishop up?"

"The one and the same." The unlicensed, disgraced alcoholic sawbones didn't ask questions and only took cash, but I couldn't criticize his work after the Ryan fiasco six months ago. His bedside manner sucked, but I guess you get what you pay for. He represented healthcare in Ryan's underground economy crib sheet.

The other guy Doc Crock had patched up, Bishop, was also on the list. He was a corrupt cop I knew from the last scheme and a long-time colleague of Ryan's, if that was the right word. He was back at the Pennsylvania State Police barracks, still managing the property room, last I heard.

And on and on. The list had places to get cars, fake IDs, hacking services. And this was interesting: a couple other doctors. But they weren't there to treat gunshot or knife wounds that would be inconvenient to report. These names had notes like "Off the record Scripts, NOT opioids." Or, "Pain meds okay but last resort only, not a regular source."

I started to understand. Ryan was no dealer. These were sources for compassionate, albeit illegal as hell, medicine. And I again saw the man that had come to the door asking on behalf of his sister. He'd even told me the liquor store where he worked.

I also remembered my own mother, long ago, during her own battle with cancer and getting screwed over by her insurance company. We were only in high school, but Ryan, a born hustler, had already built a network. He'd taken the old bottle of the drugs that had been helping Mom and a week later brought her a refill, along with making us both swear we didn't know anything about where we got it.

Mom probably lived a year longer because of those drugs and I almost decked the smug doctor who'd sung the praises of the crap substitute drugs the insurance still covered.

Ryan never asked me for a dime.

I thought again of Beet, and how there was no way Ryan could be making money from lending such small amounts with such favorable terms.

There were plenty of fences on the list for stolen merchandise. I also saw another sort of list with things Ryan apparently knew that others wanted. He was a sophisticated middleman.

Rollie traced his finger down the list.

"I know this guy," he said. "He's a second-generation hitter for the Irish. I knew his old man before he went career goon right when I joined the service." Rollie pointed to another name, with plenty of notes: "Likes dominant women, growing coke habit, can go too far on a job." Then a star next to "Collects baseball cards, needs Yastrzemski rookie. Can use bottles of Green Spot 10-year-old to soothe pissed off O'Briens. Don't get him weapons, be careful, MEAN guy."

There were more, but I saw a couple of patterns now. Ryan was always looking to help people who could help him, if not now, then down the line. And then there were a good number of other people who couldn't have been of any imaginable use to Ryan; sometimes, it appeared, he was just being a nice guy.

Rollie shook his head. "What the hell are you supposed to do with all this?"

"Beats me, but you're looking at a lifetime of networking." I was impressed, and more than a little freaked out. He couldn't have reached out to *all* these people and mentioned me, could he?

"That little pest will be back before you know it. I can feel it," Rollie said. "We ought to get him back here and check out the stuff for this project."

"I suppose so." It was ten o'clock at night by then. My head was reeling. I put away the list Ryan had made for me and called Tom.

CHAPTER 8

Tom must have been circling the block, as quick as he reached Rollie's front door. I'd have mentioned for him to be careful in this neighborhood, but I knew better than to worry. He lived in war zones and never got a scratch.

"Took you long enough," he said. "I was beginning to worry there was a different code nobody had ever heard of."

Rollie stretched and yawned. "I'm an old-fart triggerman, not a hopped-up cryptographer."

"Fine. Thanks for all the work, chap. What does it say?"

I spread out the papers on the dining room table. "It looks straightforward, at least as far as it goes. The goods …," I paused. "What *are* we talking about here? If it is drugs or something like that, you can forget it."

Tom looked like he was going to fly apart with all our clumsy delays. "No, of course not."

I waited for him to go on and when I saw he didn't intend to I felt my temper come on hot. "Listen, you little twerp. Stop playing games. What the fuck is it that's so worth all this crap?"

"If this is how you behave now, I can't imagine how Ryan thought you could help under fire."

"You know better than that. If I really lost my temper, you'd be headed for the emergency room."

"Don't be a mug, it doesn't suit you." Tom shook his head. "A real professional would know better than to ask, but if it helps, it is a satchel, and inside are dozens of cracking big diamonds, large fat untraceable gemstones worth a fortune. That bling is what makes Mr. Beautiful such a lovely."

Ah.

"And before you get on some high horse about 'Now just you wait a cotton-picking second here, sport ...'" Tom always could do a really funny, Southern American accent.

"Cotton-picking?" Rollie said.

"I never said that." I smiled. "Hey, relax. However he made his dough is sand down the hourglass, or whatever they say. I don't care that much and since you brought it up, I am NOT a professional."

Tom frowned. "Yes you are, mate, but you have a lot of work to go on your game." He returned his gaze to the paper. "Right. Me, I make sure the package gets out of the Sand Box. It will come here, hidden inside a truck, and wait for us in the Philly port."

"And then?" I pointed. "You and I access the port and the Delivergistics section. You'll have the paperwork needed?"

"Yes, yes." Tom sounded impatient. "That's been arranged."

"Sounds so simple. You could just mail the stuff," Rollie said. "They once did that with the Cullinan diamond. They—"

"What a gripping yarn that must be," Tom cut in. "If only we had time to hear every detail." He rapped the table. "There's nothing simple about getting the package here, but yes, this part should be routine." He looked expectantly at me.

"Okay. And then we remove the package and the truck driver acts as courier?"

"Not quite," he said. "The package is built into the truck itself, so you will drive west until we stop in Johnstown, Pennsylvania. We make a stop and extract the package. After that, we meet our contact and if all goes well, we'll proceed with the exchange."

Now we were getting somewhere. Or at least Tom was. "Okay. Ryan can't be here for this great plan. You sound like you have things nicely in hand. I think if Ryan trusted you this much, you can take it the rest of the way."

"I don't understand," Tom said.

"Shoe's on the other foot, huh?" I hated to admit I was enjoying the moment. "Take it away, 'mate.' It's all yours and Bob's your uncle or stepfather or whatever you want him to be."

"Come again?"

"You did the hard part. You might as well finish it off."

"This was Ryan's part. I can't …" Tom pinched the seam on his pant leg. Maybe even along with some skin, trying to stay calm. "Thanks to his paranoid machinations I can't complete the mission without your help. I thought I'd been clear."

"It's a straight shot from here. You said so yourself. This isn't my deal and never was." I raised my hand to block the next objection. "Tell you what, I'll bring you to meet the contacts along the way. Then I will find a trustworthy driver. Shoot, he doesn't even have to know what he's carrying, does he?" That was a trick Ryan had pulled on me a couple times over in Iraq, taking advantage of some surplus cargo space when we carried supplies and personnel into hot zones. Once I found out, I dropped him to his knees with a gut punch. We reached an understanding after that.

Tom frowned and spoke slowly, like he couldn't believe his ears. "You do grasp that you are to hold on to Ryan's half of the fee?" Tom locked his gaze on me.

"You hold it. He trusted you this far. This is your baby."

"Don't tempt me." Now his eyes glittered in a way that told me he was already doubling the payday in his mind.

"Go on! Live large, dream big," I patted him on the head. "So to speak." Then I turned serious. "Ryan never got around to asking me to do this. *He* was the hustler. I'm just a guy who is trying to learn from my mistakes."

"But your share would come to—"

"A bunch, I have no doubt." I tamped down the greedy-but-dumb part of my brain. "But if I may waste my breath, I'd warn you that 'easy part' and 'can't miss' are famous last words for a reason."

"Easy is a curse uttered by ignorant outsiders unaware of the planning that goes into one of these operations," Tom said.

Rollie spoke up. "And you know the one about no plan survives contact with the enemy? The kid wants out. Surely you have enough flexibility to handle that?"

"This *is* the flexibility. I was supposed to be working with Ryan, remember?"

"I think you've figured out his plans weren't so perfect after all," Rollie said.

"Yeah, well I wasn't involved in that, was I?" Tom's cheeks puffed as he exhaled a long breath. "Right. Kyle, can you agree to this much? I'll finalize the operation overseas and meet back here as soon as everything is in place. The truck will be on a transport ship and will take a week to arrive. Meantime, if the contacts over here refuse to cooperate with just me, you will join me as planned."

"I didn't plan shit, but if I say yes, will you go away?"

Tom smiled. "I wasn't sticking around for the tea."

CHAPTER 9

FISHTOWN: TWO DAYS LATER

As much as I tried to pretend that Tom had gone away for good, a pressure started to build inside my skull. It didn't help that the only news I saw about Delivergistics was bad and getting worse. The more the reports of investigations leaked to the press the less my manager or anyone with the company said. Workers like me were stuck in the dark and the paychecks that still came in were little comfort.

As a side effect, I had more time on my hands than I wanted.

I kept reading the list Ryan shared. My first impression held true: Half the contacts made him look like a scam artist or crooked middleman, all of which I suppose was true, but then the others made little sense if he was expecting to earn a buck. They read more like a cross between Robin Hood and the Make a Wish Foundation.

Invariably, those perceptions led me to think about the guy we'd shooed away who claimed to be worried about his sister. I had enough of my own problems without having to add this guy's desperate gamble. If I was his last hope ... crap.

Maybe there was still a chance to try to help him out. It was my turn to stock the fridge with beer, so I headed to the state-run Wine and Spirit store over on Girard. Aside from the brew, I wanted to see if that old guy really was there.

* * *

A bored-looking clerk glanced up when the door chimed at my entrance. He was about my age, early thirties at the youngest. Not my guy, in any case.

"Help you find something?" The store was fairly empty, as it was before noon.

I started to say no as I pointed to an enormous cardboard display of a football player with a six-pack of beer tucked under his arm like a pigskin. The figure looked like he was going to smash through a stack of cases. I decided to do my part for the home team and took a case off the top.

"Actually yes, I'm looking for another guy who works here, an older gentleman?"

"We have a couple. Do you have a name?"

I didn't bring the Ryan list with me. I'd decided to treat it like dynamite, but I checked it before I left. "Russ," I said. "No, that's not it. Ross."

The guy's eyes narrowed. "He expecting you?"

"I'm not sure. You can mention I'm a friend of Ryan's and if that doesn't ring a bell for him, then I'm sorry to waste your time."

The guy glanced around the empty store and shrugged. "I get paid by the hour."

A few minutes later the clerk returned and I recognized Russ/Ross peeking out the door to the back area.

"You can leave that on the counter and I'll ring you up," the clerk said. I nodded and walked past aisles of bright green Midori and Blue Curacao liqueurs.

The old guy pulled the door all the way open as I approached.

"You're Ross?"

"Ryan spoke to you?" I thought he might grab hold of me. The guy looked like he hadn't slept since the last time I saw him weeks ago. His curly gray hair tufted out from a balding pate like a clown's hair in a black and white film.

"I wasn't prepared for your visit last time," I hedged. "I understand much better now, but why don't you start from the beginning so there's no confusion?"

Relief washed across his face and his eyes welled up. My neck started to itch. I don't do sob scenes well. I could hear some voices joking and laughing from the back area, but far away. We could speak freely.

"My kid sister." Ross stopped, I suppose at my expression. "Kid to me, she's sixty-one. I should be retired but, well, you don't need to hear all my problems." He flashed a nervous smile.

"One at a time, anyway. So, your sister, what's her name?"

"Evelyn. She's been fighting cancer for a couple years now and the docs put her on a new chemo drug to shrink the tumors. It was working, but her damn insurance company changed the rules and now they won't pay for it."

"Ryan's not doing insurance as far as I know," I was only kidding, but I remembered that these stores were run by the state. "You get your coverage from the state working here, don't you? Can you get her a job here?" I felt like King Solomon for an entire second before Ross replied.

"She's, what's the word for it these days? Special? She helps out at the local Y but lives on her own. Flat out refuses to live with my wife and I so the state won't let me claim her as a dependent for the insurance."

"I see, so what exactly was Ryan doing for you?"

Ross handed me an empty prescription bottle. I noticed the date on the label was a year old.

"Doxitax? I never heard of it."

"Be cheaper if it said 'gold nuggets'," Ross said.

"I'm sure." I wished I could ask Ryan how he was supposed to pay for this. "So, uh, if I can find some of this, you know, somehow, what was your arrangement with Ryan?"

Ross glanced around. "Tell him I might have a line on a bottle or two of what we talked about."

I remembered from the list some mention of rare whiskeys, so I decided to pretend I understood and check later. "Right. Tell you what. I'm still new, let me ask around and if I have any luck I will get back to you."

He looked like he shrank an inch at the news the way his shoulders sagged. "She looks gray again. I think the tumors are coming back. The other stuff they have her on is sugar pills for all the good they're doing her."

"Can I hold onto this bottle? I'll get you an answer as fast as I can, all right?" Why the hell was I feeling guilty about some hustle that had nothing to do with me?

He handed it over. "Ryan told me he knew some people." Ross seemed to be talking to himself as much as me. "I promised my parents before they died that I'd take care of her ..."

* * *

ROLLIE'S HOUSE

"Kid, you know I'm no lawyer, but if you get caught, they'll lock you up." Rollie's pledge of support needed some work.

"Since when did you let that kind of stuff make you so nervous?"

"Since total strangers began to knock on my front door asking me or you to go jump into Felony Lake." Rollie's lips pressed together before he resumed. "Besides, you don't owe Ryan anything. I'd say the balance is on the other side of the ledger."

"Maybe so. But you didn't see this guy's face. He looked lost."

"Plenty of lost animals at the pound, you can't save them all."

"All right, I get it. You saw the list, looks like Ryan had his 'charities,' but I think I see the whole picture a little better. He collected favors as much as cash. More, maybe."

"Big deal. He can't use either now."

I nodded. "But not too many people know that. We have a shot to cash in some to our advantage." I was thinking out loud. I was also remembering how Ryan helped my mom and maybe I owed him one after all.

"What advantage? Looks like a creative way to land in prison. And for what?"

He had a point. "I don't know, but I think I'm going to look up Doc Crock and see if he has any ideas." I watched Rollie walk to the coat rack and get his windbreaker. "What are you doing?"

"What's it look like? I'm coming with you." Rollie grabbed his car keys.

* * *

LANSDOWNE, PA

The Blue Bomber's engine roared like a stock car's, which was exactly how Rollie drove it. The powder blue Oldsmobile Delta 88 may have looked like a geezermobile, but the fat tires and deep rumble of the crate motor V8 made it a sleeper. I slid across the bench seats and white-knuckled the "Oh shit" handle on the headliner while Rollie powered around turns.

"Next time it's for pinks!" Rollie yelled out the window to the tricked-out Subaru driven by a kid with a man-bun who made the mistake of revving his engine at the last stoplight.

"Rollie, we don't need to be smashed up to talk to the doc," I said. "Besides, I thought you wanted to avoid getting in trouble." The only other time we came out this way, both I and Ryan's friend, the crooked cop Bishop, were badly wounded and every second counted. I was sliced up like a turkey and Bishop had a slug in his ass. We'd needed the best no-questions-asked medical help money could buy.

"C'mon, kid, gotta blow out the carbon every once in a while." Rollie grinned. I swear he looked ten years younger every time he tried to kill me in this thing. "She pulls hard on race gas, doesn't she?"

We thundered up the road and I was about to point out a squad car when Rollie backed off the gas and it felt like we'd run into a giant pillow. "Not a bad job bleeding the brakes, if I do say." Rollie glanced over at the police car and nodded at the officer behind the wheel. "Just an old man scouting out some new early bird specials," he said under his breath.

"It's not too late to call ahead first."

"Why spoil the surprise?" he said. "Let's see how strong these ties are on your magic list. If he tells us to go fuck ourselves, we have a good idea we wasted a perfectly good evening pawing through that dictionary while playing codebreaker."

We passed the historic Fernwood Cemetery and turned up the next street. Rollie pulled into a driveway a couple houses down and killed the engine.

We walked over to the side entrance and I noticed the small security camera. I didn't see any cars other than ours in the driveway.

"Maybe they aren't home," I said.

Before Rollie could respond, an intercom speaker crackled to life. "Whattayawant?"

"Dr. Crocker? Hello?" Rollie spoke at the lens. "Does that camera work, or are you back on the sauce?"

"Rollie …," I said.

"I remember you," the doc's voice growled over the speaker. "Shut up and wait there."

"His customer service has improved," I said. The last time we were there, he and his live-in girlfriend nurse threw us out when we were barely off the operating table. He did work for the O'Brien's and others who needed his under-the-radar emergency medical services. When he realized we'd been in a beef with the Irish Mob, he got spooked.

The door opened a minute later and Doc Crock stood in a worn maroon terrycloth bathrobe. He was unshaven and his hair stuck out like gray straw. It was after two o'clock.

"Sorry to wake you." I wasn't sure what to say.

"Not for long. Get lost. I can't help you."

"I haven't asked for anything yet," I said. "And before you slam the door, you should know we smoked the peace pipe with our Irish friends. You can ask them yourself."

He looked around. There were some other houses close by, but mostly just small gas stations and car repair places. It seemed like the kind of place where everyone minded their own business. "Get in here." We followed him in to what laughingly passed for a waiting room, with its beat-up couches and old TV. "I don't ask them anything. They tell me when they need something, and that's it."

"Well you aren't going to get clipped for speaking to me, all right?"

"Says you." He looked us both over. "Unless you're bleeding internally, you two don't look hurt."

"We're fine. I'm here because Ryan Buckley told me you were the right person to speak with."

"He did? And when was that?"

I racked my brain trying to remember how much Crocker knew about what happened to Ryan. "He's left me in charge for now and you're listed as a good guy to know for certain hard-to-find items."

"Hard to find, huh? I hope you know better than to hit me up for a shitload of Oxy or anything like that."

I pulled out the bottle. "Nothing quite so ... recreational. This lady is hurting bad and her brother thinks she won't make it without this."

Doc Crock read the label. I noticed his eyes didn't look so bleary now that we were off the street and began to suspect some of that was an act.

"Nobody takes *this* stuff for fun. Obviously, I don't have a pillowcase of it in the closet, but I may be able to tap a source." He looked up from the label. "But we don't work off favors, Kyle."

I was surprised he knew my name, but I guess Ryan was as good as his word about preparing people for me to be his understudy. "How much?" We'd anticipated this and had stopped by the safe deposit box on the way.

"This is a year old. How long has she been off it?"

"Don't know. I assume that's the correct dose."

"That's a stupid assumption, but it also isn't my problem. I wish I could see her chart."

"How much?"

"Five grand. That's cash up front and I can have it for you by tomorrow afternoon. That should be good for a month and I'll see if we can do better down the road if that's what you want. Speed carries a price."

Actually, the number wasn't worse than what the insurance company turned down, but I figured this source hadn't acquired the pills at retail, either. I nodded to Rollie, who counted out the bills.

"Be back here same time tomorrow." He poked me in the chest. "And if I hear the Irish are still on the warpath, you can forget the whole thing."

"Always a pleasure," I said.

"Hey," he whispered.

"Yeah?"

"Tell your guy I hope they help."

CHAPTER 10

"Five more reps," Sandy growled at me right after she shoved the weight machine pin even lower on the heavy stack of iron plates.

The smell of fresh paint hung in my nostrils while I tried not to show the pain from my aching knee. "Meet the new torture chamber, same as the old torture chamber." Sweat poured down my face. I'd *missed* this?

"Keep whining and I'll start thinking you like the attention you get from this damage." Her tiny smile told me she didn't mean it.

Sandy Keane, my long-time physical therapist, at least on this side of the world, and much more recently, my sometime dating partner. The whole thing still felt strange, as I was still getting used to the idea of having an ex-wife.

I wiped my face and took a drink of water. "The muscles feel like Jell-O, but good Jell-O, you know?"

"The stronger they get, the sooner you can run." She brushed her dark red hair out of her face.

"I can run," I tried to say under my breath, but the acoustics in the new place made it easy for her to hear me.

"I meant run without setting your rehab back a month every time." She glanced up at the clock.

"Got another client soon? I can do the cool-down stretches in the other room if you like." I stood and tested weight on my left leg. It hurt, but just soreness from the exercise, not a fresh injury. A nice change of pace.

Her expression clouded, and she turned away. "I'm not sure."

She'd only been over at this new location a few months. I was one of the few clients to follow Sandy from the Roseman Institute into her own practice. It was a small space in a building she shared with a chiropractor who, I swear, went by the name Barnaby Bones.

"Something wrong?"

"Nothing." She started gnawing on her thumbnail and I realized she'd taken most of them down to the quick.

I should have noticed that sooner. "I'll do my cool-down by walking around the block slowly. Come with."

"I should stay." She looked at the clock again.

"How about we talk here? You're sure everything is okay?"

She shook her head and when she didn't speak, I saw she was on the verge of tears. I didn't know her that well but got the sense that was rare.

"We won't go far. I don't move that fast. If they show up, we'll see them. Come out and some nice fresh Philly air."

She forced a smile, which I appreciated. I took her hand.

On the steps I glanced back to make sure we'd secured the door and saw movement in the window under the painted sign for the chiropractor. The curtain was pulled back and a thin-faced man in his fifties stared directly at us. Barnaby Bones, if that was his real name, and not a trace of a grin, like the chipper guy on the sign.

Sandy jumped right in. "I've been an idiot."

"Impossible."

"Don't be so sure."

"If this isn't about us, can you catch me up?"

She looked at me while we walked. "Remember how Barnaby got me all those referrals?"

"Yeah and I still don't know how you call him that with a straight face."

"Because it's better than 'Dr. Bones.'"

Fair enough.

She continued. "Anyway, I was so busy being excited to cover the rent that I didn't see the pattern."

"What pattern?"

"All the referrals that came through Barnaby were from the same doctor and insurance company."

I thought about that. "But if they were all from the same guy, that might make sense. Is the insurance company legit?"

"As far as I know. We didn't use them at Roseman, but that was half the reason I wanted to leave there in the first place. I wanted to take on as wide a range of clients as possible."

"And the insurance company paid?"

"So far. Better than yours, who still might bag on me."

I stopped her. "I'll get you paid, even out of my pocket, don't you worry."

She waved it off. "Listen. The patients are diverse enough. When I went back and looked at the treatments, they are all soft-tissue, kind of subjective aches and pains."

"You think they were faking?"

"Not necessarily, but I couldn't prove it if they were."

"That hardly makes you an idiot," I said.

"No, but how about when my mentor-buddy Barnaby popped in a couple weeks ago and mentioned that Dr. Park had other places to send these clients?"

"Unless …?" I'd started to get the picture.

"Unless I could come up with a, how did he put it, 'finder's fee' for clients. All in cash, of course."

"Ah, hell. I'm sorry, Sandy."

"It gets worse. The prick actually looked offended when I said the words 'Insurance fraud.'"

"Truth hurts."

"And it looks like I'm the collateral damage."

"Huh?"

"He flat-out warned me that loose talk like that was dangerous and reminded me, with copies of records of all the clients I'd treated from Dr. Park, that he would be happy to testify all about my involvement if I said anything."

"You didn't know." It sounded feeble to my own ears.

"I'd hate to argue that in court, and I don't exactly have a rainy-day fund for a top shelf lawyer."

"So, where did you leave things?"

She sighed. "A standoff, I guess. I told him no more referrals, no more Dr. Park, no anything. I could build my business on my own." Her eyes welled up. "Tough talk, huh?"

I hugged her. "A tough lady. We'll get you through this."

"I don't think so. Now he wants to raise the rent."

One of the reasons for her move to open her own shop was learning about the space here next to the chiropractor that was offered at below-market rates. I was beginning to see why.

"How much?"

"Enough. He said the 'adjustment,' I guess that's supposed to be chiropractor humor, in cash, was to make up for my uncooperative nature."

"Weasel. How about I see to it he needs more than a bone crusher?" I was kidding, but only because I knew she wouldn't want that.

"Aren't you sweet? But then I'd have nobody to take me out and he'd still have that sword over my head." She shook her head. "I'm going to have to start over again, probably in a different state. Maybe Jersey or Delaware."

My head was spinning with names from Ryan's list. Some ideas started to percolate.

"I hate to tell you that might not make a difference. I think insurance crimes might be a federal thing." I was outrunning my legal knowledge fast, but I remembered reading something about it when I was worried that I might get cut off for my injury.

"Wonderful. The kicker is that he has two different rental agreements from me, including one that says I'll pay the higher rate."

"How?"

"I told you I was an idiot. He slipped in an extra form on me when I was signing and I read the first one but didn't check the second. Now he has a version with my real signature."

"Son of a ..." Now the wheels were really spinning in my brain. "Where does he keep the contracts?"

"I don't know, in his office I guess, unless he took it home. Why?"

"Do you know where he lives?"

"No. He's very secretive. I don't even know his original real name, he even uses Barnaby on his contracts. What are you thinking?"

"Me? Nuttin'. I just noticed a long line of black cats that are about to cross his path, that's all."

CHAPTER 11

ROLLIE'S PLACE

I didn't get back to sleep the remainder of the night, but once the sun came up hunger shoved me out of bed.

Rollie topped off my coffee and listened to me tell him about Sandy's situation.

"Slimy. What's the old one about a deal that's too good to be true?"

"Yeah. He thinks he has her. Unfortunately, she agrees."

"Am I hearing you right? You're going to let that crap stand?"

"That hurts me, Rollie," I said. "Of course not. Just trying to establish the rules of engagement."

"All right, the world makes sense again. I'm in."

I hadn't thought I could keep him away. "I guess we can't shoot the bastard," I joked. "But other than that, there's only one real rule."

"Yeeees?" Rollie asked.

"Don't get caught."

* * *

LANSDALE: DOC CROCK'S PLACE

"Any problems?" I asked Doc Crock after he invited me inside.

"My whole life is a problem," Doc said. "But I'm guessing you meant the meds. Money always talks. I have them."

I was ready to roll and stood waiting. "I think this is the part where you hand me what I paid for and I'm on my way."

He looked at me like I was nuts. "No, this is the part where I offer you a beer or some tea or whatever and we talk about the Eagles or the weather or whether or not you're getting laid these days."

"Huh?"

"Ryan said you were bright. Now would be a great time to start acting like it."

"You lost me."

Doc's face hardened. His jaw set and he stared at me. "Does the term 'low profile' mean anything to you? The neighbors mind their business, but if cars show up for five minutes and then drive off, what does that look like?"

Oh, yeah. "Like a drug deal?"

"There's the gray matter I was waiting for. And they'd be right, wouldn't they?" Doc shook his head. "If you're going to stand in for Ryan you better wise up quick. You want to be a sneak, start thinking like one or you're going to get pinched or clipped by someone who never took a Hippocratic Oath."

"All right." I felt just as dumb as he seemed to think I was.

"Wait here and contemplate your navel for about fifteen. I'll be back." Doc disappeared through a door. I heard the lock from the other side.

When he returned, he handed me the old scrip bottle, now stuffed with white pills. "Like I told you before, this should last a month at the rate on the original scrip. When you need more, bring this back. Give me some lead time and I can do the same for about half the cost."

"Okay, thanks." I stuffed the pill bottle in the pouch in front of the gray hoodie I was wearing.

"Not exactly professional grade, smuggler-approved, but there shouldn't be any reason for anyone to be suspicious. Try not to get pulled over."

I was just hoping to get the stuff out of my hands as fast as possible.

* * *

On the way to the state liquor store to find Ross it occurred to me that I would place Rollie in jeopardy by pulling any of this activity while in his home. He hadn't said a word, but I knew how things worked. An ambitious prosecutor could tangle the home up in some RICO case crap. Rollie could even lose his house.

As soon as I had the thought, the solution popped into my head. Anything I did that was what I thought of as "Ryan's list" stuff might as well be done from Ryan's house.

* * *

FINE WINE AND GOOD SPIRITS, GIRARD AVE.

The same lanky guy sat at the counter and the place was busier than the last time I visited. I scanned the store for anyone looking like a cop and kept reminding myself this wasn't heroin and I wasn't some dealer.

No? Semantics won't keep you out of the pokey.

Sometimes my conscience was an asshole. I thought of my mom on her sickbed and decided I could still look at myself in the mirror.

This time the guy left his post and called to the back without my having said a word. I remembered how, at the end, hours felt like days at my mom's deathbed. Any thread of hope was like gold.

Ross appeared a moment later. "Come on back, I have that special order for you."

Jeeze. Ross's eyes had such dark circles he looked like he'd put on zombie makeup for Halloween.

I stepped through the door and he led me to a small office. There was nobody inside and he closed the door. "Everything okay?"

I saw his entire world rested on that simple question. I nodded and handed him the bottle. "My guy said that's a month at the rate on the label, but without more info he can't guarantee anything."

"We left guarantee a year ago." Ross blinked away a tear. "I hope this will do." He reached inside a desk drawer and removed a dark hand-made wood box. "Teeling 33-year-old. Super rare, one of less than three hundred bottles made. Over three retail."

"Hundred?" I asked. Too rich for my blood.

"Thousand." Ross looked insulted. "I can get others, some even nicer. Ryan collected them or something, he said."

"No, that's fine. Thank you." I took the box and was careful not to drop it.

"No, thank *you*. This is a lifesaver." Ross clutched the pill bottle in his fist. He dropped his voice into a whisper. "Can I get more, you know, later?"

I hadn't planned on making this a habit. Or doing it at all, for that matter. But I just nodded.

I thought he was going to hug me so I backed out and slipped out of the store as quickly as I could.

* * *

FISHTOWN: RYAN'S PLACE

I drank some outdated instant coffee I'd scrounged from Ryan's cupboard. I needed the caffeine and didn't want to leave before my next "appointment" showed up. It had taken more convincing than I had expected to get a face-to-face, but I hadn't seen any other way.

He was a starred and circled name from Ryan's list and, if he was half as good as the emphasis implied, just the guy I needed. Sandy's situation had kept me awake all night and thinking about what she was going through burned in my gut.

I heard a light tap and looked to the front door. I didn't see anyone and thought I just wasn't used to all the noises the old house made.

Tap, tap, tap.

I realized it was the back door.

It was either a prelude to a break-in or my guy was even more squirrely than I realized.

Rollie and I had staged baseball bats by the doors just in case while we were working on the place. You never knew who might have figured the place was empty and we'd need to encourage the riff-raff to keep their distance. I moved to the door and saw a masked figure in a hoodie hovering by the back step.

My adrenaline kicked hard and I hurried as fast as I could without popping the scar tissue on my knee, another way of saying a fast walk, and snagged the bat.

The guy in the mask was barely taller than Tom, but that didn't mean he wasn't dangerous. Kids didn't need much strength to pull a trigger and this place was as good as any for a gang initiation.

By now the guy must have seen or at least heard me coming. He didn't run and I noticed both hands were buried in his pockets.

I snatched the door open with one hand and brought the bat up. I was close enough to take his head off if his hands so much as left the pockets. "Whattyawant?"

The eyes behind the mask went wide and I heard "Oh, shit" from behind the bandana. I could see it was a white guy and the voice sounded young.

"Hands, slow out of the pockets and empty, or I cave in your skull," I growled and got close enough that he'd never get away before I got in a good lick. Judging by his size one would be more than enough.

"Dude, you invited me!" the guy squeaked.

"You're VoxPox?" I didn't have a real name but hoped I would soon, as this moniker was right out of a videogame chatboard.

I saw pale pink palms come out of the pockets. No weapons and they were shaking.

Ryan, this your idea of a joke?

"Who did you expect? Are you Kyle?"

I almost told him to call me Mr. Logan but lowered the bat and turned aside. "That's me. We spoke on the phone. Ryan said it was okay, right?"

The kid had sounded older on the phone. Fear factor?

"Ryan said a lot of things," he said. "You sure you aren't going to crack me?" Jeez he sounded like he hadn't hit puberty yet.

"The neighborhood can be an adventure sometimes. Where are you from?"

The guy came into the house. "I've never been inside here before. I thought it'd be different."

I wasn't surprised. I barely saw the place even when we were tight growing up. Ryan was a private guy in many ways and weird about who met his parents. He didn't change after they were gone. The whole place was like a weird shrine.

"Are you going to lose the anarchist-chic look or what?" I pointed to the dopey bandana and hood.

The guy paused. "You don't need my real name. Why do you need to see my face?"

"Ryan told me what you look like," I lied. "You better match the description or it's 'Batter up,' got it?"

He let a sigh like the teen I expected. "Fine. But I'm not used to dealing with people I don't know."

"Tell me about it."

The guy removed the mask and I tried to conceal my surprise. Not a teen, and not a guy.

VoxPox was a young lady, probably in her early twenties. She had mousy brown short-cropped hair and a pretty face, outside of a droop on one side that went from her left eye to her mouth.

"Happy?" She had a defiant spark in her eyes.

"You can't be too careful," I said.

"I can see Ryan never told you everything."

I knew I shouldn't have felt defensive but did anyway. "Not necessary."

"Yeah it is. I don't want to talk shop while you're wondering and wondering."

"Fine. What happened to your face?" I *was* curious.

"A stroke. When I was fifteen. Believe that shit?"

"I thought you sounded like a kid, but that was when I expected you to be a guy. Your voice sounds unaffected."

"So, Ryan never said what I look like." Her smile was kind of crooked, but it seemed to suit her, like she was hiding a secret. Probably she was.

"Busted. No, he didn't."

"You're funny. As for the voice, you're hearing years of therapy and speech training. I was going to get into acting, but I'm not exactly ready for my closeup."

"It makes you distinctive," I offered.

"Ooh, I could star in the all new *Really* Diff'rent Strokes."

She'd had that one teed up and ready to go. "The droop isn't the problem, it's the chip on your shoulder, but I'm not your shrink or your life coach."

"That's good. I don't do sympathy discounts."

"Ryan suggested you for a reason, I hope. Are you as good as he says?"

"Better." She walked in to the living room. "Whoa. The seventies called and asked for their decorator back." She turned to me. "When is he coming home anyway?"

I shook my head. "Can't say. A long time, could be permanent. Things got hot for him around here. You're stuck with me for now, but I can pay."

"You've worked with Ryan over in Iraq?"

How much did this girl already know about me? "Yeah, which put me halfway across the world a lot of the time. The company is in trouble right now. I might be home for good."

"Okay. Ryan and I did a lot of barter."

"I hear that quite a bit. Let's find out if you can help me first," I said. "I guess I need a hacker."

She grimaced. "Anybody can do that. I'm a data manipulation artist."

"You just made that up."

That crooked smile again. "Not bad, huh?" She plopped into a chair and I thought maybe she was starting to relax. "Lay it on me. What do you need?"

Where to start? "My sort-of girlfriend—"

"No stalking."

"Nothing like that. Her landlord is blackmailing her and I need to get some documents. I realized snatching the hardcopies probably wouldn't do the trick."

I told her the situation and she listened with a focused stare at the faded carpet. I noticed all the wisecracks vanished while she took in the details.

"He needs his ass kicked," she said.

"Agreed. Two things about that: I went that route once with someone else and got locked up for my trouble, and even after what this jerk has pulled, I don't think that's what Sandy would want."

"Where do I come in?"

"I need someone to get into this guy Barnaby's office and find that copy of the fraud lease, but I assume he must have backups. Even if we found all the bogus leases, we still have a problem with Sandy linked to the scam clients. Those would show in the doctor's records not to mention the insurance company who paid on the claims." I stopped when she looked at me like I was nuts.

"Slow down there, sport," she said. "You want me to hack into this goofus Barnaby's system, and some shady doctor and then a big insurance company, and do what to them exactly?"

"It sounds like a lot when you put it like that." I paused. "Look, I guess I need advice as well as expertise."

"I don't want us to get on the wrong foot here since we just met." She stretched her neck and I could hear the vertebrae crackle. "Let me be clear. I'm not a ninja or cat burglar. I don't do B&E's, lock picking, any of that crap, okay?"

"I thought—"

"Never mind what you thought. I'm not saying you shouldn't have called. You definitely want me to check this dude's system. And I love solving mysteries like an alter ego. I'll be happy to snoop the doctor's stuff too, but I'm not about to go take on a big company's finance system, not without a good reason and for this, it's overkill."

"Fair enough." I wasn't a hacker, but the thought of learning what all Barnaby was doing gave me more ideas. "As long as Barnaby and the doctor have a reason to keep quiet like Sandy does then they lose their leverage. Even more so if we find out about more sketchy crap that they're into."

Her eyes lit up. "Now you're talking my language! And I'm always down for some counter-blackmail. This cat needs a beat-down, VoxPox style."

"So, we're on the same page," I paused. "You don't expect me to call you that, do you?"

She thought about it. "For right now, yeah. If we work well together, maybe my name later. VP will do. We superheroes need to protect our secret identities."

"VP it is. Tell me, if I can get you access, can you find what I need so he'll leave Sandy alone for good?"

She answered without a trace of a smile. "Do you want him to cuss, cry, or kill himself?"

CHAPTER 12

MEDIA, PENNSYLVANIA

I sat in my truck just off Route One near Troop K of the Pennsylvania State Police. After getting instructions and a wish list from VP I decided I should look up an old friend. Except Steve Bishop wasn't a long-lost buddy and we weren't really friends.

He may have been a dirty cop, but his own screwy ethics made as much sense as anything else. Once upon a time I think he had a promising career with the State Police. I suspect long before he hooked up with Ryan that he was cherry-picking choice bits from the seized property room at the barracks.

He'd expected to retire off the score Ryan plotted right before it blew up in all our faces. Half that score got ripped off and we had to split what was left. That didn't begin to account for the personal costs. That was the night I nearly got fileted with a knife and Bishop had a nice bullet wound in the ass. Yes, Doc Crock fixed up our bodies, but the damage to Bishop's retirement portfolio was enough that he wound up back in the property room, corrupt and bitter.

Just my luck.

I picked up a burner phone and used one of the several numbers for Bishop from Ryan's list. Just to be safe, I made sure it wasn't an official police line. Sometimes calls were recorded for "quality assurance."

"Who is this?" Bishop's voice growled over the line.

"Bishop? Man, time flies."

"Spit it out or I'm hanging up," he snapped.

"Are you still sitting with your fat butt cheeks on a hernia cushion?" I could feel the guy tense up over the phone. Better not piss him off too much. "It's Kyle."

"I know." I wasn't sure if that was a bluff. "How'd you get this number?"

"Our mutual friend."

"That's some trick," Bishop said. He was a charter member of the "There the Night Ryan was Killed" club.

"He left me his little black book. I was hoping for chicks."

Bishop's voice dropped to a whisper. "He said he might. I was hoping not. You didn't call to invite me to poker, huh?"

"Nope. Can you get away for a few? The coffee place just off Route One?"

He paused long enough I thought the call might have dropped. "All right. Fifteen minutes. And I haven't agreed to anything."

* * *

The diner was just busy enough that there were people coming and going all the time yet it was easy to get a table. Bishop arrived minutes later in his white unmarked cruiser.

He'd gained weight since the last time I saw him, not that he was slim to begin with. I figured he'd eaten to make up for the chunk of his ass that got shot off and had overcorrected.

Our booth was in the corner and I could see we'd have some privacy if we spoke in low tones. Bishop spotted me when I waved and approached. He dropped into the seat and the leather on his gun belt creaked. "You're the last person I expected to hear from."

"I missed you, too. How's tricks?"

"Why'd you call?" Bishop's face tinged red, easy to spot over the pasty skin. His eyes locked on me and I recalled it was a mistake to underestimate him.

"Might have a project for you."

"Better be good."

"I don't know how you and Ryan handled things, so I guess I'll lay out what I need and you tell me if you can help or if I'm going too far."

"Go ahead," then we both clammed up while a waitress poured coffee and left us without a word. Bishop was a regular.

"Did you ever work with one of Ryan's people, a computer jock?" I wanted to be careful here, as Ryan knew many people but they didn't necessarily know each other.

"He worked with several, but the best was a guy who went by VoxPox. Hacker shit, but the info was scary good. I never met him in person. Why?"

That he got the gender wrong told me I was right to try to keep things compartmentalized. I suppressed a shudder, as small mistakes could get people killed in these circles.

"In a second," I said. "Someone I'm dating has gotten jammed up with a slimy landlord. He tricked her into giving him some leverage and is trying to keep her quiet and skim some cash."

"I guess your divorce went through, huh? This one must be hot, for you to jump on the favor train." Bishop sat forward.

"Yeah, Beth is doing well on the other side of the country in Colorado. Sandy and I hit it off and we'll see. She messed up, but it shouldn't become a career ender. And this guy is a real piece of work."

"Do tell."

"I called you because I cooked up some payback for what he's up to now." I gave him the quick version like I did for VP.

"So, tell the Irish he dug up evidence or something and now wants to go to the Feds." Bishop brushed his palms together in a "That's that" gesture.

"I'm not trying to get him killed."

"Picky, picky. You want nuance, it'll cost you more than a cup of coffee." Bishop smiled.

"I've got nuance. VoxPox came up with an open-ended campaign that's going to keep him busy."

"But—"

I almost said "She" and caught myself. "He said you could help score a treasure trove of data fast." Ryan had made keeping track of all the balls in the air look easy. "He also wants something in trade that only you can get for me."

"If you're talking accessing the state database, he probably could do it easier than me. Or safer. They are real hard asses about logging searches and I have to be careful."

"Nothing like that, but you'd still have to be careful. You might get a kick out of it all the same."

"Let's hear it."

"VoxPox has a nifty gadget that he needs you to plant in Barnaby's computer."

"I'm not a hacker," he said. "Why doesn't he do it?"

"I'm not either and asked the same thing."

"And?"

"VoxPox said he's 'not a frigging ninja,' and I have to say that sounds about right, but I really think he doesn't want to get his hands dirty with fieldwork."

"In other words, dopes like us can do the break and enter, is that it?"

"Pretty much. The good news is that the hack is on a simple flash drive and all we'd have to do is find the computer, pop in the stick, power up the PC for five minutes and shut it off again."

"Sounds easy enough as far as felonies go," Bishop said. "What does the hack do?"

"I don't know exactly, but he said it would give him a back door to the computer and he'd have the whole hard drive copied and all trace of the intrusion gone like he was never there."

"And then the games begin?"

I nodded. "But the less you know about that, the better."

"I see. Well, what is the something in trade only I can do?"

I hesitated and made sure we were still safe to talk. "A dozen PA driver's license blanks."

"You're shitting me."

"Nope and the truth is I have no idea what they are for. That's his payment for the caper." I felt strange even asking. "But if you can't, I can scrape up some cash."

"Why don't you just handle the break-in, and pay him in the first place?"

A fair question. "'Break' is the operative word. I can get through the door, but I don't know lock picking and I'm pretty sure his office has an alarm."

As I spoke, I could see a glint in Bishop's eyes that told me to discount his grumbling about the task. The "king of the storage lockers" was maybe a little bored with his kingdom.

"I have a few conditions," he said. I waited. "You're part of the lookout team. And I'm not doing anything until you get me specs on the alarm. VoxPox should be able to dig that up via billing and whatnot. You can get a head start by going by the dork's office and checking the alarm company's displayed warning sign."

We'd never exactly gotten along, but it was way better to have this guy on my side rather than against. "You got it. And what is it going to cost for your help and the other stuff?"

"I need a favor, if Ryan trusted you enough with his connections."

"What favor?"

He stared out the window and spoke just above a whisper. "Not here."

"I thought you'd want everything up front. You're extending me credit?"

"You're talking to a cop. I can always just arrest you." He pushed the bill my way and stood up.

* * *

FISHTOWN

I figured there was no time like the present, so on the way home I turned off on Girard Ave and swung by the entrance for Barnaby Bones Chiropractors and Sandy's Physical Therapy of Fishtown. Although Sandy was sharing space rented from Barnaby, the place was really two converted row homes repurposed in this mixed-use neighborhood. Sandy had a different account for her alarm system, otherwise I would have gotten the code from her.

As I rolled past, I didn't bother to stop. Both of them were likely busy and all I needed right now was to get the company right. Sure enough, at both entrances there was a visible, stop-sign-shaped placard that read in white letters: "Protected by Klaxon Sentinel."

"Not for long," I muttered and turned the old truck for home.

CHAPTER 13

FISHTOWN

"Are you sure this piece of junk didn't go through the crusher once?" Rollie said.

We were sitting in an absolute wreck of a Kia. The back seat smelled like a family of mice had died in it. Still, the outside was clean, more or less, and most of the doors matched.

"Beggars can't be choosers," I said. "And again, I must remind you that you insisted on coming out here tonight. This heap is the last legal thing about the night."

We were waiting for Bishop to show up. I hoped I wouldn't sweat through the coveralls I was wearing.

"How am I supposed to get in trouble sitting at home?" he asked. We'd watched Barnaby get into and drive off in the new Volvo that Sandy told me about.

"Got your phone?"

"Yeah, but if there's trouble, I'll hit the horn on this beater and pretend it got stuck. You guys cheezit if you hear that."

I liked it. "I have to hand it to old Mike. He came up with this pretty fast." The shady garage in Conshohocken was on Ryan's list and I'd seen him work with the guy before. Ryan referred to him as a "dealer for disposable cars."

"What did it cost you?"

"That's the funny thing. Mike said all we had to do was bring it back, unless there was trouble. Then we're supposed to set fire to it and lose his number," I said. "That and to tell Ryan that they were all even."

"Ryan's 'favor economy' strikes again eh?" Rollie said.

I glanced up the street and saw the van approach. "Here he comes. How do I look?" I pulled on the white painter's cap printed with the BugsOff logo.

"Like a man on a mission."

Bishop pulled right into the driveway in a white van marked with same exterminator logo. He jumped out and I clamped down on my laughter. He looked like he'd been poured into the coveralls.

I wore glasses with clear lenses and a mustache. I doubted the neighbors, if any noticed, remembered what I really looked like, and half the block was shops or offices now closed, anyway. Still, the last thing I needed was an accurate description.

Bishop had gotten with the program and had a dark wig to cover his gray hair and shades along with fake muttonchops. He looked like Elvis in a bland jumpsuit.

"Thanks for meeting me out here. Had to get the work order from the office," he said for any eavesdroppers while he pulled a pump sprayer from the van.

"Pop gave me a lift," I played along. "They saw the nest in back?"

"Yeah." Bishop moved fast to the back entrance. Dress-up was fun and all, but this was serious shit if we got caught.

At the back door facing the alley we had relative privacy so we could speak as long as we kept our voices down.

"The geek is good." Bishop meant VP. After I gave her the alarm company she'd come up with the account and we knew the exact system. "If he's great, we'll find out."

I stood with my back to the rear door and blocked anyone from seeing Bishop crouched over, working on the lock. He had a gadget in his pocket with little alligator clips dangling from it.

The lock didn't give him any trouble, but the hard part was next. As soon as the door opened, we both could hear a high-pitched tone. I saw the sensors on the door. The system was waiting for the owner to enter the code.

Bishop stepped inside. "Find the computer," he said. "I got this. We have sixty seconds, but if my toy doesn't work, we'll have to bail. Too bad VP didn't get the code."

"He told me there were tripwires all over those files," I said. "Not worth the risk."

I stepped around him and headed for the front of the office. I passed a room with a table and posters of skeletal and muscular systems. I was here for another system. Maybe next time, Barnaby.

I glanced back at Bishop and heard the whine of a power screwdriver over the steady tone of the security panel. VP had confirmed that there were panels by both entry doors.

The clock in my head got to about forty-five seconds and I saw the light on the panel by the front door flip to green. I headed straight to the office area and the desk next to a set of locked metal file cabinets. There was a monitor and desktop computer in plain view.

I wondered what on Earth I'd do if Barnaby came back and hoped that we'd hear Rollie honking the horn.

Under the desk I could see wires and plugs leading to a power strip. I flipped the switch when I remembered that VP said it was vital that the unit be powered off when I plugged in the flash drive. I took out the stick and found the USB port. I popped it in and made sure it was seated properly.

I hit the power switch back on and listened as the machine whirred to life. The screen flickered and I saw a black screen with a blinking cursor. I was expecting the usual Windows power-up. Now a numbered list appeared item by item:

1. Good job so far
2. Wait five minutes
3. Did you wash your hands after using the restroom? J/K
4. Are you sure it has been five minutes?
5. Power off, remove flash drive, and tiptoe out the doe. Thank you for flying Hacker Air.

Smart aleck.

I must have waited six minutes just to be sure, and I hadn't needed to use the bathroom until she'd brought it up. I wasn't about to touch anything I didn't need to, though, and I wore thin gloves in any case.

During the wait I could hear the hard drive working so it was clear there was more than cute messages on that flash drive. I pocketed it and made sure to remember to close the office door again.

Bishop was waiting by the back door. The open panel box looked like it was wrestling a tiny electronic octopus that grabbed connections with its toothy clips. "All good?" he asked.

"I guess we'll see. Nice job on the panel."

"Don't thank me yet. I need to reassemble this in under a minute after I reset the system."

"Want help?"

"Nah, you'd get in the way. I'll meet you outside."

I stepped out of the place and stretched like I'd been actually working. A moment later I heard a chirp and the screwdriver then Bishop slipped out the door. I blocked the view again while he relocked the door.

"Hope that worked."

I felt like we'd been exposed for an eternity, but in fact it'd only been about fifteen minutes from when Bishop arrived.

"Always nice to get in a little overtime," Bishop said to the night air.

I glanced at the corner to see if Rollie was agitated, but he sat placidly at the wheel. "Thanks. I owe you."

"Damn right, you do. I'll be in touch." Bishop scratched one of his sideburns.

At the car I got into the passenger side. The door creaked in protest. Rollie spoke without facing me. "We happy?"

"We done," I replied. "I'll have to hear from our friend to know if it worked."

Rollie cranked the car and for a moment I thought I'd used up all my good luck for the week. The engine caught and rough idled until it decided to smooth out and get us out of there. "Don't pay her if it doesn't work," he said.

Rollie knew about VP's gender.

I had to trust somebody.

CHAPTER 14

RYAN'S PLACE, FISHTOWN

The next afternoon I answered the back door knock at Ryan's house with a lot less drama. VP wore her anarchist getup and carried a laptop case under her arm. I let her in.

She took off the mask once she was inside and played with the drawstrings on her hoodie. She looked around. "Hey, you didn't have to pick up the place for me."

I'd hardly touched the room, aside from dusting enough area to sit and work at the table. "I didn't, but there are some MonStar energy drinks in the fridge."

"You shouldn't have."

Did she just blush?

"We're still rounding up the other stuff for you," I said, "but I'm dying to know, did it work?"

She dug the neon green can out of the refrigerator and I heard it open with a faint hiss. She held another can to me. I took it and opened it.

"Of course. I wrote the code myself."

"Nice Hacking for Dummies instructions, by the way."

She gave me a light version of her crooked grin. "Lots going on in the background. I ghosted his whole drive and swept up afterwards. He has some passwords and encryption on the drive."

"Was that a problem?"

"It saved me time. That told me where all the good stuff was. The encryption itself was a joke."

Impressive. "You got into all of it?"

"Kyle, I told you I knew what I was doing. Yeah, and once I had all his logins it was cake to get the whole picture. The dude is pretty messed up."

"In what way?" For the first time I wondered if I should consider Barnaby a physical threat to Sandy.

She shrugged. "For starters, his real name isn't Barnaby."

"I had that figured out," I said.

"Yeah, but it is legally recognized, so he can hide behind it when he wants."

"I don't understand."

"It's lawyer stuff, but basically he can run his bone-cracking operation and keep his real life separate."

"But—"

"That's only for a surface look, like online profile stuff. I have the source. So, you want to know his real name?"

"If it's not too much trouble." The sarcasm just slipped out.

She ignored it and pulled out a sheet of paper and slid it across the coffee table. "Meet Mr. Mason Oliver, age fifty-seven, originally from Patterson, New Jersey. Was married, wife deceased, no kids."

I glanced at the paper and it had the basic information, including his social security number, followed by a listing of several addresses. "What are these? Chestnut Hill, and Strawberry Mansion. Wide range of neighborhoods."

"I know which one I'd want to walk around in after dark," VP said. "And where I'd rather have a house to live in."

I caught her drift. "The place in Chestnut Hill is his home?"

She pulled out another page, this one a satellite picture printout of a huge stone house with a large yard and pool surrounded by a stone wall. "The Beauregard Estate, two acres, and ten thousand square feet. Ideal digs for a bachelor, don't you think?"

"I didn't know bone-crunching paid so well. What about the Strawberry Mansion ones?" I studied the addresses. "Are these all next to each other?"

"Good eye. Yup. The dude owns a whole block down there." She took out another set of papers.

"Rentals?" I flipped to the pictures. Apparently, the Google camera cars weren't afraid to buzz through the 'hood to map the region. "Are these current? They look like they could be condemned."

"Right? These pictures are a couple years old, but do you want to put a bet he wasn't sinking all his dough into renovations?"

"Slumlord?"

"That's where the smart money is stacked," she said. "To be fair, you might want to cruise by there to make sure."

"This was all in his computer?"

VP gave me a crooked grin. "In *one* of them. He's kind of paranoid, it took a bit to find the second system at the house."

"I thought you didn't do fieldwork," I said.

"I don't. He left the door open so I walked right in."

"I don't understand."

"On his office PC. Turns out Mr. Oliver has a smart home and I found an application that showed me all the remote controls."

"Really? And his alarm?"

"Yup, that too, but that isn't the coolest. I piggybacked onto the login and it let me plant software and ghost that drive as well."

"Okay, you *are* good."

She stood and took a little bow. "Barely slept, but it was so worth it."

We clinked energy drink cans and I took a swig and felt my face grimace. I'd had plenty of the things over the years, but never got the taste.

"This guy is a big-time douche," VP said. "I mean, you still have to pay me, but I'd take this asshole down for free if I knew about him."

"How does this guy have time to manage all these rentals and run his practice, not to mention his insurance scam?"

She pointed to the dilapidated buildings. "Even if he puts in minimal effort, he'd have to have a manager. I found a guy on the payroll. Based on the deposits, he does okay."

"You have access to Oliver's bank info?"

"Of course. There isn't too much on the manager, just a name and bank. Franklin Smith. He's pretty low key, looks like. He lives in one of the units as far as I can tell, but it could be a front."

"I'll definitely have to go by there. In the meantime, do you think you could pull up a list of the clients for the Barnaby office?"

"Easy. And before you ask, here's the address for that Dr. Park guy who it looks like is feeding him all that business."

"Do you hack brains, as well?" I smiled. "Don't tell me you were able to get his records?"

"Nope." She pulled out another flash drive. "But I did cook up another sneak-attack program."

I saw the address for the man's office. Downtown. Pulling another late-night break-in might be pushing it. It'd be harder to get in and out, I noticed, and we'd have a building guard to get past. I explained the difficulty.

"I can't help with that, but I did some tweaks and this bug infects an active system. All you have to do is cut the power, put the drive in and power it back up. It loads fast and puts up a bogus crash screen. When you see that you are all set. When they power it back up it will boot up and run like normal, but I'll have my back door."

I was getting an idea. "So, all I need is a couple minutes?"

"If that."

"If I got it, do you think you could get the same list of clients?"

"I don't see why not." She nodded. "I bet you could get the guys to turn on each other if you wanted."

"The name of the game is leverage."

"Don't worry. Bonesy-boy's going to have so much shit thrown at him he won't know where to turn."

CHAPTER 15

STRAWBERRY MANSION, PHILADELPHIA

Rollie rode shotgun with me while we drove over to check out the rental places in the Strawberry Mansion neighborhood. Despite the benign-sounding name, the area could be one of the toughest in Philly. I figured my old truck would fit in okay and Rollie, while not actually packing a shotgun, did have his old .45 tucked under his shirt.

"Turn right up here." Rollie pointed to the next intersection.

The trash-strewn streets were barely wider than an alley. Cars pressed to one side and battered plastic chairs guarded precious open spots. Public parking or not, I wasn't about to take my life in my hands over stealing one of those spaces.

The state of the tightly packed rowhouses went from bad to worse and the boarded-up places made me think of a mouthful of rotten teeth.

"This is the block." Rollie checked the addresses.

"I saw nicer places in Baghdad ghettos," I said. People sat on narrow stoops and wandered the sidewalks eyeing the passing traffic with suspicion. I saw black, brown, and white faces, the only common thread being evident poverty.

Open windows and the occasional battered window A/C units told me that when heat waves crashed onto this street it would be sweltering inside some of the spaces. Luckily, it was a mild morning.

"Hey, one of the units is available," Rollie said.

He was right. Several homes down from another house owned by Oliver/Barnaby that looked in good repair, I noted the "For Rent" sign. I double-parked the truck and put on my flashers, then stepped outside.

Rollie slid over to the driver's seat. "I'll circle the block. Try to stay out of trouble."

As I circled the truck, several Hispanic women looked me. I wasn't exactly dressed for success in beat-up jeans and an old T-shirt. I had a battered baseball cap and hadn't bothered to shave this morning.

I pointed at the sign. "Is this still available?"

Two ladies just stared at me. Quiet neighbors, one for the plus column.

"You live here?"

"Si."

"Cuonto cuesta?" I dredged up my high school Spanish to ask her the rent.

"Demasiodo." Too much.

I couldn't tell if she meant something like if you have to ask you can't afford it, or that she felt like she was getting ripped off. She pointed to the well-maintained place and I gathered that might be where I could find the manager VP had mentioned. Smith. It was clear she wasn't interested in a long conversation. She glanced at the other lady and they went inside and locked the door without another word.

"Gracias," I said to the faded white door.

I couldn't resist a closer look at the rental unit and since it didn't seem occupied, I tried the door, which opened, to my surprise. I figured it was an invitation so I stepped inside.

The smell hit first. I got a whiff of fresh paint as I stepped onto a drop cloth but the mildew, stale onion and fried fish reek lingered underneath. More drop cloths covered an old couch and a peek told me it was as ratty as I'd guessed. "Hello?" The place was small enough, I figured my voice would carry. Aside from street sounds the place was quiet.

Even so, I stayed in character. I went to the kitchen and saw right away that one of the burners on the electric stove was missing. Wires dangled from the ceiling and a faint ring of grime told me that was where the smoke detector used to be. There was an old refrigerator that kicked off its compressor in greeting.

Battered cabinets lined the walls and some of the doors canted down due to missing hinges. I tried the water tap at the sink and it coughed out rusty water before running clear. The hot water side just kind of groaned at me.

I decided to check the basement. The door creaked, but enough light spilled down to confirm the steps and let me find the light switch. A naked bulb lit the rest of the way, giving the roaches a chance to scatter.

I didn't see a washer or dryer, but there was a furnace and a hot water heater, the latter drooling orange-tinted water toward a corner. Mildew spread across one wall and old mouse droppings dotted the floor.

I'd seen enough.

The stairs were thick boards nailed to the riser and one in the middle gave a loud creak when I put my weight on it.

"Who's there?" A deep voice boomed from the kitchen.

My heart jumped. "Hello? I saw the sign."

"It don't say come in, do it? Get up here, I got a gun."

Great. I led with my hands before I stepped into the kitchen. "Don't shoot. I'm sorry, I just wanted to see the place. The door was open."

Dwarfing the small kitchen stood a big dude with graying hair wearing painter's coveralls and carrying a blocky Glock in his hand, thankfully at his side and not aimed at my head. "You really wanted to ask about the place?"

"I think I'd like to change my shorts first." I offered a weak smile.

"Clever. The place isn't quite ready, but if you want to fill out an application, we can go down the block to my office. I'm Franklin, and you are?"

"Scared of guns." I noted he hadn't put away the pistol. "Jack Skipper."

"When are you looking to move?"

"In the next couple of weeks. Everything happened kind of sudden and I need something quick. I just started looking today. How much?"

"Just you?"

My flimsy cover story wouldn't stand up to a third degree, but he was still between me and the door. "No, my girlfriend and her kid. Is that a problem?"

"Nothing's a problem if your money is green. It's eight-fifty a month, for two bedrooms, first and last month's rent up front. Cash is best."

I wasn't an expert, but that was cheap even for around here. "Not bad."

"Let's get you an application." He stepped aside and let me by, but that damn pistol was still in his hand.

Just as I headed toward the front of the place, I saw another figure silhouetted in the front doorway. "Kid, you still in there?"

Rollie.

"Who's that?" Franklin stepped back and now gripped his gun with both hands. It was by his head, pointed at the ceiling.

"Whoa, that's my uncle."

"So you say."

"We startled the manager," I called out to Rollie. "He's got a pistol. Don't freak out, Uncle Dave." I hoped Rollie would take the hint to keep his own piece hidden.

"We're double-parked here, kid."

"Okay, be right there." I continued to the door and turned to Franklin. "Can I meet you at your place? The one on the end, is it?"

"I never said which one. Why can't he park while you get started?" He took a step forward.

I was almost running for daylight at this point. "You should see him drive. I better do it. But maybe lose the heat, huh? I don't do business like that."

He didn't waver. "Sure thing. Just let me see your driver's license."

Damn.

"No problem. It's in the truck." I fought the urge to flat-out sprint.

"I'll bet." He leaned in the doorway, his right arm behind the frame.

Rollie had already made it to the truck and if I knew him, his own gun was in his lap now.

Another car turned down the street and honked. I'd never been so happy to block traffic. I gave the driver a big apology wave. "Be right back," I said to Franklin.

I made the truck, put the thing in gear and barely avoided screeching the tires.

"Does this mean you're not moving out after all?" Rollie flicked on the safety and tucked the .45 back under his shirt.

* * *

ROLLIE'S PLACE

I used a burner phone to reach Bishop. He seemed glad to speak to me, so things must have been slow at the property room. I caught him up on what VP had found out about the real Barnaby and our trip to see his properties.

"You should see these places," I said. "I can't understand why anyone would live like that."

Bishop laughed. "What were you expecting? The Four Seasons?"

"No, but there are laws for basic service. I doubt half the systems worked in that place. Don't they get inspected?"

"Give me the addresses again," Bishop said, and I felt a glimmer of hope.

I read them to him.

"Hang on." I could hear him tapping on a keyboard. "Well. You can forget that. The guy from Licenses and Inspections is Dexter Davis. L&I handles housing codes and violations."

"So, what's the problem?"

Bishop lowered his voice. "Because he makes me look like a boy scout. I'll give up beer if he isn't on the take big time from our guy."

"You should have seen how crowded some of those places were." I shook my head. "It's fucking criminal."

"You have a real squeamish conscience sometimes, Kyle. Life's not so simple. Think it through. You said some of the places are holding multiple families?"

"No question."

"There's rules against that, too, and who do you think is choosing to ignore those? Not to mention try going down there wearing an ICE jacket and see if they don't scatter."

"But—"

"But nothing. Sure, the places might be dumps, but they're still a roof over their heads and they aren't chained to them. Maybe packing the place makes it affordable and if you rock the boat too much all you'll end up doing is getting them arrested as well, maybe even deported."

"There's nothing anybody can do?"

"I'm no crusader. But that doesn't mean you have no options if you just have to get involved."

My mind had already returned to Ryan's list.

CHAPTER 16

FISHTOWN, OFFICE OF DR. JOO WON PARK

The three-story building a couple blocks off Girard Avenue held a bunch of private medical offices, including dermatologists, dentists and, on the top floor, a rehab specialist. I was glad that it was a relatively small office and hoped at wasn't filled with cameras. Even so, we were prepared. I wore a greasy baseball cap with a wig and a generic Eagles sweatshirt. Rollie had an antique flesh-colored hearing aid that he'd fuss with so it made squeaking sounds. I was glad I didn't have that squealing assaulting my eardrums. He, too, wore a wig that gave him silver hair and I wondered how close it was to his actual hair color if he didn't get his dyed.

"You sure you don't know this guy?" I whispered to Rollie while we walked toward the door at the end of the hallway.

"I only look senile in this getup, Kid," he said. "But I may need an audiologist when we're done here."

"Whatever you say, Uncle Al."

We reached the door and stepped inside.

A low-pitched electronic chime announced our arrival. A middle-aged lady sat at a reception desk and tapped on a keyboard. She looked up. "May I help you?"

To my disappointment I saw another guy already in the waiting room. I wondered if they could be found on the client list of Barnaby Jones. No matter, we were prepared.

"Yes, my uncle has an appointment? For his sore back?"

She frowned. "With Dr. Park? Are you sure? What's the name?"

Rollie looked around the room, doing his best confused old man bit.

"Albert Kennedy?" I glanced over at Rollie. "Uncle Al, you told me Thursday, didn't you?"

Rollie looked at me like I was nuts. "Of course. Today is Thursday, the sky is blue and I served in the Air Force. I don't need another memory test, just something for my damn back."

"I'm sorry," the woman said. "I have no record of a patient named Kennedy. Do you have an insurance card?"

"Sure, no problem." I lowered my voice. "Sorry, he may have forgotten to call."

Rollie looked over at the man slumped in his chair. "You here for shrapnel too?" The guy stared at his phone like he wanted to fall into it.

The receptionist clicked icons on the screen. I leaned over and saw the desktop case for the computer. "It's not in there, is it?" I pulled away.

"I don't see anything at all in here. Is he a new patient?"

Rollie's hearing aid shrieked while he fiddled with the button. "Lady, I'm not a new anything. Is this guy going to patch me up or what?"

I shook my head and kept my voice low. "I probably should have made the arrangements. He's getting worse. It's not your fault."

"We work by appointment only, but I could put you in the system and we could call you when there's an opening. Do you have his insurance card?"

"Uncle Al? Do you have your card?"

"What card?" Rollie said.

"The one in the glove box I told you not to forget when we got out of the car."

"Then whose fault is that?" Rollie flopped down in a chair. "Oof. That second egg sandwich was a mistake."

The receptionist looked torn between being amused and wanting to call the cops.

I looked at her and shrugged. "Can I leave him here and go get it? I had to take off work today and ..."

She shooed me out the door.

I waited in the hallway for a couple minutes. When the door opened and the patient from the waiting room hurried out, I walked toward him feigning being out of breath.

"You don't want to go in there," he said and pinched his nose closed.

"Don't tell me that he ..." But I could already tell he sure did.

"I think he needs a different kind of doctor." The guy took the stairs.

Just inside, the sulfur stench of the stink bomb hit my nose with its full, room-clearing pungency. I heard the arguing in a back room.

"You can't be in here."

"I'm a vet. Let go of me."

I stepped around to the reception desk and switched the machine off. I popped in the flash drive, then powered it back on while an accented voice tried to reason with "Uncle Al."

"Sir, you have the wrong office. This is not the VA hospital."

The system lit up and once it flashed a system error blue screen, I knew it was safe to remove the flash drive. I'd let her reboot it. Once she did, VP's magic would go to work.

"Hello? Uncle Al?"

"Back here," the receptionist called out. I followed the sound to a back room where Rollie was struggling with a lean, gray-haired Asian man in a lab coat and the woman from the front.

"Call the police," Dr. Park said.

"Please don't. He gets confused. I'm sorry." I took Rollie by the arm. "Come on, Uncle Al. We'll go home and get you cleaned up,"

I pulled a laminated card from my pocket. "Do you still want his insurance?"

* * *

"How long does that crap last?" I paused to listen before leaning my head out the open truck window like a dog on a car ride.

"I wish you could have seen their faces." Rollie had barely stopped laughing to draw a breath. "It'll be gone in an hour or two."

"VP's program better have worked. They won't forget us anytime soon."

* * *

ROLLIE'S HOUSE: ONE DAY LATER

I was in the backyard checking Rollie's jacket for remnant stench when VP called on the burner phone. I'd had that phone with me all morning. I picked up the jacket, having passed its sniff test, and went indoors to take the call.

"Please tell me that worked," I said.

"Dude you're gonna have to learn to trust me." VP sounded excited.

"It's working? Anything good?"

"Pure gold, my man. I got everything and can track up-to-the-minute communications. Well, those go to a dark site and I get them from there."

"That's great, but anything I can use?"

"Of course. You didn't tell me what you did to plant the drive."

"I thought you didn't care about 'fieldwork.'"

"I said I don't do it, but let me live vicariously. Just before I called you, I checked and this morning Dr. Park sent a really snippy e-mail to the local VA hospital about some crazy patient. He wanted to know if they knew anything about him and why did he show up in his office."

"I'm guessing they won't have any idea what he's talking about." I told her about our little mission.

She had a contagious laugh. "Love it!"

"What else did you find?"

"You owe me for some more energy drinks, but I found the shady patients and almost fifty of them match the ones sent over to our boy Barnaby."

Now my brain started whirring. "Is there contact info for those patients?"

"Sure. Names, addresses, phone e-mails, the works," she said. "What are you thinking?"

"Can you prepare a couple info bombs for me? One containing everything that can go to a reporter contact I have, one for the DA and one for the insurance company. And I need a second one with all the properties he owns under his real name so we can make it easy for our friend in the media to connect the dots."

"I can do that. When do you want me to drop those?"

"I don't."

"Say what?"

"Not unless we have no choice. I'd like to avoid any collateral damage to Sandy for one and the people in the houses for another."

"So, what then?"

"We turn up the heat until he realizes we're serious and he better get the hell out of Dodge if he doesn't want to go to jail." That gave me another idea.

"Won't he just cover his tracks? And don't desperate people get dangerous?"

"He doesn't scare me." But I thought about staring down the barrel of Franklin's gun. And Sandy remained an easy mark for retaliation. "I'm going to see if Sandy can take some time off, just in case."

"I don't know," VP said.

"About what?"

"You think she'll hit the brakes on her new business on your say-so? And does she know how deep you're into this?"

She had a point.

"Not everything." A wee understatement. "But I'll make sure she understands what I'm trying to do."

"And if Barnaby wants to push back?"

"He won't know about you, if that's what you are worried about."

"It wasn't. I know how to cover my tracks." I realized that included me, as I still had no idea where she lived.

"He's a businessman," I said. "We just need to make sure he understands when it is time to cut his losses."

"He's a piece of garbage. You can't think a simple ultimatum will work."

"We have to show him he has no choice. We're going to hit him where he lives," I said. "You said you got into his home network via his smart apps?"

"Yup."

"Can you also access those controls?"

She laughed. "Hell, yeah!"

"Those poor people in the row-home have no air conditioning. Maybe the Mason Oliver Estate can get a taste of that."

"Yes. Hang on." Keyboard flurry. "Okay, I'm in. I just cut off the A/C. It's supposed to get warm today."

"I don't trust the weatherman. Can you fire up his furnace, too?"

"Ooh, good call. It says it can go to ninety."

"One way to find out." I grinned. Now my mind was racing while I thought of all the neglected repairs over in the Strawberry Mansion places. "What else does he have on there?"

"Let's see, a hot tub ... oh, and a pool!" she almost yelled.

"It's huge, I saw it. Does it have a 'soup' setting? I can bring by some carrots and onions." I couldn't help but laugh with her.

Another thought occurred. "Hey, won't he see all this mayhem, like an alert on his phone?"

"Great point." She sounded disappointed, but only for a second. "At least, if he got an alert. I'll have to cook it up, but I can screen-grab a peaceful shot of his systems and have that show if he checks it."

"Perfect."

CHAPTER 17

MEDIA, PA: ROUTE ONE COFFEE SHOP

I had drained my cup and left a tip on the table when I saw Bishop pull into the parking lot. He parked at the end of the building away from the last window. I hustled outside and hopped into the passenger side.

"How'd it go?" Bishop asked. I think he was as interested in what we were doing to mess with Barnaby as he was in making sure his own butt was covered.

"VP is a real pro." I had to remind myself to watch those pronouns. Maybe that sort of deception would eventually become second nature. If it did, would that be a good thing? "In and out and all traces removed."

"How soon before he feels the heat? I hope you are being careful."

"I imagine when he got home last night, he wasn't too happy."

"Why?"

I recapped the smart house hacks.

Bishop laughed. "So much for careful. VP moves quick."

"I kind of liked the poetic justice of making him feel the heat, literally."

"Just be careful while you're poking him that he doesn't feel the need to poke back. He'll know it was you, eventually, won't he?"

"By then it'll be the least of his worries." I noticed a briefcase in the back seat of the car but decided to let the guy move at his own pace. "According to VP we've got dozens and dozens of names of people who are in on the fake claim filings. With that, on top of all the housing he's been running like it's the Third World, I think we can get him to back off."

"That's all you want him to do?"

"Not all. We're trying to figure out the best way to play it," I dodged.

Bishop shrugged. "Make sure you check with me before you move on anything that might get back to me." His gaze drilled into me and any trace of easy banter had vanished.

"Of course." I didn't want Bishop involved any more than possible. There were more than enough chefs for this stew.

"Now, I'm sure VP will want to get paid."

"But not before you do," I jumped in.

"I'll have the license blanks in a couple of days and will let you know. I did the locksmith bit on credit, didn't I?"

"True," I admitted. "And said you'd let me know how you wanted the rest."

"The rest is in the back seat." He hooked a thumb at the briefcase. "When we're done, you're going to take it with you."

"What's in it?" Wasn't this supposed to go the other direction?

"Part of my retirement that was interrupted when Ryan screwed up and got himself killed."

"How am I supposed to fix that?"

"I was stupid to count on such a large payday, but greed does a number on all of us, wouldn't you agree?"

"No need to rub it in," I said.

"Actually, I think I do. See, while you are running around cashing in on all your friend's schemes, some of us had to go back to our jobs." Bishop's jaw flexed.

I was about to protest, but it was clear Bishop wasn't going to hear me.

"But I had my own deals going. Frankly, you already know far more than I'd like, but that's spilled milk under the bridge, as they say."

"Nobody says that."

"Shut up. I need you for this part. Over the years I was able to skim some items off of bust and property logs. Dealers that get killed tend to leave plenty of non-cash goodies behind."

"You don't worry about audits?"

He shot me a look of disgust. "If what is logged in matches what is found on the audit, all's right with the world. Let's just say some colleagues didn't excel in counting when they processed crime scenes."

"I get the picture. Who's to say how much was found in all the confusion of a raid or the aftermath, right?"

"You have the right idea, but a little credit, huh? Internal Affairs takes a dim view of finders, keepers and they watch for that."

"Makes sense."

"However, the right people can be discreet and smarter than the average IAD bear."

Bishop was warming to his topic. I guessed there weren't many people in his life he could speak to this candidly.

"But why do these clever folks with sticky fingers need you?"

"Part of being sneaky involves managing expectations."

"Huh?"

"Say a midlevel dope dealer gets raided on a good warrant. What do you expect to find at the place?"

"Drugs, cash, guns, I guess. Cars, jewelry ..." Now it clicked. "Okay, small expensive stuff."

"Good. All of the above. And as I said, these are all things everybody expects, so if most of the cash disappears it looks wrong. Ditto all the items you mentioned. Guess where IAD looks when it is out of whack?"

"The arresting cops."

"Correct. And to their credit, the bastards, they are sneaky too."

"Yeah?"

"Say some dumb rookie pockets a stash of gold chains, or 'just one' bundle of Benjamins, and nothing happens right away?"

"He'll do the same the next time or worse."

"Bingo, only now he's being surveilled and will get nailed dead to rights."

"So, the moral of the story is don't steal?" I smiled.

"I'm not talking about ripping off widows and orphans here. The scumbags we shave had no right to the stuff in the first place and these are items that the state would sell off. They'd only waste the dough. Trust me on that." Bishop wasn't losing sleep on this point.

"Okay for your conscience, but for those that see it differently?"

Bishop shook his head. "You should see some of *their* houses. Paragons of virtue, my ass."

"All right, so how does it work for the non-dummies?"

"I mentioned expectations. That cuts both ways."

"How so?"

"Let's say another dealer gets taken down and the team finds the drugs and cash and whatnot they thought they would. Good show, right?"

"I guess."

"Now suppose that someone found a great deal more? An amount of cash way higher, or where they thought they might find several expensive watches there were dozens squirreled away in another hiding place?"

Aha. "So, it's more a target of opportunity?"

"Isn't everything? Sometimes you take the balls as pitched and other times you swing for the fences. Now, my non-dummy colleagues have done this for a long time and know the expectation game better than the IAD does."

"I get it," I said, "but still don't see where they'd need you, exactly."

"If we're talking excess cash, they don't. They know enough to be discreet." Bishop held up a finger. "But none of them are dumb enough to get caught with a bunch of items if IAD ever wants to look up their skirts."

"Why wouldn't they just pawn them?"

Bishop stared at me. "Weren't you listening? If anyone saw them hanging around places like that, the red flags would fly like crazy. Besides, pawnshops are much cleaner than in the old days."

"They give them to you?"

Bishop coughed. "Give?"

"They sell them to you."

"Pretty much," he said.

"Last I checked, you're still a cop, and one who works in the property division. IAD knows this as well."

"Ya' think?"

"Aren't you worried you'll be the one holding the bag?" That thought flowed to me. "And why shouldn't I worry about the same thing, assuming the case has what I think in it?"

"Young grasshopper, so much to learn. Now you know why I went through this exercise. I do get audited by IAD. I know about that. I also get surveilled. Not often anymore, but it happens."

"How do you know that?"

"Ryan wasn't the only one with connections. I know before the teams even get the assignments. When they come, the books are as clean as ever and they could search anywhere and never find a thing. Mind you, I'm talking precautionary audits. If they really suspected me it might make life harder, but I'd still have a little warning."

"I see how you'd get involved in the process, but you said yourself you already know people like Ryan did. What do you need from me?"

"I know the best places to get quick cash for them, but pawn shops that can pay top dollar know who I am and won't touch anything I bring in."

"Why not?"

Bishop shook his head. "Think. They know I'm a cop in Property and may well have a veritable entourage of cops tailing me. They have good reputations and messing up with me would get them shut down."

"I see. But I'm okay?"

"You're nobody to IAD and you're okay with Ryan in their eyes. That's worth a lot." Bishop reached behind him and lifted the briefcase over the seats and dropped it in my lap.

Heavy. I peeked inside and saw fat watches and rings encrusted with gems. "Aren't they going to say something to this much stuff at once?"

Bishop handed over a sheet of paper. "Ryan knew everyone on there. There's half a dozen who pay well. Spread the wealth, though, huh?"

I recognized the places from Ryan's lists. "You understand I'm not a jewelry expert? I might get crushed here, then you'll think I ripped you off or something." I thought about what it might take from Ryan's remaining stash to just pay Bishop and be done with it.

"Your ignorance has been baked into the cake. They think you're acting for Ryan, and he knew jewelry. I also know what's fair." Bishop smiled. "And you hurt me to think I wouldn't trust you."

I took the case and opened the door. "Just have the blanks ready. How the fuck did my life become one big scavenger hunt?"

"Live the dream." Bishop strolled toward the diner.

CHAPTER 18

FISHTOWN: RYAN'S HOUSE

I sat in Ryan's place with the briefcase full of loot between my feet and studied the sheet with the pawnshops. They were all local and even clustered on South Street not too far from the house. I compared the list with the contact names Ryan had left me.

It looked straightforward enough. Ryan had developed relationships with the contacts and apparently, they had an understanding. I knew pawnshops could be scrutinized at any time over dealing in stolen goods. And that's what I had, a big old bag of swag. Regardless of whether the last owners were drug dealers, I sure hadn't come by the stuff legally.

On the other hand, the stuff here may have never had an honest owner. Maybe Bishop had a point, that in the big picture the items weren't going to be missed. It'd be one thing if he'd gotten it from a burglary ring, then everything would be eligible to be returned to the rightful owners.

I sat there and let the thought sink in, imagining Ryan hitting me with his little grin and nodding in approval. I also imagined how Sandy would feel at the moral gymnastics I was going through to get Barnaby out of her life once and for all.

I'd have to leave it at imagining, because I wasn't about to tell her. What would I say? It's all okay because at least I didn't beat him up or do something worse?

That last sent a chill down my spine. This was Ryan's world. It looked like the same neighborhood I grew up in, but here was an underbelly I hardly recognized. Money ruled and debts were paid in cash or blood.

As I stared at the fancy watches and glittering jewels it occurred to me that for a couple of these baubles I could go a little deeper into Ryan's list and make Barnaby disappear for good. Shit, I could probably get it done with just one of those bottles of fancy Irish Whiskey in the right hands. Scary.

So, was I looking for a medal because I only wanted to be but so much of a crook? Maybe not but, sitting all by myself, I liked the idea that I had some control over what happened next to people I cared about.

* * *

SOUTH STREET: KING'S PAWN

"Is Mort in?" The shop was lined with cases displaying merchandise and brightly lit by harsh fluorescent light tubes buzzing overhead. The air smelled like camphor.

The heavyset balding guy with curly hair along the sides of his head peered over reading glasses at me. "Who's asking?"

There were some customers down deeper in the store getting an electric guitar appraised by a woman with bleached blonde hair that looked white under the lights.

"My name is Kyle. Tell him I'm a friend of Ryan Buckley's."

The guy disappeared into the back of the store and returned a couple minutes later.

"C'mon back." He held open a swinging half-door that interrupted the long row of lit glass cases.

I followed him through a door to the back of the store. I heard it lock behind me as my eyes adjusted to the dim light.

"I'm here," I heard a squeaky male voice call out.

I glanced at a desk piled with papers and saw an old leather-backed swivel chair. A small man with fuzzy gray hair and a crisp white shirt and a black bow tie waved to me.

"You're Mort?"

"In the flesh. You look just like Ryan described you. Welcome, please sit down."

"Thanks." I took a seat in the vintage wood desk chair across from him.

"Ryan said you might stop by. How's he doing?"

I never knew quite how to play that, but at least I expected the question. "I haven't heard from him lately. I don't want to say too much, but he left town under a bit of a cloud and it could be some time." I felt like an asshole, but what else could I say?

Mort pressed his lips together and nodded. "Always a gambler. I tried to tell him to rein it in."

"He's never been big on taking advice."

Mort smiled. "He must have known something was coming. He told me so much about you. I've never heard him trust someone without question."

"He's not as smart as he thinks." I was relieved that the guy got the joke, even though it was true. He had a chirping laugh like a bird call.

"Did he ever tell you what he did for me?"

"No. I know some things, but mostly I'm learning as I go here." That sure was no lie.

"When you talk to him, tell him Jacob made honors again and he's talking graduate school."

"Okay."

"My grandson. He almost didn't get into U-Penn at all because of a stupid mistake on my part."

"What happened?"

"Jacob borrowed my car one night and got pulled over, speeding I think, but the officer spotted something and asked to search the car. Jacob, bless him, had nothing to hide, or so he thought."

"Uh-oh."

"Yeah, uh-oh, the police found a loaded gun and arrested him." Mort tapped himself on the chest. "It was mine. I'd forgotten all about it. Stupid, I know."

"Damn."

"A conviction would have wrecked his scholarship, maybe his acceptance. I felt awful."

"Sounds like things worked out."

"Thanks to Ryan. The lawyers wanted to talk about plea bargains, but Ryan told me not to worry, that he knew someone who owed him a favor. Poof. Charges dropped." Mort brushed his palms together. "He wouldn't take money, just said I owed him one and that was that."

"That's Ryan."

"Yup, but enough history. How can I help you today?"

"He said if I needed to move some things to come see you."

"Say no more. What have you got?"

"Watches and a few rings." I'd worn a heavy leather coat with deep pockets and brought only a portion of Bishop's stash. He'd told me to spread it around, so this seemed like the safest approach and I didn't want to wander up and down Pawn Shop Row with a briefcase.

Mort already had his jeweler's loupe out and was examining the watches. "Submariner, Oyster and a very nice President." He glanced up. "Are they on a list?"

"A list?"

"A hot sheet? Reported to the police?"

I hesitated. "Not as far as I know."

"I can see you are still learning." Mort smiled. "It's kind of a myth that pawnshops are full of swag. Stolen goods. We'd get run out of business and probably straight to prison."

"But Ryan—"

"Is a special case, and because he said you are to receive all accommodation, so are you. But understand." His smile dried up. "Never send me anyone. This is for you alone. Maybe I know some people as well. You notice we are talking back here and not at the front counter."

"I did pick up on that, yes." Now I felt like this was a big mistake. "Maybe I shouldn't have come. I don't have any paperwork for these and I can't vouch for them."

Mort held up his hand. "I can check on the items myself. If they're dirty I'll know and handle it accordingly. I will have to adjust the payout, of course."

"Sure. I'll leave you my number."

"I have it."

"You do?" How much had Ryan told him, anyway?

He nodded. "Ryan always brought the outlaw in me back from the past. He never burned me. Don't worry, I won't get hurt on these. But only come to me."

That raised a question. "About that. I have some more, but there are some others on my list."

"I bet I could name them all. I just meant for when you come here. That's a smart approach, just make sure you stick with only the ones Ryan told you to see." Mort scribbled furiously on a piece of paper. "Give me a minute." He got up and went through another door deeper into the shop.

When he returned, he stepped over to me and the top of his head barely came up to my neck. He handed me an envelope thick with bills. "Count it here before you leave," he said.

I pocketed it. "Trust is a two-way street, Mort." We shook hands.

* * *

And so it went. I'd reload my coat with more of Bishop's ill-gotten gains and make my way to the next store on the list. Each place was different, some dark and close, others wide, bright and expansive. But the ritual was very similar. Invariably, I'd ask for the person on the list and once I gave my name (and Ryan's) I'd be escorted to a back room like a long-lost pal and greeted by the owner. They came in different shapes and sizes and all had stories of ways that Ryan had helped them. One mentioned unreasonable payments to the Irish Mob that Ryan had managed to get lowered. I couldn't imagine what I'd say to the O'Brien brothers that might pull off that trick, or even not get my teeth kicked in.

Another insisted I thank Ryan for getting his daughter a translator job over in the Middle East. I wondered if Tom knew about that one. I'd have to ask him when he came back into town next week.

Unlike Tom, who I couldn't wait to see so I could get him out of my hair on his smuggler's quest, I didn't have the heart to tell these folks that this was a very temporary gig for me. As soon as I got out from under the contortions necessary to make sure Sandy was safe and everyone involved was satisfied, I was looking forward to just driving a truck where all I'd have to worry about was the occasional IED.

* * *

FISHTOWN, ROLLIE'S PLACE: LATER THAT EVENING

"How much?" Rollie asked after I told him of my adventures on Pawn Shop Row.

I held the bag up. "Better than 60K. There's gold in that thar gold," I said. "The bank is closed, do you have somewhere safe to hide this? I'll buy the first round at Kelly's."

"Thirsty work, was it? Yeah, but make that the first couple." Rollie took the bag and disappeared down to the basement.

"Ready?" I said when he returned. I pulled on a light windbreaker.

Rollie chose his leather bomber. "Yup, booby traps are all set."

Sometimes I couldn't be sure if he was joking, but I figured the cash would be safe enough.

* * *

FISHTOWN, KELLY'S KORNER

The bar had several things going for it. The owner, Dave, was an old friend and the fact that the joint was within walking (or staggering) distance didn't hurt. The place felt like a comfortable pair of shoes.

As soon as we got inside Dave saw us and grabbed a pitcher, allowing us to head to toward the lights over the pool tables.

Two hours and a couple pitchers later, Rollie was on the verge of taking me out in another game. He'd sandbagged for a few games and now moved in for the kill.

"Once a sniper always a sniper, huh?" I'd met Rollie right here over a year ago, and when Beth kicked me out of our house, he was the guy who offered to take me in.

"Steady hands, what can I say? You should be ashamed of yourself, trying to hustle an old man out of his pension." Rollie had sunk his last solid ball and set up the eight ball perfectly. But then he looked up from his cue stick. "Company."

I followed his gaze to see none other than Barnaby Jones, a.k.a. Mason Oliver, in the skinny flesh. He stood in the center of the room scanning the patrons until he spotted me.

"Isn't that the mope bothering your girl?" Rollie asked.

"How the hell did he find us here?" I muttered.

Barnaby didn't even look at Rollie. "I need a word. Outside?"

Rollie glanced at me and I gave a tiny head shake to let him know I'd be okay.

"You got it."

It occurred to me this might not be the safest move. Barnaby was half my size, but I knew firsthand he had employees who packed guns.

Barnaby led me just around the corner. I could see parked cars lining the streets and while we had relative privacy, there were people walking around.

"What kind of game do you think you're playing?"

"Hold on. How'd you know to look for me here?" I was determined not to let him control this conversation.

"You must think I'm stupid. You were poking around Strawberry Mansion."

That couldn't be a lucky guess. Franklin must have helped him fit the pieces together. "Just trying to see how the other half lives. You ought to try it sometime. Some of them live like crap. Maybe if they had basic amenities, you know, that actually worked?"

"What do you care? And who do you think you are to stick your nose in my business?"

Heat crawled up my neck, the leading edge of a temper storm. "What, you don't like it when someone has inconvenient information about you?"

"A threat? What are you going to do, report code violations?"

I remembered what Bishop had told me about the man in charge of inspections for that section of the city. "You're into more than that. We both know it."

"So *that's* what this is about. Did Sandy tell you she was all for our arrangement at first? She got cold feet, but I have detailed records of all the people she worked with." Barnaby was too smug and it only pissed me off more. All at once I knew the best lever to play against him. It was like a pressure valve released the building fury in my chest.

"She told me enough." I let doubt creep into my voice. "You jacked up the rent over it."

"The rent never changed, she just opted out of another way to pay is all. And I made clear to her that throwing accusations around can lead to all sorts of backfire."

A powerful urge to punch him in the face melted when the hairs on the back of my neck stood up. I learned in the Sand Box to pay attention to those warnings. Barnaby wasn't alone. Of course, he wasn't.

"Drop the rent back and leave her alone."

"Or?" He smirked at me. "You'll make my lights come on at night? Open and close my garage door?"

"Sorry your house got haunted."

"Not anymore."

I moved closer to the front of the bar while facing him. "I tried. But if you want to show how smart you are, Mr. Oliver, you might ponder what else someone might have learned in your system besides how to play with the pool heater." I slipped back inside.

Barnaby didn't follow me back inside and I could swear that last remark hit a nerve. He wasn't dumb and I couldn't help but worry that I'd underestimated his toughness.

The next move would have to be for keeps.

CHAPTER 19

FISHTOWN, ROLLIE'S PLACE: THE NEXT MORNING

I half-expected to see Franklin or some other goon on the doorstep when I woke up to a thump, but it was just the *Inquirer* on that chilly morning. Even so, I was sure we hadn't heard the last of Barnaby, which was okay because he for damn sure hadn't heard the last of us.

"Send Bishop my love." Rollie plopped the bag of cash on the kitchen table, forcing me to grab my mug of coffee.

"You could send it yourself, but he gets weird about surprises at meetings."

"You could have stopped at 'gets weird'. He was already awake, I take it?"

"I think I woke him up, but it's funny how chipper people can be when you have wads of dough for them."

"I gotta do the gutters today. You going to be around to help?"

"That's my cue to make something up. But yeah, I do have somewhere to be after I meet with Bishop. Be good to get this out of our hands. Can you wait until this afternoon?"

"Hey, if you're too busy," Rollie started.

"Will you let me go up the ladder?"

"You have a bad knee and weigh more than the Blue Bomber. Any other dumb questions?"

"Yeah, why doesn't a retired guy in his seventies hire somebody instead of climbing the walls like a kid in boot camp?"

"Ladders are cake, try it with a full ruck and a rifle on your back."

"Just wait for me." I wanted to avoid anything that could place him at risk, though he'd only get mad if I brought that up.

* * *

MEDIA, PA

Bishop had insisted that I use a burner phone and now that I'd chucked another cheap phone in the trash, I was off to meet him. Did they sell these things by the crate?

This time he had me meet him in the parking lot of a community swimming pool, closed this time of year. He got out of his car carrying a briefcase identical to the one on the seat next to me.

He got in my truck and tossed his case on top of mine. "Let's roll."

"Good morning to you, too. Where are we going?" I put the truck into drive and eased onto the quite residential street.

"Doesn't matter. I just don't want to sit there and have the neighbors think we're on a date."

I tapped Bishop's case. "More? How many of these will make us even?"

"Depends. How'd you do?"

"Over sixty. And they took all of it." It was a ton of cash to me, but I had no idea if that was enough.

"Okay for openers." Bishop cracked a smile. "Kidding. I knew I was right to go this route. Nice job, your end is in the case. Six blanks, just like VP requested."

"So, we're good?"

"For this? Yeah. But I'd like to move some more down the road and if we're even-up on favors, you can take a cash cut. Ten percent, same as Ryan got."

"That much? You're joking," I said. Six grand to chat up some of Ryan's old pals? Not bad. Then again, damned costly if I got busted.

"It's still worth it. But between you and me, I prefer the favors."

"How many of those baubles do you have lying around?"

"None of your fucking business," he snapped. "Kyle, don't ask people shit like that. It makes you sound like a rube. Or a rookie cop with a short life expectancy."

Adrenaline, half anger and half embarrassment, pulsed through me. "I *am* a rube and I didn't want to do this crap in the first place."

"There wasn't a gun at your head this time and wouldn't be the next. With Ryan gone we all have to make adjustments."

"I wish I never worked with him in the first place."

"Hey, I wish my gut wasn't so big that I can't see my cock when I take a leak. What's your point?"

"This all feels like it could spin out of control any second." I felt like I was just babbling.

"Isn't that half the fun? Besides, why are you complaining? You wanted to fix Barnaby's wagon and be the knight in tarnished armor for your girl, and now you can."

"I guess you're right. It's just I didn't seek this as a lifestyle. Ryan did. I just want to be a truck driver."

"Suuure. Who has to go all the way to the Sand Box to play dodge 'em with terrorists and wishes he could beat the shit out of scammers without consequences."

"Gee Dad, when you put it like that, what's a few more felonies?"

"That's the spirit," Bishop said. "Take me back to the car, I've got a mattress that needs stuffing."

* * *

PHILADELPHIA PORT

While it felt great to get that cash off my hands, I still had those driver's license blanks to get to VP. At least they were a lot less conspicuous. I'd catch up with her soon enough. She hadn't seemed in too big of a hurry and now was a good time to check in with my real job.

Delivergistics had offices here and in Virginia Beach. The mercenary stuff, especially the weapons and such, were stored south, but up here we housed more of the trucks and other equipment. My boss Cliff managed logistics for the company and the local office was down at the port where he could juggle assets and stick them on a train south if necessary. The cargo ships came practically to the door.

I pulled to the guarded gate and flashed my ID to the guard. "Here to see Cliff." He gave me a nod and went back to checking his phone. Things looked quiet.

I parked and noticed a few trucks being moved. Not nearly enough for me to get called in. This was union work. They only looked the other way when we were too busy for them to staff it. How much they paid them off was well above my paygrade.

Inside the converted tin-roofed repair building I said hello to a few people I knew slightly. Being one of the overseas workers meant most of my time was spent in country or at home. These folks were the faces behind the paperwork.

Today, they all looked like they'd just come back from a funeral.

Cliff's door at the end of the hall was open and I saw him sitting at his desk with a couple manifest sheets, comparing lists.

His thinning hair looked several shades grayer than just a few months ago. His face was drawn like he'd lost some weight. I knocked on the doorframe and he nearly jumped out of his chair.

"Christ, Kyle, you trying to give me a heart attack?" He pointed to an empty chair in from of his desk.

"I was in the area and thought I'd bug you in person this time."

"Good to see you. Wish it was under better conditions." Before I could settle into the chair, Cliff pointed behind me. "Get the door?"

"Sure." I stepped over and closed it.

"How's the knee?"

"Fine. Itching to work a clutch, you know?"

"You and every other driver. I wish I had better news."

"Do you have any? That you can share? I can keep a secret."

He gave a thin smile. "Most of it won't be secret long. The papers have a few details wrong, but the gist of the whole investigation is heading us into a ditch." He took off his glasses and cleaned them with his shirt.

"The papers make it sound like we're a goons-for-hire mercenary gang run amok," I said.

"The longer this goes on, the more it looks like they have a point, at least about one group of the operations."

"Last I heard it was still allegations."

"You didn't hear it from me, but it seems like they are zeroing in on a few individuals with a history of this."

"You're not just talking about the Market Square Massacre, are you?"

Cliff shook his head. "Once that story broke many more allegations popped up. Some were nothing." He paused.

"But others?"

"They're still gathering whatever hard evidence they can find— which is not much—but it doesn't look good, Kyle."

"Shit. We've all read about how one of our security squads went berserk while on convoy. I know it can't be like what they say, that they opened fire on a crowd for no reason, but that doesn't make it a good shoot either. What other stuff have you heard?"

"Enough that it looks like someone on our side popped off without justification and the rest of it went down fast," he said. "Too many bodies for anyone to ignore and the Iraqi government is demanding some scalps."

"So, our guys get thrown under the bus?"

"Like I said, this incident opened up other fresh investigations, and I have to say there may be a pattern."

"You think we slaughter locals for the hell of it?"

"I never said that," Cliff said. "You may not work in the security division, but you know better than I how rough it can get out there. And I back our guys unless there's an ironclad reason to doubt them." He dropped his gaze. "Not a word," he whispered.

"What?"

"The more they looked, the more they found, but not with most teams. One group had almost ten times the fatal incidents. I hear that was because they always volunteered for the hairiest missions."

"Spear-tip Company?"

"The press will love that one. Amazing that nickname hasn't leaked yet. It will soon. Yeah. And the reports explain a lot of what happened and stress that the men in Spear-tip Company are very good at shooting back."

"But—"

"But marksmanship alone doesn't explain everything. You never heard this here, but I understand they discovered several cases where the victims never fired their weapons."

"How'd they know?"

"Fired AKs at the scene, only once they looked for them, no fingerprints. Nearby, a kid found a buried stash of rifles. Same number as the victims, and their fingerprints on the stocks. Unfired. As if the other guns had been planted on the corpses."

"Holy shit." I thought about it. "But isn't that good? They have the guys they suspect and that's not the whole company. *We* sure as hell had nothing to do with it."

"Nobody is looking to throw us in jail, but if the case keeps building like this the company is going to be crushed."

"Why aren't the killers arrested and then they pay the price?"

"They are building the case, but the local prosecutors will pounce on a chance to get Delivergistics booted out of the country. Sued into oblivion too, if they can."

"When I came in here, I was looking for a quick yes or no about work picking up," I said. "You know how to cheer a guy up."

"I'm in the same boat. Maybe this looks worse than it is. They'll get the bad actors and the show will go on," he said. "If this goes in the shitter, we'll need drivers over there and back here to offload the gear and move it. Maybe to an auction block."

"Not the kind of overtime I was hoping for, boss," I said.

"You and me both. Look on the bright side."

"There is one?"

"Maybe the hard asses will confess and take all the heat for themselves."

I inhaled and puffed out my cheeks to show Cliff I'd be holding my breath for that.

CHAPTER 20

FISHTOWN, RYAN'S HOUSE: TWO DAYS LATER.

Still no work calls from Cliff and I was almost ready to check with Bishop to see if he had any trinkets, just to break the monotony. Rollie made me feel like a teenager by suggesting that I could help him with chores around the house if I was bored. Of course I pitched in, but I was itching for some movement, if only to meet with VP and get those driver's license blanks out of my hands. But she'd stalled, told me to wait until she'd earned her pay.

I got the sense she didn't like going out in public more than necessary. She also didn't like talking on the phone, which made life difficult. I was accumulating a stash of burner phones and it was a pain in the ass keeping track of all the damn numbers.

She finally called me back and I picked the squawking phone from the row of bland flip-tops. "Where have you been?"

"The Bahamas, working on my tan."

"Hilarious. Are you ready to meet up or what?"

"What. Definitely what. Are you driving right now?"

"Nope, I'm home. What's going on?"

Her voice sounded strained and tense. "It looks like our guy isn't taking things lying down," she said.

"I hadn't heard from him since he confronted me at Kelly's, so I figured he must be up to something."

"Yup. He changed all his passwords, but I had that covered. My bug sent the new ones to me. He tried to delete the records of all the bogus clients, but I already got those."

"Are you getting anything new?"

"Hard to say. He's really cryptic online. He always was, it looks like, but he has moved some money around. I'd say he's spooked."

"What did he say?"

"It was more what he didn't say. He reached out to some contacts and only asked them to call. Otherwise most of the old activity is shutting down."

"Any ideas on what that could mean?"

"My guess is he might be rebuilding a new system, one I can't see, and since he still has this one, he's trying to plant a tracer to catch me. I also think he might be looking to reach out to some muscle."

"Be careful." The last thing I wanted was to bring heat on her directly.

"Same to you. He knows you. I play with some of the best corporate cyber security teams just for practice. I'll see him coming if he tries to back-trace me."

"I think we have what we need already," I said. "You can bail on the hack if you want."

"Yeah, we have plenty to get him in hot water. I have all the contact information and the stuff from the doctor, who so far is clueless to his hack. I've got everything ready for a dead drop remailer to the media and any authorities you want. The insurance company would also probably be interested. Hard copies and electronic versions all covered with their IP addresses."

"Can you get me a copy and hold off on dropping the bomb until I try something?"

"Sure, why?"

"I may have a way to keep Sandy out of it and avoid official entanglements that might have authorities asking too many questions."

"Do you mean about where she got this info?" she asked.

"Something like that."

"Don't worry about me. I'm expert at staying out of sight." She sounded confident.

"I'm sure," I hoped I hadn't insulted her.

"One thing," she said.

"Shoot."

"Don't wait too long. This info is a weapon, but the more Barnaby pokes around you and your, um, life, the harder it will be to hit him without getting caught up in the blast."

She made a good point. If I wanted mutual destruction all I had to do was go back to plan "A" for Ass-kicking. "Fair enough. Give me a day and I'll either talk to you or if not, turn the key and launch all missiles."

"With pleasure." She sounded like she was about to hang up.

"Wait, how do I get your payment to you?"

"With some goon on your tail? You don't. Later. I know where you live." This time she did hang up.

* * *

I reached Sandy at home. She sounded a little surprised to hear from me. I called sometimes, but usually I'd work in my small talk during physical therapy sessions.

"What's up?"

"This is going to sound strange, but is there any way you can call out sick for maybe a week?"

"You're right, it does, especially since you know I'm a sole practitioner. Unless you have tickets to Paris?" She sounded like she was smiling.

"If I did, would you take the week?"

"What's really going on?" Not smiling.

"Your situation with Barnaby."

"What did you do?"

I wanted to deny, but that wouldn't be fair and was no way to build in any future relationship.

"I did some digging, and found out he's not what he seems."

"What is he?"

"He's every bit the scammer you found out, but he's also a rich slumlord with a mansion and apparently another life under his real name of Mason Oliver."

"Sounds like more than a little digging. How do you know this?"

"It's a long story, but remember my friend Ryan, the guy from the neighborhood I work with over in Iraq?"

"Charming, too slick, that one?"

"That's him. He had a lot of side hustles, lots of contacts, and he left town leaving me to help him tie up some loose ends. He forgot to tell me, but I had to help him anyway."

"Why and what's that got to do with me?" The tension in her voice elevated the pitch.

"I'm going along because some innocent people would get hurt if Ryan didn't keep his promises. That's not important right now. What matters is that he put me in touch with some people who were able to do the kind of digging I never could."

"You don't need to do any of this."

"Well, I did. I also checked this guy's properties myself, and you should see the way these families were living. They can't complain or they might lose where they live or even get deported. See? He's got them boxed in, like he's got you."

"What are you going to do? Call in a favor and get him beat up?"

"Of course not." I didn't add that I'd enjoy doing that one myself. "My contact got evidence that, used properly, will solve your problem for good."

"If that means getting him busted, then your solution will get me swept up in the crowd. Or had you forgotten?" Now anger lowered her tone.

"Of course not, and if my plan works that won't happen. But he may feel cornered for a time and I don't want him to, um, lash out."

"Yeah? And you expect me to just hide? Well, if you really have all that evidence and want to help me, just give it to me and I'll turn it in and make a deal. Maybe they'll take it easy on a first offender."

I'd been afraid of that, and as much as I admired her courage, I still didn't know what this guy was capable of doing in a pinch.

"Please don't do that. I'll make him understand this wasn't your idea and whatever happens to him is on him, not because of you."

"Kyle, don't be stupid. He won't believe it anyway. The way you talk, he already knows something is up,"

"I'm sorry. You're right, and I just did to you what Ryan has been doing to me."

I figured this would be the part where she hung up on me. There was a long pause and I almost thought that she had.

"You said you had a plan. Tell me everything."

So I did.

CHAPTER 21

FISHTOWN, ROLLIE'S PLACE: THE NEXT DAY

I helped Rollie clean up after breakfast. It took longer because I kept going to the front of the narrow house to peer out the front window. The cramped street was lined with cars I recognized belonging to neighbors.

Parking in the city was always a bitch, but at times like this it was helpful, as it made stakeouts a pain in the ass for outsiders.

"Remind me not to start any long-winded war stories," Rollie said as I walked back into the kitchen. "You're jumpier than usual."

"Okay out back?" I asked, not for the first time. I'd relayed that VP had warned me that Barnaby might be looking to sic some hired muscle on us, but he didn't seem spooked by it.

"No. Last night the wind blew more hemlock leaves from the Andersons'. I swear I'm going on a stealth mission of my own to cut that fucking thing down."

"I'll get them later and put the bag on their doorstep," I joked.

"Nah, we'll toss it out of the Blue Bomber into Barnaby's pool." Rollie chuckled. "How long do I have to look over my shoulder this time? I'm old, you know, and my neck gets stiff."

"VP should be sending her e-mails out to her media contacts soon. Something tells me Barnaby is going to be working this weekend."

"Think that'll be enough to call off the dogs?"

"He wanted escalation, he got it," I said. "I could have tried a shot across the bow by showing him a little of what we have."

"Warning shots are for dead men or POWs," Rollie said. "That shitbird doesn't seem like the type to take hints. Tip your hand and he'll figure a way to wriggle out."

"You're right. Better to be subtle as a two-by-four."

Thump!

The sound came from the basement.

"What was that?" Rollie asked.

"You doing laundry?" The old machine had its moods.

"Nope." Rollie opened a cupboard and reached high. When he turned around, he had his old slab-sided .45. He pulled back the slide and confirmed the gun was loaded, then crept to the door leading to the cramped basement.

I killed the kitchen light and followed close behind while Rollie opened the door slowly and listened.

Nothing at first, then a soft shuffling sound.

Rollie moved faster than I expected and in a blink the old guy was down the stairs and pointing the weapon in a solid two-handed grip. "I see you back there. Hands right now, asshole!" His voice would have done a drill instructor proud.

"Don't shoot," said a muffled voice.

"I said hands," Rollie boomed as I tried to hurry down the stairs without wrecking my knee. "Ah, shit."

I got to the bottom and saw Rollie appear to relax some. At the other end of the room, wedged between the wall and the washer, was Tom, looking anything but serene.

Cool air blew in from the tiny cellar window that was still open. One pane had been carefully removed. Tom must have pried some lattice free and crawled under the back deck to reach the window.

"Son, just what the fuck do you think you're doing?"

"I'm back."

"Did you see a 'no dwarves' sign out front? That door works."

"No time for jokes, mate. We need to talk. All of us."

Rollie flicked the safety on the pistol and shoved the gun in his waistband. "Upstairs. We'll talk all right, and then you're going to fix my damn window."

* * *

Tom peered out at the street in front of the house like he'd caught my paranoid bug.

"Sit down," I said.

"Have you seen anyone watching?"

"Why would you think we might be watched?" Rollie and I shared a look. "And what's with the cat burglar entrance?"

"Sorry, I didn't mean to spook you," Tom said to Rollie. "What have you seen?"

"Nothing yet. We think a private eye is scoping us, but how would you know about that?"

"I don't. The merch is on the way," Tom said.

"Okay, but weren't you going to call us first?"

"No chance. I had to sneak out of Iraq and land far away from Philly." Tom rubbed the back of his neck.

"Back up. You said the stuff for Mr. Beautiful is on the way?"

"Yes. But things are a little more complicated."

"Here we go," Rollie said.

"Hold on," I said to Tom. "Let me save you some time. Those are *your* complications, not mine. We've got more than enough on our plate. It sounds like you've been through a lot and I think you deserve all the reward."

"No, you don't—"

"Hush. I've thought about it and whatever my end was, don't even worry about it. And hang on to Ryan's. If you're ready, I'll line up the contacts and make sure they'll work with you. But that's as far as I'm going."

"Mate, I'd love to indulge you, but you haven't got a choice." Tom pointed to Rollie. "Neither have you, and for that I am truly sorry."

"How's that?" Rollie said.

"When I returned to Iraq, I got word that our plans had leaked to some people who decided to poach the stones."

I felt a sinking in my gut. "Who?"

"Grist and Mauser."

"You've got to be shitting me." Now I felt like I was going to puke.

"Friends of yours?" Rollie said.

"Definitely not," I said. "They're the security contractors who are the focus of the investigations that may take down the company. Almost as sneaky as they are brutal. I know them by reputation and because they took point for some of our hairiest convoy runs. Grist is the ranking officer, ex-intel, tough and mean. Mauser is a brick wall of a guy, just as tough and downright cruel. A true predator."

"It's more than that," Tom said. "Ryan and I worked with them on some side hustles. As you say, right good lads to have on your side when your back is against the wall," he added.

"I wasn't part of any of that."

"No. And once Ryan and I saw just how rough they could be, we decided we didn't need that sort of heat and we stopped working with them. There were enough hustles to go around and we stayed out of each other's way."

Tom continued. "Not long after we stopped partnering, we met Mr. Beautiful and began to gain his trust."

"If they never knew about it, what changed?" I asked. "I know Ryan could keep a secret."

"I don't appreciate the insinuation that I couldn't. You know who we're talking about. The investigations are like a vise, and slowly but surely they are closing in on those two and their men. They're desperate and it appears they want to run for it, but first they've been collecting debts and favors and not taking no for an answer."

"I'm not going to like where this goes, will I?"

"No mate, you're not," Tom said. "One of the men I was going to use to get me into Tikrit got squeezed and shared what he knew. Not the whole plan, we never told anyone everything, but enough to get Grist's attention." Tom looked at Rollie. "Grist was a captain in Army Intelligence and he has a network of informants that put our own to shame."

"How much did he learn?" Rollie asked.

"Grist was smart enough to figure out we were going to move something valuable and relatively small. He didn't know who the client was, but he got his hands on the courier I was going to use this week to retrieve the package in Tikrit."

"What happened?" I said.

Tom didn't answer right away. Rollie left the room and brought him some water.

Tom's hands shook so hard he almost spilled the drink before he could gulp it down. "About a day before the move I received some hints to watch out. It was clear that my contacts knew more but were too terrified to do anything but hint."

"What did they tell you?"

"It was bits and pieces that I had to put together, but I figured out that we might get hit. I wasn't sure when or where. Just to be on the safe side, I sent a message to Mr. Beautiful's people to relocate the stones, but I sent the courier to the original spot in Tikrit."

"What was the guy picking up?" Rollie asked.

"A bag of marbles in a tamper-proof case."

"Why?" I asked.

"While the courier was away, I slipped out of the Green Zone and into another area, not quite as safe as the spot in Tikrit where I sent the courier. Or so I thought," Tom said. "I went to an area north of Tikrit called Al Mu'taridah that Mr. Beautiful and his crew picked. It was easy to find, but better, I could be sure I wasn't followed."

"What happened to the first courier?" Rollie said.

"I'm getting to that," Tom said. "I decided to play it safe and send another contact to meet with the first courier for the exchange. Originally I was supposed to be the one at the meeting."

"You changed your, mind? Why?" Rollie pressed.

"Call it instinct."

We all knew about that.

Tom continued. "Anyway, in the meantime I managed to bring the real package to the Delivergistics supply depot where I met my people."

"And the decoy meetup?" Rollie was hooked now.

Tom's shoulders sagged. "I had the pickup man on my mobile. He reached the location expecting to meet the first courier carrying the bag of marbles. Instead he only saw a bag sitting at the meet spot. From his description, it was much larger than I expected and I tried to caution him, but he opened it straight away."

"IED?" I always jumped at the sight of any unexpected packages over there.

"No. The first courier's head. My man lifted it out and said marbles spilled out of the mouth."

"Jeez," Rollie said.

Tom looked into space while he spoke. "Then I heard a commotion I thought must be bystanders reacting to a bloke's noggin on display and spitting glassies."

"Not?" I said.

"Shouting, angry voices in broken Arabic and the phone being batted about," Tom said. "I called out the man's name, but knew it was over the instant I heard who'd torn the phone away from him."

"Grist?"

Tom shook his head. "Mauser. Sounded like he expected me. 'Tommie boy,' he said, 'We need to talk.'" Tom tried to take a sip of water before he realized the glass was empty. "My throat went dry and I didn't think I'd be able to answer, but I heard my voice say that we had nothing to talk about."

Tom accepted a refill from Rollie and took a long sip. "He disagreed," he went on, "and made it clear it was a one-time offer to beg for mercy." He drained the glass.

"You want something stronger, son?" Rollie said.

"I don't drink and better get through this." Tom smiled, but it never touched his eyes. His thoughts were still back in Iraq. "I asked Mauser if that would be my head next if I said no. He said, 'If you don't give it up, it'll be your own balls going into your mouth. Where do you want to meet and hand it over?'"

Beads of sweat formed on Tom's forehead and I hurried to the kitchen to refill his water. I could've used the scotch Rollie had offered, but returned to let Tom finish his story.

"You told them something to get out of there," I said.

"I named some intersection outside the Green Zone to buy some time, but I'm sure they didn't believe me." Tom took the water and gulped some down. "At least the stones were in place and I didn't need to return to the motor pool. My men there already knew how to hide them."

"So, you packed up and hightailed it?" Rollie asked.

"Not a chance. I left with the clothes on my back until I could reach one of my bug-out kits."

"No shit?" I said. "Boy scouts have nothing on you." I thought about it. "Good thing. I bet they or one of their people were watching your room as soon as you hung up."

"They were. Once I got clear and was organizing to slip out of the country, I called one of my insiders who confirmed it. Over the next few days, I got the rest of the bad news."

My stomach did a slow barrel roll.

"My man told me that Grist and Mauser were leaning—and that's being kind—on some of our people about Ryan."

"What would they know about Ryan?" I felt confused.

"They know they can't reach him, which is common knowledge, but the problem is that they learned you are the American contact for business stateside, at least until Ryan comes back."

"But that's not true. I never—"

"Aren't you?" Tom asked. "From their perspective, what will your denial mean to them?"

"Fuck, Tom! These men are killers."

"But if they want those stones so bad and are so connected," Rollie said, "won't they learn where they are anyway? Why didn't they just grab them from the motor pool or wherever you put them?"

"You forget, the investigations are tightening for them. The stones were well hidden and they no longer have access to the area where they are secured. They would need days to search unless they knew exactly where to look."

"And you said the package is already enroute to the States," Rollie said.

Tom grimaced. "Yes, but it gets worse. Just after the package departed for the cargo ship, Grist and Mauser volunteered to self-deport back to the States while the investigations continued. Delivergistics was more than happy to get them out of the country."

"They're coming here?" I said.

"They're based in Virginia Beach with the rest of the military contractors, as you know." Tom looked like he might cry. "But I learned that they have had unauthorized access into the Delivergistics personnel files for years."

"Son of a bitch. So, they not only think I run Ryan's little empire, but they have my fucking address."

Tom pointed at Rollie. "Actually, *his* fucking address, mate. That's where they send your mail. And they likely have Rollie's name, as well, I expect."

"Ain't that some shit." Rollie shook his head. "These bozos aren't coming home on a container ship, are they?"

"No. The ship will arrive in a week. I'm told they are to fly back in two days. We have a little time, I think."

CHAPTER 22

ROLLIE'S PLACE

"Hang on," I said. "Time to do what, exactly?"

"To prepare for their arrival." Tom gave me his best "dumb question" look.

"We don't even know they are coming here."

Rollie joined in. "Aren't they in enough trouble already? Why ask for more, messing with an old man like me?"

"Because they are desperate. Right now, they are only suspected of a number of terrible crimes, but we know the charges have merit, based on our own experience. It's only a matter of time before they will be locked up."

"Sooner the better," Rollie said.

Tom shook his head. "It'll be too late for us, mate. Don't you see? The diamonds are their last big caper before they vanish. We have their retirement fund, savvy?"

It made sense. I took a deep breath. "I thought I was out before, Tommy old stick, but you are quite right. I've seen those two at work and I have no interest in being on the wrong end of either of them." My thoughts clarified as I spoke and I held up my hand to silence Tom's protest. "What's more, even if I was all in on this goofy crusade, I'm not about to have Rollie dragged in."

"You don't get it."

"Sorry, *you* don't. Rollie saved my life once. Getting him hurt or killed isn't my idea of how to thank him."

"Then you have to help me," Tom said.

"No offense, but you and Ryan cooked this fiasco up. Give me one good reason not to hand the damn things over to Grist if he and his psycho attack dog show up."

Tom's frown was deep enough to shut his eyes. "Why stop there? Why not turn the stones in to the police? Wash your hands of the whole bloody mess, yeah? Send those blokes to the station to collect."

"No need to invite an anal exam from the law," I said. "And if I have to pick who to piss off, respectfully, those guys scare me more than you do."

Tom smiled. "Good. They should. Now think it all the way through. If you give away the stones, what do you imagine Mr. Beautiful will think about that?"

"Fuck him," Rollie said. "Next time use Western Union."

"Neither of you know the man. We'd never have worked for a dedicated Jihadist, but he's hardly an innocent. Mr. Beautiful has more resources than this shipment alone and he was known in Iraq as a man willing to protect his interests." Tom pinned his gaze to me. "He knows who you are, and has been led to believe he can trust you. You want to think twice before tossing that in the rubbish bin."

"And if I decide to take my chances?" I sounded tough, but I already knew that living life looking over my shoulder got old fast.

Tom continued. "You *do* know Grist and Mauser. After what they did to my courier," Tom glanced up at the ceiling, then back to me, "what do you think they might do to you or him to gain your cooperation, or to ensure your silence?"

An obvious question that sent a chill through the room all the same.

"So we're fucked either way?" Rollie said. "And I thought it was going to be a boring year."

"There's a third possibility," Tom said. "We win."

"I thought that would piss them off," I said.

"Oh, most certainly. However, if the prize is no longer available and if we deliver for our client, they may decide there is no point in retribution. We might just become less important than their efforts to stay ahead of the authorities."

"That's a big if," Rollie said.

"I truly regret you became involved through no fault of you own," Tom said, "but if we're to gain purchase on even this reed of hope it will take all of our combined skill."

"No need to flatter," Rollie said. "You had me at 'There's no choice, sorry about that, guv'nor.'"

Rollie was getting a gleam in his eye. Not good. I wanted to figure a way to keep him far from the action if there was going to be any. Tom, it appeared, had other thoughts.

I turned to Tom. "Let's assume for now that they are coming. What do you see as their move?"

"When we planned this out, Ryan and I saw the Delivergistics facility as a natural and convenient entry to the country. We hadn't expected many problems from that point forward and you see how that's worked out, but I think our venue can play in our favor."

I'd been thinking the opposite. "If Grist knows the package is coming to Philadelphia, to our base here, doesn't that help them?"

"Yes and no. It does tell them where to begin, but the same problems they faced in Iraq apply here. They are known to the corporate security here and won't be permitted on the facility."

Rollie leaned forward in his seat. "From what you've said already, these two don't sound like the permission types."

"No. But they still don't know exactly where to look, the shipment coming over is large. It wouldn't be possible to search it all in secret."

"Riiiight. And why go to all that trouble if you can drop in on the one of the planners who can lead you right to it?" I fought the urge to look out the window again.

Tom nodded. "Exactly. That's why I think their first move when they get up here is to come to this house, looking for you or anyone who knows you."

"Nothing pisses me off more than getting run off my own land," Rollie said.

"Rollie," I said, "this is no time to go all Alamo on me. These guys are pros. I doubt they'll just knock on the front door."

He stood. "I didn't say we'd be here when they arrive, just that it pisses me off. C'mon kid, pack a lunch, we're bugging out."

* * *

FISHTOWN, SCORPIO PHOTOGRAPHY STUDIOS:
SEVERAL HOURS LATER

I shouldered my bug-out bag, which consisted of little more than dumping my laundry basket into a borrowed duffel bag along with everything related to Ryan's list and a shaving kit. I'd need to pick up a new toothbrush, but if those assholes searched the place maybe they'd see mine in the third-floor bathroom at Rollie's place and think we were coming back.

I stared up at the stone walls of the old church. Years ago, it had been sold and converted into a photography studio owned by one of Rollie's old friends. Not all that long ago the tower roof had served as a perch for an old sniper to ply his trade, watching over me while I was on a rooftop a couple hundred yards away saving Beth's life the night Ryan died. Another tale I couldn't discuss in public.

"Drop your bag anywhere, kid," Rollie said. "I need help with this footlocker." He stood at the side door. Next to the church the property had a small fenced-in parking area. We'd taken the Blue Bomber and left my truck at Rollie's place. If Grist was into the employee files, he likely knew what I drove.

I stepped inside and adjusted to the classic architecture and the scent of darkroom chemicals in place of candle wax and incense. In one corner, tarps and background screens made up the portrait area. "Sal still does his pictures old school?"

"He does them every school. The digital stuff is upstairs and you should see when he goes super-vintage and takes shots with real flash powder. Crazy bastard keeps trying to dress me like I'm in some damn western." Rollie lifted one end of the footlocker.

"That I'd like to see." I picked up the other end. "Damn, Rollie you fill this with lead bricks?" He just looked at me and I realized it was a dumb question. "Why'd you need to pack all your rounds?"

"This is nothing. But it ought to be enough."

"I wish I could promise it was too many," I said. "How long did Sal say we could stay?"

"No worries there. He's gone for a month on a European tour, unless he comes home early with some models for a private shoot."

"This is damn generous of him."

"We'll keep his fridge and bar stocked. You have to help patch any bullet holes."

"Not funny."

"I was serious." He backed his way to what I was thrilled to see was an elevator that had been added. Framed photos of elaborate foods covered the boxy exterior of the structure all the way to the ceiling. "I meant it when I said I hate bugging out in the first place. And I can't even get mad at you for starting this shit."

He put his end down inside the wood-paneled elevator car and we rode it up two floors, where it opened into what must have been the administrative building. Now it looked more like a luxury loft. A huge picture window with sliding curtains overlooked the former chapel level.

"Looks like a corporate box at a stadium," I said.

"Yeah. Old Sal broke through in a big way. I'll show you the gallery and shop downstairs later."

"Not to look a gift church in the mouth, but are you sure it's a good idea to have a public access area while we are hiding?"

"Don't sweat it kid. The gallery will stay closed until he gets back. I don't see how your guys will make the connection, but even if they cruise by and want to ask questions, the place will be quiet as a tomb."

"Nice choice of words." But that reminded me. "Let's move it on the unpacking. We have to warn off friends or anyone that might come by the place. If Grist stakes it out, they might be the ones getting grilled."

"Good point."

I left Rollie to unpack his arsenal but hoped like hell it wouldn't come to us needing it. Grist and Mauser were a two-man wrecking crew. I knew which end of a gun to point, but I didn't do much shooting and was never all that good. Not that I wouldn't try, if necessary. Rollie, on the other hand, joked about his age, but I saw firsthand that he could drill anything with his rifle, as long as he got the chance to aim.

I didn't think Grist could know about Rollie's background, so there was that, but we were going to focus on avoiding them if at all possible. A two-way running gunfight seemed like a recipe for suicide.

At least Sandy wasn't part of this mess, but that made me think of who was most at risk to get caught up.

If these goobers even show up. Maybe Tom was wrong.

I tried to believe that, but the smell of paint and darkroom chemicals snapped me back to reality. I dug out a burner phone and thought it was dead when I couldn't get a signal. It showed a couple bars when I stood near an exterior window.

VP picked up right away. "Yo, you psychic or something?"

"Something, I guess. What did I almost miss?"

"Hello? I'm in the missile silo and about to turn the key. Every file I have on that skunk will be pinging the inboxes of the press and after that the DA's office. Right at the top I have a promise for every paper and station in town to get the same thing in one day." She sounded like a kid on Christmas morning.

"I hadn't forgotten." Except I had a few other developments vying for attention in my addled brain.

"I'd begun to wonder, but you only said to wait a day," she said. "I'm bouncing the address all over. He'll know you had something to do with it, but good luck proving anything."

"Yeah." My mind began to race. "Hey, can you hold off on the whole info-missile thing one more day?"

"Only if you tell me why," she said. "Remember what I said about info going stale. Our boy is sure to be trying to cover his tracks."

"If you send that, don't you think Barnaby will come running to me?"

"Like the proverbial scalded cat, but I told you—"

"I know. I'm not doubting that you covered our asses. I just can't have him coming around Rollie's place." I thought quickly. "You either. Not for anything. That goes double for Ryan's place."

"Wait, what?" Her confusion poured out of the phone.

"One of Ryan's adventures has just grenaded and I'm holding the bag." I gave her the minimum essential details.

"These guys scare you that bad?" VP said. "You never mentioned what's in the package. Enough for these guys to get that rough?"

"They do and it is." I wasn't embarrassed to admit it. "They're not shy about hurting anyone they need to if it will get them what they want. Including Barnaby, you, Rollie. Anyone."

"Shit. Okay, I'm in."

"In what? Did you miss the part about them being killers? And our client, if that's even the right word for it, will blame me if anything goes wrong, so I don't even get to choose the coward's way out."

"So, you need help."

"This isn't fun and games with thermostats." I told her what happened to Tom's now headless courier. "And I've seen the aftermath of a couple of their firefights. More like slaughters, a big reason they are in trouble and why they are all the more desperate."

"Desperate people make mistakes. And I'm not crazy. I don't want to meet these characters, but you can't be everywhere at once."

"Meaning?"

"Meaning I can help you keep an eye out for them so you guys have a chance to see them coming."

I knew if they made a move that we didn't anticipate, it might be our last mistake. "What kind of help?"

"I'm thinking out loud here, but if you're worried about them staking out where you live, how about some cameras? We can hook them up discreetly and I can let you know if they show up. Maybe you guys are all worried for nothing."

"I'd love for that to be true, but ..." She'd given me an idea. "You'd be able to watch those cameras from home?"

"Sure, wherever, really. And I could call you as soon as something happened. I could record the surveillance as well and review the footage so I could get a few winks of beauty sleep."

"So, no way they'd know where you are? Can you only monitor your own cameras?"

"Are you thinking traffic cameras? I have something else to follow a moving target, but I'd have to be a lot closer."

Interesting, but not where I was going. "I was thinking more like the security cameras at the Delivergistics site in Philly. There's a whole network of them. If Grist and Mauser can't find us, their next best move is to head over there."

"Nice! Yeah, if I can get into the system, I can hack the cameras. I have a bunch of extra monitors. This'll be sweet."

"I'll see what I can do to give you a head start into the security system at Delivergistics." I just remembered. "But you'll have to really cover your tracks. These guys aren't just knuckle-draggers. They have an in to the personnel files and know my work schedule. I don't know the extent of their computer sophistication, so try not to run into them online either."

"This is where I'd usually act insulted, but considering what you already told me, thanks."

"Can you print me up enough info for me to prove to Barnaby that we have his balls in a vice?"

She gave an overdramatic sigh. "You're no fun anymore. I guess so, if you're sure you want to spoil the surprise."

"He'll be plenty surprised. I need him to believe me so he doesn't run into a buzz saw. Can you get me the cameras? Are they hard to set up?"

"Not if you know what you're doing. I'll take care of it."

"No way. You can't go near the place."

"Thanks, Dad. I have some techies who can do it and they love to play spook, so anyone watching for you guys won't have any idea what they're doing."

"I want to keep the circle tight, here—"

"*Now* I'm insulted," VP cut me off. "All I'll tell the techs is where the cameras need to go and to be discreet. I'm also adding a few so even they won't know what the real surveillance subject will be."

"That's not bad. You're on."

"Apology accepted. Get your meet set up with Barnaby, and I'll have a 420 courier drop off an envelope at the church. I'll address it to the studio and have 'Photos - Do Not Bend' on the envelope."

"420?"

"Stoner bicycle messengers. They're like chill Kamikaze, but they get it done. You'll have the stuff in a couple hours. The cameras will be up in a day or two. Is that cool?"

* * *

Scorpio Photography Studios: Two Hours Later

Sure enough, a young white guy with thick dreads of what may have once been dirty blonde hair but now was mostly just dirty showed up. Rollie signed for the thick cardboard envelope. I gave the guy a ten-dollar bill and got a "Thanks, Bro" in return.

"A punctual stoner. What's the world coming to?" Rollie chuckled as he handed me the envelope. "Here you go, kid. Hope it's enough to keep that asshole away from my casa."

"Maybe we'll catch a break."

"If we need to save up luck, let's spend it on the psychos who could kill us." Rollie locked the big wooden doors.

"Do you need me for anything else before I head out?"

Rollie waved me off. "Go in peace."

CHAPTER 23

FISHTOWN

I sat in my truck and waited. I didn't think it would be long, since one of the benefits of being a scammer like Dr. Park allowed for good control of one's hours.

At 6:15 p.m. he came out the door and I pulled right across the back of his Mercedes.

"Hey, I'm leaving! Move your truck." He sounded like I wasn't the first inconsiderate double-parker he'd seen in Philly.

I shut off the engine and hopped out with papers under my arm.

He took a step back and I thought he was going to bolt. Not good. He may have been older, but I no longer did speed without making my knee feel like it was on fire. "Hang on Doc, Barnaby sent me."

I wasn't in disguise, but I could see the confusion on Dr. Park's face. I must have looked familiar from our visit to his clinic the other day and his brain was trying to figure out why.

"He didn't want to use the phone, understand?" I gestured to the papers like that was supposed to mean something to him.

He stopped and looked at me again, caution and confusion battling it out in his expression. "Who are you?"

I glanced around before speaking and lowered my voice. "The referrals. He told me to get over here and warn you before they come."

"Who and what are you talking about?"

"Dr. Park, there's not much time. I think they tried to find Barnaby already, you know, over at *Mr. Oliver's* house." By now I was almost whispering and he had to step closer to hear me.

"You work for Barnaby?"

"Oh my God, yes! He didn't call ahead, obviously. That's not a good sign."

"What is this about?" I knew I had him or he would have run back to his building by now.

"Bayshore Insurance, they figured it out. Their rep had these on him." I handed over a list of the bogus clients and some copies of the claims filings.

"How did—"

"Do you know Franklin?" I wasn't sure if the name rang a bell, but it would sound good when he called Barnaby later. "It doesn't matter, he also works for him and I guess Barnaby panicked. Franklin knocked the guy cold and we took these off him."

"Knocked out?"

"I know, right? Digging the hole even deeper, but no going back now." I shifted on my feet like I was itching to get away myself.

"I didn't—"

"Me either. Look, I don't know what they are going to do with him and I don't want to know. But you can bet that's not the end of it. Bayshore is onto us and the cops can't be far behind."

"The police?"

"Here, see for yourself. They already made the connection between you two." I gave him the rest of the papers. It wouldn't take more than a glance for him to see that someone sure had all the info to bury them both.

Dr. Park looked like a trapped animal. "What does he want to do?"

I shrugged. "This is the end of the line for me. I think he wants you to get out of town. Maybe destroy your records first, but it's probably too late for that. I'm gone, and you best forget all about me. Last bit of advice, off the record." I had his undivided attention. "If you do stick around, Barnaby might think you decided to cut a deal. You might want to get one of those remote car-starters," I looked down the street and headed back to my truck.

As soon as I pulled out of the way, the doctor burned rubber on the way up the street.

* * *

Sandy called right in the middle of my short drive to Barnaby's office. "Hey, is he still there?" I asked.

"Yeah. He's yelling at someone on the phone. You found Dr. Park?"

"I think we stirred things up nicely. I'll be there in a minute. Did you lock your door?"

"And turned out the lights like I went home. Do you really think this will work?"

"We'll know soon." I turned onto their street.

* * *

FISHTOWN: BARNABY BONES CHIROPRACTORS

I pulled up and he opened his office door before I could even knock. Almost like he was expecting me.

"What have you done?"

I strolled in like I owned the place. "Yes, I'd love to come in for a drink."

He closed the door. "You take a lot of chances."

Mason Oliver glared at me. His face was brick-red, going on purple, and the smug demeanor had disappeared.

I tossed the second copy of his records at his feet. I didn't see a weapon on him, but I thought it would be wise to make sure he realized it wouldn't be a good idea to blow me away on the spot. "Says the guy whose empire is built on fraud."

He picked up the papers and shuffled through them, then glowered at me again. "What did you tell him?"

"Who?"

"Who do you think? Park! How did you get these?"

"I'd love to banter with you all night, but I have bigger problems than you." I took a seat in what was his waiting room. We had the place to ourselves. "This isn't a negotiation."

"No? What would you call it? Park just called and said that *I* sent you to him."

"I'd call it presenting you your terms of surrender, and considering I don't want a nickel from you, they are more than fair."

He laughed. "You don't want anything?"

"I didn't say that. You let me know there wasn't going to be a reasonable solution, so I went forward with an unreasonable one."

"What are you talking about?"

"You're out of business. Forever, at least around here. Whether or not you stay out of prison will be up to you."

"Is that a fact?" His face was still flushed, but I think his survival instincts were beginning to kick in. Good.

"It's all there. The clients Park sent you, complete with contact information. And the bills to Bayshore Insurance."

"So?"

"You have a better poker face than Dr. Park. He hit the roof, and by the end had the distinct impression that you were going to bump off the investigator and that he might be next. I expect he'll be difficult to reach in the near future, though he is probably considering a chat with the DA's office."

"And if they have no idea what he's talking about?" Barnaby gave a thin smile. "And what if he's right and the 'investigator' does disappear?"

"You think *I'm* the key? It's already arranged. Whether I live or die, this is going to the media, the DA and especially, how could I forget, all the stooges you bribed to file the claims in the first part. Are you prepared to mass-murder nearly fifty people just to avoid insurance fraud charges?"

"You wouldn't dare. They'd bring your girlfriend in too."

"I told her that, and can you believe it? She didn't care. She's willing to take the hit. And before you get any ideas that will make me get violent, she doesn't have any copies of anything. They are already at dead-drop sites."

He paused a long time trying to figure a way out.

"I almost forgot all the property you're neglecting," I said. "That's going to make for excellent television."

"What do you want, you bastard?"

"Same as what I told Park. You gone. You are out of the Pennsylvania business. Go quietly and you can save your money—well, most of it. And better still, you aren't a legal scalp that an ambitious DA could try to parlay into higher office."

"*Most* of it? So you do want money."

"Not for me. If you go quietly, you are going to repair all those broken-down systems in Strawberry Mansion."

"Like hell. Do you forget I know where you live, too, and your girlfriend?"

I held my temper. It wouldn't help to start bouncing him off the walls. This way was better. "That's what I thought." I took out a final sheet of paper. "My people found where you tucked the laundered profits under the mattress." I handed it over.

"What?" Barnaby scanned the paper that showed account numbers and balances across a half-dozen bank accounts. His face went pale when he saw the second sheet with the new banks, complete with all information where he'd transferred large sums as a precaution.

"If you decline my offer or try doing anything to myself or Sandy, that money is gone."

Barnaby shook his head. "Bullshit. You're just a truckdriver."

"I'm just as impressed as you are, but why don't you go online and check the current balances for yourself?"

He dove to the receptionist's computer and his fingers danced across the keyboard. One account after another, and by the time he was done his face looked closer to plum-colored.

"You stole it! I'll see you in prison with me. It'll be worth it. I'll have you shanked."

"Don't blow a gasket, champ. *I* didn't do anything. I'm just a truckdriver."

"You—"

I held up a finger. "Buuut, I could probably put in a good word to some people I know who could restore those ill-gotten gains, less the cost of capital repairs at Strawberry Mansion, of course."

"Who do you think you are, some kind of modern-day Robin Hood?"

* * *

I circled the block and saw right away that Barnaby had left, maybe forever. Whatever he did next would be as Mason Oliver, at least until he could cook up another bogus identity.

I went to the other doorway and tapped on it. I was glad to see that Sandy peeked out before opening it. She gave me a big hug and I stepped inside.

"It got quiet," she said. "What happened?"

"A ton. I certainly gave him good reason to leave both of us alone."

"So, what's the problem?"

"I also gave him good reason to strike back, and I can't say which way he'll go. He's smart, but he's also arrogant and I don't think he's used to push back."

She crossed her arms. "You're not going to tell me to go into hiding again, are you?"

I took a deep breath. The excitement of confronting Oliver had been a fine distraction, but changed nothing about the certain threat posed by Grist and Mauser. I took her hand, which she allowed. "Sandy, I'm sorry if my trying to help made things worse."

"It'll be okay."

"I hope so. I really do. I can't tell you what to do, but you need to hear some things about me and when I'm done you may never want to see me again." My heart was pounding in my chest but it felt great to have someone to talk to, even if it was for the last time.

"What are you saying?" She looked nervous.

"Oliver ... Barnaby, whatever, called me 'just a truckdriver.' It's not that simple. You understand?"

"You seem to have some, interesting acquaintances." I appreciated her gift for understatement.

"That's one way to put it. Most of them were Ryan's people, but I seem to have inherited this crazy network he built."

"What do you mean, inherited?"

No going back now. "Ryan isn't away, or hiding. He's dead. The world doesn't know it, but now you do."

"I don't understand."

"Nobody else can know this, but I trust you and need you to trust me. I'm going to tell you as much as I can without putting others in danger, including you. And me."

"You're scaring me." Her hand shook and she pulled it back.

"I'm scaring me, too. I wish I could say none of this was my fault, but that would be a lie. Ryan was planning on sharing his weird empire with me but got himself killed before he could let me in on it. That said, I joined him once on a simple deal that almost got me killed and caught him in the end."

"Who killed him?"

I shook my head. "It's better you don't know, but they play by rules that he broke. I was a small cog in the operation. Fast forward to today and he drops all these schemes in my lap along with the oddest assortment of characters who can help pull them off."

"Why not say no?"

"I wanted to do just that, but funny how one thing leads to another and before I knew it, I was in deeper than I realized. But along the way, I think I'm helping some people."

"Like me?" She was hard to read.

"Yeah. I'm sorry, but not for what happened to Barnaby."

"You better tell me what you did to him. All of it."

"That's fair. I'll share that and more, because you have to understand what I'm going to ask."

And I did. I told her about my lifelong friend Ryan's second, hidden life in which he built a shady but not thuggish empire. We worked together in Iraq. When my marriage was falling apart and I slugged my wife's new boyfriend, throwing my career onto the rocks along with everything else in my life, Ryan offered me a chance at a once-in-a-lifetime scam. It was victimless, he assured me, the "perfect crime"—which of course went completely sideways.

I told Sandy how the goons the scam double-crossed kidnapped my estranged wife Beth and used her to get me to help them find Ryan. At that point I'd have done anything to save her. To his credit, Ryan, with a lot of help from Rollie, Bishop and others, was able to figure out a risky way to get Beth back. By then we couldn't have returned all the money we'd scammed if we wanted. In the end Beth was safe, Ryan was dead, and the goons we'd initially worked with had broken some of their own group's rules and got themselves killed as well. Sandy's eyes widened when I showed her the long scars from the knife attack that almost killed me that night.

As for the current business, I told her about VP's hacking and the break-ins and all we learned about his business. I mentioned the guy at the liquor store and his sister with cancer and explained what I'd begun to learn about how the oddball underground economy of favors operated.

Then I told her how we'd hacked Oliver's accounts and drained them.

"You don't expect to be able to keep it, do you?" she asked.

"I don't want his money. Other than twisting his arm to do the right thing for his tenants, it's just leverage."

"How do you expect to stay out of prison?"

"Great question, except it turns out when you rip off crooks, they tend to avoid calling the authorities. And when the authorities are just as crooked, you can also use that."

"I suppose," she said. "But why keep getting involved?"

"An even better question. One thing leading to another is just an excuse. I'm not that blind. But now I get to the reason I am going to ask—even beg, if that's what it takes—that you go into hiding for a week, maybe even two."

"I thought I made it clear you don't get to tell me—"

I held up my hand. "I'm not. But I am praying you will change your mind."

And I explained the big deal Ryan stuck me with and how things that once were so simple had gone horribly awry. I pulled no punches when I shared what Tom had said about the headless courier and what Grist and Mauser were capable of doing to anyone in their way.

She'd gone pale by the time I was done. I guess that was progress.

"If these people are so dangerous, why are you sticking around?"

"I'm not."

"Sorry?"

"Not exactly. I'm underground, for all intents and purposes. Rollie and I are holed up for the duration and you won't see me again until it is all over."

"Where?"

"Can't say. You don't want to know. I've told you more than I should about everything else. But for your safety, the less you know about this, the better. These guys are animals."

I told her about VP monitoring Rollie's place. "Hopefully we did enough to keep Oliver away," I said. "Not that I expect him to appreciate my concern for his safety."

"He called you Robin Hood, huh?" Sandy leaned in and kissed me. "Two weeks. Come back safe and you have to help me build my client list back." She smiled. "Unless I decide you're crazy by then."

CHAPTER 24

FISHTOWN

It was already light out by the time I left Sandy's place. We'd talked through the night at her office and no sign of Oliver returning. I'd insisted on driving her home, but she declined my offer to help her pack. She didn't say where she would go to lay low and I didn't ask.

As I rolled through my neighborhood, avoiding Rollie's street by a couple blocks, I remembered that I shouldn't be using my truck at all from now on. With Grist and Mauser having access to personnel files and who knows what else in the company database, that likely included the vehicle info for my company parking pass. At least there'd be no mention of anyone named Sandy.

On the other hand, speed was important and there were plenty of old red trucks in this part of town. Mostly I didn't want to think that they were already here hunting for me.

But they would be soon.

I turned up Girard and felt my jaw clench when I approached the intersection where Cream of the Cup sat. Right in front of Milosh's shop paced a short man wearing a sandwich board ad for the place, complete with their stoned cow logo. Even before he turned around, I felt a sinking in my gut. I reached the curb just as he faced me.

"Beet, what are doing?"

He smiled at me. His puffy lips were starting to return to normal. "Hi, Kyle!"

The bruises on Beet's face were in greens and reds, but most importantly, all healing and nothing fresh. His trademark Spock T-shirt had bright white blotches on one shoulder.

"Why are you here?" I asked him.

Beet looked confused. "Working, just like you wanted. He said that's how you wanted it."

"Who?"

Beet jerked his head toward the shop. "You know. The boss." He lowered his voice. "He doesn't want me to say his name."

Crap.

"After I work off the debt, he said I could do other stuff for him."

"Like what?" The words jumped out of my mouth and I shut off the engine.

"Stuff. He said you'd know."

Anything I could imagine filled my face with hot blood. "Sure. Is he in yet?" I opened the driver's side door and it screeched on a hinge I kept forgetting to oil.

Beet rummaged through his pockets. "No, but he said to give this to you."

I took the crumpled paper and opened it. The handwriting inside was fine cursive so neat it looked like a calligrapher had taken dictation.

> *Idle hands are the Devil's workshop, wouldn't you agree? He's working out well and I'm certain he'll be up for promotion in no time. You'll have to step up if you want to take his place. Nothing wrong with a little healthy competition, is there?*

It wasn't signed, but I'd read the whole thing in Milosh's accent all the same. His English was way better than he let on in person. But Beet himself was the real message.

"Beet, I'm glad you're able to help out like this, but I need you to listen carefully."

"Dad would be proud. I'm taking care of my business." He pointed to the white spots on his shirt. "See? I got the bloodstains out by myself. Bleach to the rescue."

"That's great. But listen. You can't come around Ryan's house or where I stay either for a little while."

"Okay, but why?"

"I have to go out of town for a little while and …" I knew that wasn't enough, I'd only made him curious. "There have been some mean guys hanging around and I wouldn't want you to run into them without me there." Close enough.

Beet nodded. "All right. But Milo ... I mean, the boss could probably help with that."

"No. Promise me until I get back that you won't do any different work besides this. Wait if he asks you to do any other jobs, understand?"

"Nope." Beet stared at me. I fought the urge to yell. Then he grinned. "But I promise."

"I'll be back soon. Tell Milosh I'm coming back to work it all out. I got his message. Use those words."

Beet held up his hand and gave me Spock's trademark split-fingered Vulcan salute.

* * *

SCORPIO PHOTOGRAPHY STUDIOS

I spent the rest of the day dropping in on anyone I knew well enough that they might conceivably be moved to stop by Rollie's place. Most had no idea there might be danger and I didn't want to make things worse, so made up excuses. By the time I got back it was dark and the streetlights cast pools of light. I didn't think anyone would be hiding in the shadows, but I'd have put more floodlights on the grounds if I didn't think the change might draw attention.

It was going to be a long week.

Rollie had been busy. He pointed to a pizza box. "Grab a slice, kid. How'd you make out?"

I wolfed down a large piece in three quick bites and filled him in.

"I got my sewing circle of friends covered. Didn't take long. Being a cranky hermit has its advantages," he said. "Think that prick Barnaby got the message?"

"He was rattled, to say the least, but I hope he thinks straight when he calms down."

Both of us jumped when the front door erupted in a loud, rapid cadence from the heavy iron door knocker. Rollie relaxed first, while I was still wondering where to find the nearest gun.

"That's the secret knock I gave the shrimp. The whole neighborhood probably heard it."

Tom stepped inside. He carried a cardboard box full of burner phones. "I think I hit every shop on the East Coast." He handed Rollie a set of keys. "Thanks for the wheels, mate. You know your way around a wrench, but it gobbles petrol like nobody's business."

"And if you scratched it, you're going off the steeple."

"No worries."

We got Tom caught up.

"Good. I'm going to alert the contacts for the handoff of the package."

"I thought I was supposed to handle that," I said.

"They will only work with you face-to-face. This only tells them to expect us."

"We don't even have the item in hand," I said. "Isn't it a little premature?"

Tom looked at me like he thought I was a fool. "Right. I'll tell him we have to dodge some psychopathic bandits who followed us here from Iraq, but we're sure to give them the slip."

"Fine, tell them whatever you like and then you can let me know how we are going to give the psychos the slip."

While Tom left for a quiet pew on the ground floor to make his calls, he'd given me an idea. I reached Bishop on one of the burners and arranged a meet after his night shift. I didn't say for what over the phone, but since we never chatted about sports it was safe to assume he knew it would be business.

* * *

The next morning, I took my truck out to the diner I used to meet Bishop. Later today I'd have to catch up with another old contact of Ryan's and get some anonymous wheels. For now, I figured it was safe enough because if Grist and Mauser knew how to find me in the suburbs, I was dead already.

I didn't see any signs of being followed and when I reached the diner, I found Bishop sitting in his usual spot nursing a cup of coffee. I caught the waitress's eye and took a seat across the table.

We exchanged pleasantries until the waitress poured me a mug and I'd passed on a menu. The place wasn't too crowded so we were able to chat as long as we kept our voices down.

"Is it bigger than a breadbox?" He reached for another sugar packet.

"Is what?"

"Whatever you want from me."

"I'm not really sure. I guess what I really want is your professional opinion."

"Oh good. If it's professional, that means I get paid."

The banter worked my nerves. "Whatever. Got a Ryan special that has gone sideways and I'm in a jam."

"There's a first." Bishop hunched over his mug. "Do tell."

"You can look up the news stories of the problems at my company later, that will catch you up. Short version is that the biggest troublemakers are back here stateside and looking to… inject themselves into a standing arrangement I inherited."

"Once more, for the hard of comprehending?" Bishop said, shaking his head.

Now I almost whispered, "Two mercs, heavy hitters, under suspicion but not yet indicted, know about a Ryan deal and want it for themselves."

"They're here?"

"If not, they will be soon. They play for keeps."

Bishop nodded, taking my meaning. "So, maybe let the big dogs eat. You said it isn't even your deal." He tore the packet and dumped the sugar in his mug.

"It's a big deal."

"Gotta be alive to spend it, no?"

"You got that right and, believe it or not, I'd like nothing better than to walk away from the whole thing,"

"Buuut?"

"The people waiting for the package aren't exactly saints and have been counting on getting their hands on it. They aren't known for their senses of humor."

"So, you're caught between Iraq and a hard place?" Bishop cracked up.

"My dead friend getting me killed is funny?"

He caught his breath. "Not if it actually happens, I guess. And I'd have to get a new helper for my collection." Banter aside, he *was* listening.

"The guys coming in wouldn't believe I was out, anyway."

"Since you are screwed either way, what did you want from me?"

I explained about Tom and how Ryan had staged the deal to require both of us.

"Ryan was a hard cat to figure out," Bishop said. "I assume he meant well here, but what a mess." He shook his head. "Where's the package now?"

I told him where we were expecting it.

Bishop thought about it. "They'll watch the place. Anyone asking your network about where Ryan is? Lately, I mean?"

"Not as much as I would have thought. Seems he greased the skids for me well in advance."

"So, you are the man for the job after all. Like it or not."

"Definitely *dis*like," I said. "Any thoughts on how to get through it without ending up like Ryan?"

Bishop sipped from his mug and stared out the window at the parking lot as if he hadn't heard the question. "These guys," he said at last. "How many are we talking?"

"Two principals, for sure, but they have a network too and may have backup."

"From what you describe, this is going to be their last hurrah before they scram. That implies they will want to travel as light as possible. The bigger the force, the harder to hide the movement."

I felt better for a moment. "Maybe, but they are bad enough."

"I'm not trying to underestimate them, I'm trying to put myself in their place. They don't know where exactly the package is hidden?"

"No, but they'll know the shipment and when it will arrive here in our port in Philly."

"Then if they can't find you or someone you can't do without first ..."

I explained how we'd taken precautions.

"Good enough. As I was saying, barring the chance to sweat you or yours, the next best play is to watch the port and if they can't swipe the stuff themselves then wait for you to show and hit you once you moved out."

"Are you saying you'll cover us on the way out?"

Bishop stared at me. "I'm not getting my ass shot just to play nice guy and I don't need to remind you I'm not a gun for hire. Besides, I thought you had one of those."

"If you're talking about Rollie, you have him all wrong," I said, though I'd be lying if I hadn't thought about him covering us if necessary.

"Yeah well, I'm not volunteering to go toe-to-toe with hardcore shooters, thanks," he said.

I told Bishop how VP was going to be able to monitor the Delivergistics cameras with my help.

"Smart," he said. "I have to meet him some time. He does good work."

"He's shy." Hiding VP's gender wasn't getting easier, but it was the least I could do.

"That gives me an idea. Give me a day or two and I can have a couple numbers you can give him."

"What for?"

"Some guys on the force that I trust. When the shipment comes in, I can have them make sure they are in the vicinity and if VP spots something going down, he can call, and the cavalry will be on the scene in no time."

A spark of real hope flared and winked out as fast. "You can't let them know what's going on. The circle is getting too big already."

Bishop smiled. "A little paranoia is good for staying sharp, but don't go overboard, Kyle. I don't want to poach your deal and neither will my guys. They won't know anything other than someone I know wants some discreet additional security."

"No offense intended," I said, "but if something does go down, won't that lead your own guys into a trap if they don't know what they're up against?" I wasn't keen on leading strangers to slaughter.

"You're thinking like a sneak, which is good, but keep going and think like a poacher. My boys will come in loud and proud, sirens blaring and calling for backup."

I pictured it and tried to imagine what even a ruthless version of me would do. "You think they'll bail?"

"Of course. What, they're going to start a shooting war with the cops? They'd have to know their faces would be on camera and just getting away clean will be hard enough."

I grinned. "Sounds like a hell of a diversion."

"Nothing but the best." Bishop stood. "Thanks for the coffee."

CHAPTER 25

The sound of one of the burner phones ringing was a welcome break from watching Rollie and Tom try to cheat each other in cards and argue whether to listen to Sinatra or Arabic rap.

It was VP calling and I left the room grateful for such spacious exile quarters. "What'cha got?"

"Hey. Not sure. There's a guy in front of Rollie's place." She was monitoring the cameras she'd installed to watch the front of the house.

It was late morning and sunny out. "Early for the mail."

"No delivery. The guy is big, wearing a knit cap and a windbreaker. When he rang the doorbell, I could see he was wearing gloves."

"Jehovah's Witness?" I joked, but my heart was speeding up. VP had good instincts.

"The body type is all wrong for the hulking one of your dudes. This one is big, like an old football player, you know, with a gut. I think I can see some gray hair."

I thought about anyone else who I might not have warned away from the place and immediately thought about Ross, the guy from the liquor store. He should have enough medicine for his sister now, but maybe he had another sister. No, nobody'd mistake him for an athlete.

"Shit," VP said. "I knew he wasn't right."

"What?"

"He just peeked in the window, like he wanted to see if anyone was coming, then looked around, and now he's going around the side toward the backyard."

"Can you follow him?"

"Lemmie switch to the one in the back yard," she said. "Got him. He's creeping to the back door. Whoa, there's another one following him."

I felt my stomach drop. "Can you make out guy number two?"

"No, he's got a hoodie on. First guy is busy crouched by the door. Gotta be picking the lock."

"Do they look like they're working together?" Grist was too lean to be one of this pair. Maybe another team member?

"Can't tell yet. The guy at the back door can't see Hoodie. I'm on split screen now. Hoodie is taking his time reaching into his pocket and ..."

"And what?"

"Son of a bitch! Just lost the camera in the back. I think Hoodie might have shot it with something."

"Seriously? Can you still see the front?" I wondered if the whole feed had gone offline.

"Front is fine, and that's weird. A pedestrian is strolling by, not acting like a gun went off." The cameras were video only, no audio.

"Maybe a suppressor? Are you sure it was destroyed?" By now Rollie and Tom had overheard snippets of my side of the conversation and were now standing in front of me. I almost put VP on speaker but remembered Tom didn't know anything about who she was. That was her decision, if she wanted to let him in.

"I'm sure. It was fine one second and Hoodie raised something from his pocket and the next moment it was out."

"They could still be working together. Can you still see Hoodie?"

"No, he ran around the corner of the house to the backyard."

"Ran?"

"Yeah and he's built like a linebacker, and not an old one. It could be one of your dudes, Mauser was the big one, right?"

"Yeah. But you said the other one is older and dumpy?" That didn't sound like Grist.

"Like he was buff back in the sixties ... oh crap. They're definitely not working together."

"How do you know?" I said, but VP talked over me.

"Dumpy is walking back around the corner and Hoodie is directly behind him, like 'stick 'em up' close. Dumpy looks like he might puke."

"What about Hoodie?"

"He's got a facemask on and is keeping his head down. But he's large and in charge here, and he's walking Dumpy across the street. They'll be out of camera view soon."

"You recording this?" I didn't know what else to ask.

"Oh yeah. The back-door stuff as well."

* * *

While we waited for VP to check her video recording, Tom, Rollie and I tried to make sense of what had just happened.

"The important thing is now we know for sure those knobs are following through on their intention to nick our shipment." Tom paced up and down the center of what used to be the main chapel of the church.

"I want to know who that was trying to bust into my place," Rollie said. I could tell he was fighting the urge to go back and investigate, even though this was exactly the reason we'd bugged out in the first place.

But I was struggling with the same impulse.

"The way Mauser went after him means he wasn't part of their crew. They were right on top of your house, weren't they?" I said. "When VP called, I was worried it might be Oliver, but that man was far too large and—" It hit me. "Damn! I think that's Franklin."

"Franklin? Who's that?" Tom asked.

"He works for Oliver. He pulled a gun on me. Follows that he'd be the guy Oliver would send if he wanted to scare me or look for some leverage of his own. And that's just what he'd want to do. I go and show Oliver I have all this evidence on him, and instead of surrendering he just has to double-down, maybe try to get something on us."

Tom stopped pacing. "Tell me you didn't leave that sort of prize behind?"

"Hell, no. But that's beside the point. What do you think Grist and Mauser will do with this poor bastard?"

"That's the poor bastard's lookout, isn't it?" Tom looked back and forth between Rollie and me. "Isn't it? This Oliver bloke can't know anything about where we are now, can he?"

"No," I said. "And neither would anyone he sent. Even so, there's no way Franklin knew what he was getting into when he went snooping."

"And we care because …?"

"Maybe the guy isn't a friend," I said, "but to be fair, I'd walked in uninvited to the house in Strawberry Mansion. He was just doing his job."

"Maybe so. But now?" Tom pointed out.

"On another day he'd probably get my gun in his face," Rollie said.

"I remember the feeling," Tom said.

"Grist and Mauser are going to do a hell of a lot more than threaten the guy," I said. "Come on Tom, you know better than we do that Franklin is about to get tortured or worse and he doesn't even know anything."

Rollie looked at me hard for a minute, then shook his head. "Cripes. Never thought I'd feel sorry about a flunky busting into my home." He sighed. "We gotta try."

"Try what?" Tom said, his voice rising. "Presenting yourselves to the chaps hunting you? Keep your eye on the prize."

Rollie scowled. "My prize is getting to sleep in my own bed without being killed. Kid," he said to me, "let's go on offense. We know where these guys are, more or less. Can Bishop see to it that the cops are around when I swing by, say, to pick up my mail?"

"What good would that do?" Tom said. "Mate, if you had seen the way that pair operate, you wouldn't be in a hurry to put yourself in their hands. Kyle should know better, but he's thick."

"I've seen what they can do and I'll be damned if some dumbass landlord gets mutilated just because he has the bad luck to work for Oliver." I wished I knew what to do about it, but whatever it was it had to be quick. "What are you thinking?" I asked Rollie.

"As fast as they reached my place, I figure they had to be close," he said, "but not in a car, or VP would have seen them."

"Good point. So, they're holed up close. Like maybe across-the-street close?" I was thinking about the small apartment building across the street.

Rollie shrugged. "Last time I checked, kidnapping was illegal in Fishtown."

"That's it!" I said.

"You're going to file a police report?" Tom said. "Rather high-profile, not to mention peculiar, given the fact that you're across town, don't you think?"

"VP will." My mind raced. "She can hide the call better and describe what happened in detail."

"So, the police arrive and knock on doors, ask questions, then what? Do you really think Grist and Mauser will be so easy to catch?" Tom paused. "Wait, did you say 'she'?"

Crap. "Not now, Tom. You're right, they won't catch anyone, but I bet you we have a good shot at interrupting them and maybe even flushing them out. There's only five or six units in that little building."

Rollie grinned. "They'll be trying to avoid the cops, not some shitkicker in an Olds."

Tom shook his head. "Right, if there's no talking you out of this, then I'm going with you to protect my investment."

"I'll call VP," I said. "Rollie, fire up the Bomber."

Tom grabbed Rollie's arm. "Don't chance it. If they already know your car, we're through."

"We're pressed for time here," Rollie said, "and Kyle's truck will give us away for sure."

"No worries. Ring your mate and I'll be out front in a jiffy. Be ready." Tom slipped out the big wooden front door to the old church.

"Did he just wink at you?" Rollie asked.

"Sure it was for me?" I pulled out a burner phone and called VP, deciding this wasn't the best time to tell her about my gender reveal slip-up.

* * *

VP couldn't wait to use her voice changer and spoofing software to report the kidnapping. I was glad she was on board, but had to wonder again if this was a stupid and futile gesture. Even if it was, we had to try.

Rollie ducked into his bedroom and came out with his .45 strapped to his hip. He pulled on a light jacket to conceal the weapon. "I'll take the front seat. You tell the little guy where to turn from the back. You see our boys, don't keep it a secret."

Tom pulled up in an old, faded brown Toyota Corolla. The horn sounded, like a nasally whine.

"So much for high-speed pursuit," Rollie said.

"We won't be mistaken for the cops, that's for sure," I said. "Let's hope I can fit in the back."

We crammed into the car and I told Tom where to go for the fastest way to Rollie's. It wasn't far.

"When did you get this?" I asked Tom.

He seemed puzzled by the question. "Just now."

My heart sank. "You stole it?"

"Borrowed, mate. I wouldn't be caught dead keeping this thing."

"But—"

"Look, I haven't nicked many cars since I was a lad, so I'm not current on the latest techniques. These were always a breeze to pinch."

"You get pulled over," I said, "we're all going in for car theft."

"It won't be for speeding," Rollie said.

"We drive on the right side of the road in this country," I reminded him. "And try to avoid the sidewalks."

"In-flight entertainment. Lovely." Tom followed my directions in one take.

CHAPTER 26

NEAR ROLLIE'S PLACE

I'd checked in with VP on the way and she said the cops thought one of Rollie's neighbors had called in the activity, didn't want to leave a name.

"Grist and Mauser have probably high tailed it by now," Tom said.

"If so, then we're safe to go look, aren't we?" I said. "Maybe it's a longshot, but how many safe hiding places do you think these two have to scurry off to?"

Tom considered it. "Fair play. If they are going to sweat this bloke, they'll need a place to do it, and they can't have been in town long."

I wasn't surprised that we reached the neighborhood before the police. They hadn't been given much to go on, but I did hope they'd show soon.

In the meantime, we drove as slow as we dared up and down the nearby streets, especially by alleys. Nothing.

The first cruiser rolled past about fifteen minutes later. It crawled by the spot VP had said the guy got grabbed.

"That's it?" I said. We were parked down the next block. We'd figured Grist and Mauser must have been even closer to Rollie's place, so we decided to linger.

A second police car pulled next to the first and the cars blocked the street while the officers chatted outside their driver side windows. We couldn't hear what they were saying, of course, but the casual gestures spoke to the lack of urgency. The second car drove off and the first parked in a yellow towaway zone and a single officer emerged.

We watched as he crossed the street and as luck would have it, he went straight to Rollie's porch and rang the bell.

"That door better not open," Rollie said.

Nobody opened the door and the officer shrugged, wrote on a small notepad, then crossed the street again.

"Where's he going?" Tom said.

"He's checking the small apartment building right across the street. It only holds a handful of units. Most of the residents are pretty old, maybe they even saw something."

"Half of them are out of it. Good neighbors and they mind their own business." Rollie frowned.

"What?"

"None of those old folks would simply allow someone to camp out and watch our place," Rollie said.

I shuddered. Rollie was right. One guy in particular, Mr. Thibault, belonged in assisted living, but was too stubborn to make the move.

"Not voluntarily." I racked my brain. "We can't go without checking on them."

"Isn't that what your police friend is doing right now?" Tom asked.

"Only if he knocks on every door. They think they are investigating a report of a possible kidnapping."

"How will Grist and Mauser react if the officer comes knocking?" Tom said.

"Say nothing and hope they go away?" I felt doubt creep in as I spoke the words. "Then take off as soon as the coast is clear?"

"And if they decide to respond more aggressively?" Tom's question lingered in the air while we waited five minutes that felt like five hours.

Finally, Rollie broke. He checked the pistol holstered in his waistband. "I didn't sign up for this to get someone killed." He reached for the door handle.

"Rollie wait. If we—" I didn't get a chance to finish my thought because we all saw the door to the apartment building open.

Two men emerged, hoodies up over their heads. One was broad-shouldered and hulking, the other lean and tall. We couldn't see their faces, but that wasn't necessary.

"Why not grab them right now?" Rollie drew the gun and held it low.

"No!" Tom and I yelled simultaneously.

"Mate, you do *not* want to start a firefight with these two. Especially not with one pistol."

"You might be surprised what I can do with this thing," Rollie said.

"They won't be," Tom said. "They're ready for a scrap. Look at them."

The two men moved with a practiced ease that took me back to the Sand Box and watching operators take down a door on a house raid. They each kept a hand inside a pocket and scanned the street, then split up without warning. The big guy, who I assumed was Mauser, walked around the corner out of sight. Grist stood near the empty patrol car.

"Think we can take this one?" Rollie wasn't usually so antsy. I was used to the calm, patient sniper.

"Where's the cop?" I asked. "The place only has one staircase. Not even an elevator."

"What's he doing now?" Tom said while Grist walked around to the driver's side of the cruiser and produced a set of keys.

"Oh no," Rollie said. "Those have got to belong to the cop."

Grist hopped into the car and started the engine. The way it was parked, it was a block away with its nose pointed in our direction.

Part of me wanted to see the cop charge out of the building, but the smarter half knew that the police academy hadn't prepared him for a guy like Grist, who could kill him without a second thought. If he hadn't already.

The police car rolled toward us.

"Rollie, stay put," I said. "He may recognize you."

We all scrunched down in the tiny car and sat frozen while the cruiser rolled by at a moderate pace.

Tom stared up at the windshield.

"Think he made us?" I asked.

Rollie peered at the side mirror and spoke in a calm voice. "Start the car, Tom." The contrast between his earlier excitement and this icy tone told me shit was about to get real.

"Right." Tom sat up and turned over the sewing machine of a motor. His eyes were on the rearview. "He's on the radio. No, it's a phone."

By now all of us were sitting up and peeking through the back window. We all saw the car slow, stop, and then saw the white reverse lights.

"Get us out of here," Rollie said. "Back up and take the first left."

"That street goes the wrong direction," Tom said, but he'd already pulled onto the narrow street. In this area, many were one-way.

"We're only going one way and that's far from this asshole," Rollie said. The gun was in his lap.

I looked back and sure enough, the patrol car had reversed by the intersection and turned to follow us against the grain of the one-way street.

"Left at the next one and—Look out!" Rollie pointed at the delivery van heading right for us with its horn blaring and headlights flashing.

"I'm not blind." Tom sawed at the wheel and jammed the brakes, which squeaked like panicked mice.

If we'd been in anything larger, we'd have swapped paint with the van and the line of parked cars on the other side as we squeezed through.

"Grist'll never fit." Tom grinned and the little motor strained to accelerate.

Tom was half right. While Rollie barked out directions for us to reach Girard Avenue, we all heard the siren. I turned in the cramped seat to see the lights on the stolen cruiser on full display as the wider vehicle scraped and muscled its way past the now stopped van.

We reached Girard Avenue and turned right, catching a break in traffic on the wide thoroughfare. Grist popped out after us, using the lights and siren to make his own breaks. The powerful cruiser leaped toward us.

"You may get your shootout after all." Tom wasn't grinning anymore. "I can't outrun him."

"Sure you can." Rollie craned his neck to keep an eye on the cruiser. "Use the whole road."

And Tom did just that. He swerved left and right, and even jumped the curb when there wasn't room and sent pedestrians scattering.

Still Grist came on and I thought Rollie would start shooting past me when the car banged into our rear bumper.

The police car's PA blared behind them. "DON'T BE STUPID, TOMMY." Wham! "DOESN'T HAVE TO GO LIKE THIS." Wham! The rear end fishtailed and the back trunk on the flimsy car crumpled.

Rollie pointed at an oncoming truck. "Cut hard left across this guy. It's gotta be close."

Tom saw what he meant and nodded.

I heard more sirens, but it wasn't Grist this time. Two real police cars were coming up fast toward us, from up behind the truck.

"Now!" Rollie yelled.

If the truck hadn't already been slowing for the cops coming up behind him, I think we would have been T-boned. As it was, the driver locked up his brakes and we just slipped past. The truck's grill looked close enough to reach out and pat the chrome Mack bulldog.

I looked to see if Grist had been crazy enough to follow us through the turn down the side street, but instead realized that he'd bailed and continued straight. Both police cars had e-braked into bootlegger one-eighty-degree turns to follow Grist up Girard Avenue.

"Slow up, Tom," I said. "They both went after Grist."

Tom backed off a little and we were able to drive clear of the area.

Rollie smiled. "Where'd you learn to drive like that?"

"University of They'll-cut-your-hands-off-if-you-get-caught." Tom smiled back, but I didn't think he was joking.

* * *

SCORPIO PHOTOGRAPHY STUDIOS

Tom pulled to the back of the old church to let Rollie and me out before he returned the "borrowed" vehicle. We were five minutes away as the crow flew, but crows didn't have to dodge a pair of psychos.

Part of the hour had been creeping down side streets listening to the growing din of sirens from police cars, then fire trucks. We also had to keep an eye on the sky as a police chopper circled near a thick plume of black smoke.

"He must have torched it," Tom had said. "Pity he wasn't inside."

We were desperate to find out what was going on in the apartment building across the street from Rollie's, but we knew better than to cruise past. The best we could do was call VP, who let us know about the police and ambulance activity from the perspective of her cameras.

She couldn't see whether the people getting loaded from the apartment building into the ambulances were alive or not.

At the church, Rollie got out of the front seat and I unfolded my aching limbs from the confines of the cramped back seat. "Tom, wait a minute," I said.

"Shake a leg, Mate. This ride isn't a healthy look for me anymore."

I nodded and rushed past Rollie to get inside.

We all knew the smart thing to have done was ditch the car as soon as we were clear, but we agreed to return the car. We'd left a lot more than a scratch on the old thing and while I didn't know the owners, this was their property and the best they could manage.

Back outside, I handed Tom an envelope with "Sorry for the mess" scribbled on the outside.

Tom peeked inside and whistled. "You sure?"

"Just leave it and get back here safe." I didn't care if it was enough for the owners to buy a better used car. They hadn't asked to be part of our crap.

"We're coming with a posse if you don't," Rollie added. He'd made Tom say where he was going.

* * *

Thirty tense minutes later Tom knocked on the door and came inside. He was sweating and considering the climes he was used to I didn't think it was from exertion. At least he grinned when Rollie suggested now might be a great time to take up drinking.

"Just some of your floor-sweepings tea, thanks."

Bishop finally returned our call. I put it on speaker.

"I think you people need to look up the meaning of 'laying low,' because you're doing it wrong," Bishop said over the burner phone.

"At least you can't say we're being paranoid," I said.

"Nope," he said. "That base is covered."

"C'mon, what's going on with my neighbor?" Rollie said. It had been all we could do to convince him not to check up on him this afternoon.

"I figure you saw the breaking news reports," Bishop said.

We had. The helicopter footage of the burning cop car was particularly compelling.

"I talked to my friends in the Philly PD. Officer Vinton is doing fine and was released. The word is that he got clocked as soon as he came into the old guy Thibaut's place. The old man called out for help and it was lights out. He never got a good look at his attacker."

"It was two of them," I said. "What about Thibault and the property manager?"

"The old guy is pretty confused and had some dehydration. It looks like your friends had him tied up and blindfolded while they used his apartment. He can't ID anybody, unfortunately."

"But he's okay?" Rollie said.

"Yeah. Traumatized, but they didn't work on him like the other guy."

"What happened to him?" Tom said.

"The guy, named Franklin, was lucky you guys stirred the pot when you did. He only lost one tooth and got a broken nose. Any idea why they'd lean on him like that?"

"What did he say about it?" I said.

"He *says* he was just looking for an old friend and must have been at the wrong address and doesn't want to say any more. My pals in blue don't believe him and think he's some sort of burglar, but they are buying that he can't ID the dudes who snatched him."

"So, the cops are in the dark?"

"The cops are beyond pissed at what somebody did to one of their brothers and then made them look like jackasses by shaking pursuit and cooking their car and any evidence along with it. They hope to find more in the apartment, but it could take a while."

I felt awful about the old man and bad about Franklin, but better that it looked like we might have prevented a double-killing and that the officer wasn't seriously harmed.

Tom said, "Do they have any clue about the kidnapping tipster who kicked this off?"

"They don't," Bishop said. "They're frustrated as hell with the phone company for not being able to track the caller."

"No comment," I said. VP was good. "Is it safe to say we're in the clear?"

Bishop let out a breath. "I *think* so. The eyewitness reports are all over the place. The descriptions of your car don't match, and from what I hear, the traffic cameras never got a plate. It was pretty chaotic and you weren't the only car scrambling out of the way."

"And they aren't going to catch those psychos?" Rollie said.

"You sure you don't want to give them more to go on? They'd be all in to help, believe me," Bishop added.

"No," I said. "Crazy as it sounds, we still have a shot to pull off our deal and they'll go away on their own."

"Meaning you expect them to stick around until you do?"

"Or they stop us and take it for themselves."

* * *

SCORPIO PHOTOGRAPHY STUDIOS

A day after the neighbor rescue fiasco we hadn't budged from our fancy hideout. VP hadn't reported anything new, but she sent one of those stoner bikers over with a care package consisting of another thumb drive for me to load into Delivergistics computers when I got the chance. I wasn't about to just drop by socially and until the shipment arrived there wasn't a reason to go there. We all figured that was where we were most at risk.

* * *

TWO DAYS LATER

Time had taken on a syrupy quality that made waiting unbearable. We couldn't make a move until the next phase was in place. On the other hand, we didn't hear any more from Barnaby or the police and VP had grown just as bored as us staring at the front of Rollie's place. Aside from the mailman, no sinister visitors.

I almost didn't recognize the sound of my regular cell phone when it rang. Burner phones stood like dominoes atop my dresser.

Caller ID showed it was from my boss Cliff at Delivergistics.

"Kyle? You're not going to believe this, but I have a driving gig for you."

"Yeah?" I tried to sound surprised.

"You know the shipment we have coming in, right?"

"All that pre-eviction equipment from Iraq? You still want me to work on the yard when it comes in?"

"That's the one, and I had you top of the list like I promised, but I just got a last-minute priority request to take one of the trucks to Pittsburgh."

Tom had heard the phone chirp and was leaning in the door frame from the room I used. He pantomimed exaggerated shock. Of course, he'd forged the request and arranged for it to drop now. I didn't want to laugh, which made it harder to stop.

"Everything okay?" Cliff said.

"Yeah, it's great. You just have no idea how much I needed to hear some good news."

"Always happy to be the bearer of glad tidings. Can't promise it'll be a trend."

After I hung up, Rollie said what we were all thinking. "Unless they head for the hills, anyone want to guess where those two goons are going to stake out next?"

CHAPTER 27

I wasn't sure about the worst part of the trip. Aside from the darkness and stifling heat inside this cardboard coffin, the never ending starts and stops of the truck had me rattling around the little breathing space I did have. On second thought, the worst thing was that it had been my brilliant idea.

Like Rollie had suggested, we knew Grist and Mauser would be watching the Delivergistics site. Of course, the local guys, Cliff and the rest, had no reason to feel any heightened danger, and we wanted to keep it that way.

"How you holding up?" the driver of the big brown truck asked, as he did every time he made a stop, which was often. He was one of Bishop's contacts and for a price was willing to bend the company rules, especially for what he thought was just an elaborate prank.

"Fine," I replied again, despite sweating buckets and wanting to take a leak. By this point I decided that Bishop had lied to me that the packing tape would only work once so I had stay inside this thing for the "quick ride across town."

* * *

DELIVERGISTICS

I recognized the voice of Doug, the gate guard, when the driver finally reached Delivergistics. Judging by his tone he knew the driver and the truck was a common sight. Perfect.

Also good that the truck pulled around to a loading area that I knew was partly shielded from view, at least from the street. Cameras covered the area and if they had access to those then my stupid idea made sense after all.

"Afternoon," I heard Cliff say. "What've you got for us today?"

"The usual, I'll put it over here. And then there's this." The box I was in rocked, then tilted sharply backward and I tried not to slam into the back while the dolly whisked me off the truck.

"What the hell is that?" Cliff said.

"I'm just the messenger," the driver said. "You need to sign for it and it is supposed to go inside."

More rolling. I hoped out of sight of the street.

"'CyberPanion Deluxe Model'?" Cliff was reading off the manifest. "Gotta be a mistake, if that means what I think. We're slow around here, but not that slow."

"I learned a long time ago not to ask questions." The driver sounded like he was a having difficulty controlling himself.

I heard a door slam open and felt the dolly go up and over a metal threshold.

"Where are you taking that?" Cliff said. "It's just going to have to go back on the truck. We didn't order a sex doll or robot or whatever it is."

We had to be out of sight by now.

"I'm ready for youuuu, Cliffie." I lost it before I could say anything else.

"You gotta be shitting me." Laughing, Cliff slapped the side of the box. "Nothing deluxe about this model. Drop it into the river."

The driver helped open the box before I decided to hack my way out from the inside.

"You lost your mind, Kyle?" Cliff said as I brushed cardboard chunks off my clothes.

"It seemed funnier before they taped the box shut." I held my hand up for the driver to wait up. He nodded but pointed to his wrist. These guys were all about time, but he was my ride home. He stepped outside to wait for me.

"My truck's in the shop," I told Cliff, "and I wanted to see if this would work to get me in the gate."

"That's what this is about? You auditing our security?"

I saw the strain around his eyes. He wasn't kidding.

"No, not like that. But it is strange days, and with something coming in and us in the news so much, you never know. But I don't want to get anyone in trouble."

Cliff wasn't buying, but I didn't think he'd guessed my real reason for pulling my stunt. "Too much time on your hands isn't agreeing with you, Kyle. Let me get your paperwork and in the meantime, clean that mess up." He pointed to the box and all the cardboard scraps on the office floor. I eyed the computer terminal and promised it would be done by the time he got back.

As soon as he left the room, I pulled the thumb drive VP had given me and accessed one of the computers. She'd told me my login would be enough for the program to work and that it wouldn't come back to me, or Cliff, in any case.

* * *

"See you in a few days, and next time use the employee entrance huh?" Cliff said as I sat on a stack of boxes in the back of the delivery truck. The door rolled down and we were off.

The driver let me sit up front once we were clear of the facility (and I thought it was safe).

A few stops later Bishop met the truck and I got a lift in his cruiser.

"Thanks again. I know those guys are tracked so they stay on schedule. Hope he won't get in trouble."

Bishop shook his head. "Nah, he'll be fine and I paid him enough that a little ding in his performance won't bug him. Was it worth it?"

"It better be. I'll catch up with VP to find out for sure."

* * *

SCORPIO PHOTOGRAPHY: TWO DAYS LATER

"That's the last pallet," Tom said while we flicked through the camera feeds VP had linked to us. True to her word, the little worm I'd planted had given her access to all the security equipment at the Delivergistics site.

With VP now on point to relay all she saw from the video feeds, I figured I had no choice but to let her know I was going to let them know that she was a she. I couldn't risk a message getting garbled down the road because she was using a voice scrambler. She complained a little when I fessed up, but all in all I don't think she was really mad. It was a relief not to have to remember to cover for her.

We could see the truck listed on the manifest VP was able to pull up, along with all the other gear, spare parts and other sundries associated with an operation pulling up stakes. I felt sad when I saw all the people I'd gotten to know, doing their best to organize the material, all the while knowing that they were going to have to find new jobs. Most of them would be okay, they worked hard and were good at what they did. As for me, I just wanted this damn monkey off my back.

"Get your people lined up, Tom. Cliff will call me in to move the truck as soon as everything from the incoming shipment is inventoried, a couple days at most."

I'd have to come up with another way onto the site without getting spotted. I didn't think Cliff would fall for the UPS bit again.

* * *

ONE DAY LATER: AFTER MIDNIGHT

I was dreaming about one of the many arguments I used to have with Beth about my time away from home due to work when she started to scream at me in long trilling pulses. As my brain swam toward consciousness, I realized it was one of burner phones.

I swung my legs out from the covers and planted my bare feet on the cold floor. The phone that was ringing also vibrated and walked across the surface of the dresser in a drunken circle in time to the rings.

It was VP. "What's up?"

"Not you, sounds like."

She wouldn't call just to chat. Adrenaline kicked my eyes open. "Whatcha got?"

"Something's going bump in the night over at the port," she said. "Can you get to your computer?"

"On the way." I scooped up a couple more phones and pounded on the doors for Rollie and Tom on the way to where we had our PC set up.

VP caught me up while the guys emerged from their rooms. It hadn't taken much to rouse them.

"I noticed the place is real quiet at night, but a couple guys walked by the fence line and they didn't look like homeless types."

"It's them?"

"They picked a spot not covered, but if it's them, we'll know soon enough."

I put her on speaker and got the link to the feed working. We could see the cameras, but we were at VP's mercy as to which camera to watch.

"What are we seeing here?" Rollie spoke.

"The northwest fence line," VP said. "I think they went by the wall you see at the edge of the picture. No sign of them around the corner on the next camera yet, though."

"Too many blind spots," Tom muttered.

"Any sign the guard on duty is alerted?"

She laughed. "That dork—sorry if he's a bud—must be crashed. He hasn't switched feeds in more than an hour."

When did she ever sleep?

"Can you get us a wider shot of the yard?"

"Yeah, sorry. Here you go, this is—oh shit."

We all saw it. Two figures emerged from the blind spot to do a slow weave between containers. Two trucks sat at the front of the containers, one ahead of the other. I already knew the one with our shipment was the lead vehicle, ready to roll off.

VP gave running commentary in case she was on a camera feed we couldn't see. "Big guy over by the red container. Let me switch here. Looks like hedge clippers or something."

"Lock cutters." I recognized them immediately. "Going into the container."

Tom flipped through pages of manifest printout. "Cots, tents and furniture."

VP zoomed in the picture when the image flipped over and I could see that it was Mauser for sure. He hopped out of the container, light on his feet, like a tiger.

The next one he opened but left before Tom could even locate the list of contents.

I couldn't take it. "Can't the guard see this?"

"If he were awake. Say the word, I have the cursor over the panic button. It'll sound the alarm with all horns," VP said. "But they'll take off."

I pulled out the phone I used for Bishop and hit the autodial. "Hang on. VP, can you call the cops, anonymously, and get them on the way without scaring our guys off?"

"No problem. I can spoof the number to something local."

"I thought you could. Hit them up, let them know you saw weapons. God knows those two will be carrying, and we need the police to be ready."

Bishop picked up and I'd definitely woken him up. "Robbery in progress at Delivergistics. Word on the street is it's the cop beaters. Think you know anyone who'd be interested?"

"Damn straight." Bishop hung up.

Rollie said, "They couldn't think they'd have all night to dig around the place."

"They're over by the trucks now," Tom said.

"Poking around the back, now moving to the cab." I watched Grist mess with the lock to the door for the cab on the one in front. "They're taking it! How'd they know the right place to look?"

"The cavalry getting close you think?" Rollie asked.

VP answered, "Just got off the horn with the cops. An eyewitness who didn't want to give my name."

"VP, if they get this truck out of there, we lose, understand?" I could see Grist's legs dangling out of the open cab.

"You sure you want me to hit it?" she asked.

I saw Mauser creeping toward the locked gate, not that it would survive a ramming from the truck if it came to that.

"He'll have that truck started in another second." The instant I finished the sentence, the yard lit up with floods and shrill horns pierced the air. Grist's legs spasmed in surprise and he slid out of the cabin like he'd been shocked.

"Bitchin'." VP chuckled.

I imagined the snoozing guard falling out of his chair, but not for long. Mauser had a pistol in his hand as he made his way back toward the truck.

Now between yelps of the Delivergistics alarm, we could hear the wail of incoming sirens, a bunch of them.

Grist and Mauser seemed to argue for a moment before they decided on discretion and ran back toward where they'd made their way inside the fence line.

VP followed them as best she could with the mounted cameras. We could see some blue and red light begin to wash the walls of buildings. The last glimpse we got of the two was a street view behind the Delivergistics building. Two dirt bike-style motorcycles shot out of view, headed in the direction of the waterfront.

I called Bishop. He picked up right away, wide awake now. "Yeah, I got a buddy on the other line."

"Tell him they bailed on dirt bikes."

"They're on it. Going to do a net and ... dammit!"

"What?" We were relying on Bishop now, as our feed still showed the site and a bunch of cops talking to the confused guard. He looked familiar, but I didn't remember his name. Whoever he was, he owed us a beer. I had no illusions about his fate if he'd tried to confront Mauser.

"They turned onto the train tracks. Cruisers can't follow there. They'll have to nab them on one of the cross streets." Bishop's frustration mirrored my own.

I knew the area. There were more places to squirm past the pursuit and it wouldn't take long before the cops were spread too thin.

The rest of the chase played out on our speakerphone. Longer and longer pauses by Bishop punctuated by swearing while the police on the ground chased leads, which gave way to a report of the bikes found abandoned a mile away.

CHAPTER 28

PORT OF PHILADELPHIA

"Bet you didn't think you'd be leading a parade, huh?" Bishop said as I sat in his cruiser at the head of a four-car convoy of police vehicles on our way to the Delivergistics site.

"Not exactly low key," I said, "but I guess that's the point." At least I wouldn't have to explain to Cliff the reason for all the fuss. The break-in the other night had spooked him and I think he just wanted to get the problem as far from Philly as possible. I couldn't blame him for that.

Bishop's idea was a good one. We'd have a loud and visible presence while I got the truck away from the site and if everything looked good, the local police would drop back. Bishop even seemed like he was doing some of the officers a favor, as opposed to the other way around. Officially, the perps were unidentified, but Bishop used some of his most trusted contacts on the force to make sure the officers knew who the real suspects were and the cops wanted Grist and Mauser in the worst way.

"Glad to be of service. Those two have balls, I'll give them that, but they've got to know they blew their chance."

"We'll see," I said. "Cliff told me things are going so bad for Grist and Mauser overseas that the Philly cops will have to get in line behind the Iraqi army and several jihadi groups."

When we reached the site, I saw another marked car and suspected a couple others as being unmarked. Dave the guard let us in but checked both our IDs anyway. The rest of the police convoy fanned out onto the street by the entrance. The whole place felt on edge.

Bishop pulled up to the office. "Got me on speed dial?"

"Yup, and so you know, Rollie, Tom and VP are riding shotgun in Rollie's car, but will stay out of your way. They'll be in his old blue Delta 88."

"Rolling in the Bomber? He must be serious. Hope nobody bleeds in it this time." Bishop once nursed a gunshot wound in the ass in the Bomber's back seat.

"Amen to that, and thanks Bishop."

"Thank those two assholes for pissing off an army of cops," he said. "Get through this part and you can thank me later."

* * *

Cliff handed over the last folder of paperwork like it was contagious. "Here you go, Kyle. I hope all the motorcade you brought does the trick, but I guess you won't have to worry about being bored." He lowered his voice. "Any idea what they were looking for?"

"Who knows, with those two."

My deflection didn't seem to satisfy Cliff. The police had already told him that at least one of the guys breaking in fit the description of the man who assaulted a cop before leading a chase in a stolen cruiser. Cliff never said if he noticed that the apartment in question just happened to be right across the street from Rollie's place where I lived.

He held his hands up. "I'm not asking for specifics, I just want to know if I need to worry about World War III breaking out in the compound." Cliff paused. "Or getting kidnapped on my way home." For the first time, I noticed the outline of a pistol grip printing from under his shirt.

I never knew Cliff to be a gun guy or one to buck the company no firearm policy, so he must have been spooked.

"They'd have to be crazy to come back here. I bet they high tailed it for good. But if they didn't, they must have seen the cops and the dogs. Doesn't look like it was drugs, anyway."

"I hope you're right," he said. "Jeez, I think I'll manage a copy store next if we end up folding."

"I'll see you back here in a few days." I shook his soggy hand and forced myself to wait until I was out of his office before wiping my palm on my pants.

* * *

There were still smudges of black powder from the police fingerprint dusting on the inside of the truck. The would-be thief had worn gloves, reinforcing the impression that this was the work of a pro and not a random doper.

Otherwise the truck showed no ill effects from the other night and the engine turned over on the first try. I'd already doublechecked all the hookups and the trailer itself was empty.

The truck was destined for a yard in Pittsburgh, a short hop compared to the cross-country hauls most truckers were normally tasked with. Over in Iraq it wasn't the distance but the risk that made the difference. In other words, I felt right at home.

As I pulled the rig out through the gate, I waggled an aluminum can of energy drink at Dave the guard. He waved back. Like Cliff, I couldn't help but think he was kind of glad to see me go. I checked my mirrors and watched first Bishop, then a procession of Philadelphia police cars pull into formation behind the truck. We hadn't gotten a whole block up the street when I heard a siren yelp and one of the cop cars passed me with all lights flashing.

The driver pulled back into my lane and kept with the lights. Now all the traffic ahead of us magically parted and we cruised out of the city in style.

"I could get used to this," I told Bishop over the phone as we approached the on ramp to I-95 South.

"Don't get too spoiled," he answered on speakerphone. "These guys won't be able to stick around much past the city limits. A few will hang in for twenty miles or so. After that, it'll just be me and then only for a while."

"Well, tell them thanks for doing this much. You, too." I may have sounded disappointed about eventually losing my escort, but I was also relieved. I needed to make a couple important stops along the way to the Steel City, and discretion was going to be more important than protection.

"When I see Rollie, I'll peel off. After that, you can call. But remember, I won't exactly be right around the corner."

Bishop wanted to stay at arm's length or more so as not to be involved in what we were doing and that was fine. Our biggest danger was right now. Rollie and company knew where I was heading, so they could afford to hang well back, especially knowing I was in such good hands.

Once I'd shed my escort, I'd first be taking the truck to a non-company location that happened to be somewhat along the way. VP had uncovered an unnerving document that showed the work order assigning me to take the truck Pittsburgh. We couldn't be sure if Grist and Mauser had access to the same information, but given their specific interest in the truck, we had to assume they did.

Because of that, we were planning a more circuitous route to get to that first stop. If Grist and Mauser wanted to wait for the truck in Pittsburgh, they could have the thing once it got there, for all I cared. On the other hand, they had a tendency to express their disappointment in painful ways, so hopefully they'd just stay on the run.

* * *

DELIVERGISTICS TRUCK: ALONG I-76

The police cars had dropped back and I was reminded of the way WWII Allied bombers would lose fighter coverage during a long-range mission. Once the small aircraft hit their fuel limits they had to return to base. In this case, my buddies ran out of jurisdiction, not gas. As a state trooper, Bishop had technical jurisdiction all over Pennsylvania, but as a practical matter, the farther he got from the property room at the State Police barracks, the harder it became to explain what he was doing out here in the first place.

A short while after Bishop left my bumper, I saw Rollie drift by in the passing lane. Tom sat in the back seat and they'd been joined by VP in the front. Funny, once the guys learned she was a she, she'd come out of her shell and shown real enthusiasm to play a more active role. Now that we weren't needing to monitor security cameras and the like, I was happy to have her along. God knew he needed all the help we could get.

VP yanked down on an imaginary cord to give me the universal truck honk sign, which I obliged and Rollie faded back behind the rig again.

It felt good to know they were back there. I turned north onto a road that led nowhere near Pittsburgh and hoped the guys were being extra vigilant. They knew the way and I still scanned the mirrors more often than a kid trying to pass his commercial driver's license test. It all looked normal.

I don't know what I was expecting. A Humvee flying a Jolly Roger? Something out of *The Road Warrior*?

Nothing so sinister revealed itself as the traffic thinned then picked up when I approached Johnstown. Rollie would appear intermittently. Just before the turn into town where we were planning to stop at a Sheetz convenience store, he passed the truck with a flashy roar of his crate-motored hot rod. This meant he hadn't seen anything to worry about.

The store and most of the surrounding area wasn't set up for big rigs to park so I pulled off on the side of the road and lit my flashers. Tom got out of the car and dashed across the parking lot to the truck.

"Coast still looks clear?" I asked.

"As far as I can tell," he answered.

"Rollie knows to stay out of sight when we get to the truck shop, right?" I could have called him but preferred to stay off the air as much as possible.

"I explained how Gallagher is expecting you and I and a big truck, nothing more. The last thing we need to do is scare away the final link."

"We're close," I said, and we were. But at the same time, the air felt like it was getting thicker, as though just to slow us down.

"That we are, mate." Tom climbed into the cab to join me for the last leg of the trip.

* * *

The sun was beginning to set and I figured we'd arrive just before full dark. The roads dwindled from four to two lanes, but Gallagher's Truck Service wasn't totally in the boonies. Good thing, as these rigs were no fun on dirt roads and, if anything went wrong, I wouldn't be able to turn it around.

By the time we saw the lit sign it was dark and everything else around us was closed. We could see a solitary figure silhouetted by the light.

"Do you know what our guy looks like?" I asked.

"No, but he has our pictures," Tom said. Maybe that was supposed to comfort me, but it didn't.

As I turned into the wide gravel driveway entrance, the truck's headlights washed over a heavyset guy with bushy red hair curling out from under a baseball cap. He carried a pump shotgun held across his waist.

"You Yanks do customer service different here," Tom said.

We must have the right place. "At least it isn't aimed at us. What's his first name again?"

"Stu."

I cut the ignition and rolled down the window and showed my hands.

Stu squinted into the headlights and stepped out of the beams.

"We're closed."

Tom whispered to me and I repeated after him. "We've come a long way and have just a little further to go," I said.

Stu cocked his head and it reminded me of a dog listening for familiar words. "And?"

Tom continued.

"Ryan sent us and apologizes that he couldn't be here himself," I added.

Stu appeared to relax, though he still held the shotgun and he shifted it to his left hand while he dug out a photo from the front pocket of his oil-stained coveralls. "I didn't catch your name or your partner's."

"I'm Kyle and Tom is with me. Ryan said it was okay as long as I was here," I said as Stu digested that.

"Step out, both of you, and let me get a closer look."

We climbed down from the rig, moving slowly. This wasn't quite the welcome I expected.

He peered at me and then at the photo in his hand. He held the picture in the headlights for a better look. "You look heavier than this shot, but I guess it's you." He turned his attention to Tom. "Where's the rest of you?"

At first, I thought he meant Rollie, but he wasn't supposed to know anything about him. Then the guy's face cracked into a broad grin that revealed he still had most of his teeth.

"I suppose I sound taller on the phone?" Tom said.

"Six, seven feet, easy," Stu said and looked at me. "Last thing. You have something for me?"

I nodded and pointed to the gun. "If I may?"

Stu glanced down at the shotgun as if he'd just noticed it in his hand. He draped it over one shoulder so the barrel was pointed behind him. "Please do."

I pulled out the envelope and handed it over. We'd counted it earlier and I figured the ten grand would warm relations.

Stu flipped through the stack of bills. "That's the way we like it." He pocketed the money and headed toward the corrugated steel building. "Lemmie get the door and kindly ease her on in so we can get to work."

Tom joined me inside the cabin again. I started the rig.

"Tom, what sort of work are we doing?" I asked. "You never told me how the package was built into the truck."

"Ever swap out a diesel tank?"

CHAPTER 29

"You stuck it in the tank? Isn't that a little obvious? We're lucky the cops didn't find it when the dogs went over the truck." My nerves were getting the better of me.

"They're not drugs, and I didn't toss them by the handful to rattle about like so many pebbles. Give me some credit," Tom said as I eased the truck through the huge rollup door.

"All right." I tried to calm my tone. "So, what did they do?"

"My people did a first-rate welding job on the bottom of the tank. There's a gentle slope caused by the aluminum flap and the stones themselves are spread thin. Drugs are bulky by comparison and compartments can be detected by pros. I doubt a detective with a camera scope would notice this curve."

"Clever."

"Indeed, but what was created carefully deserves to be extracted with equal caution," Tom said. "Unless you want to take any damaged stones out of your share?"

I brought the rig to a halt and killed the engine. "Think Stu here has the delicate touch we need?"

"Let's hope so. Ryan picked him."

We climbed down from the cab. Diesel fumes lingered in the air and the engine made ticking noises while it began to cool.

Stu looked over the truck once the garage door had closed. He walked over to a side door and flipped on a row of overhead fluorescent lights that buzzed and flickered on.

"I understand you are pressed for time, so let's get going," he said. "We're doing the left tank, is that correct?"

I flicked my gaze toward Tom, who gave me a barely perceptible nod.

"Yes," I said. "And you've got the replacement?"

"Of course." Stu pointed at a cylinder-shaped object in the corner covered by a dusty tarp. "Kyle," he said, "help me move this fuel transfer pump. I have a holding tank for the diesel once we get the new piece installed."

We set up the equipment and in a few minutes, he had the pump running.

"How long until it's empty?" I asked.

"About ten, fifteen minutes. Then we'll take it off the truck and the little guy can pressure wash the insides while you and I fit the new one."

"Why do I get the dirty job?" Tom asked.

"Can you fit your arms around that thing?" Stu said. "It's only fifty or sixty pounds, but every ounce is awkward."

"Fine, fine. Go play your monster truck games," Tom said.

"When you're done, you mark the area you want me to cut and we'll fill the tank up with water just to be on the safe side."

"What we want isn't going to rust," Tom said.

"It took me all winter to grow this beard. I'm not about to singe it off if any leftover diesel decides not to play nice."

I fought the urge to look through the window in the door to see outside. I figured Rollie and VP were set up somewhere in the parking lot for a baked goods company across the street.

After a few more minutes the pump started to make a horrible gasping sound, like an asthmatic walrus. Stu shut it off, took out a flashlight and peeked inside the tank. "Good deal, then. Kyle, c'mon over. Let's get this bitch out of here."

It was kind of neat the way the tank unhooked and in no time, we'd hoisted it free of the truck and brought it to a waiting trough.

Stu handed a fat marker to Tom. "Show me where to cut and then rinse her out."

While Stu brought over the pressure washer and hooked up the hose and power, Tom pulled out a piece of cloth that looked like a small pillowcase. He turned the cylindrical metal tank until the bottom faced him. He peered in close and traced his fingers over the surface. "Ah ha." He took the cloth and spread it over the surface using the mark he'd found as a starting point. "Kyle, hold this right here, mate."

I did and Tom traced sound the rectangle with the big Sharpie. "That's it."

"All right, then." Stu gave Tom the sprayer wand and fired up the pressure washer's compressor. "Goggles on that table."

* * *

"So, what are you boys pulling out of there?" Stu asked me while we lugged the new tank into place. It was easy as a two-man operation. Would have been a pain in the ass with just me or me and Tom.

"It's not drugs, if that's what you were wondering."

"I know that. Ryan knows better than to ask me." Stu sounded insulted.

"Are sure you want to know?"

"I'm about to use a Sawzall powerful enough to grind through the tank. If you got the Mona Lisa rolled up in there, yeah, I'd like to know." He gave me his hockey player grin.

"It's not—"

"I already took ten-large for a five-hundred-buck job. I figured it wasn't Girl Scout cookies." He'd stopped grinning.

Fair enough. "Diamonds."

Stu nodded and scratched his beard. "Should be all right. As long as Tom gets his marking right."

We doublechecked our connections on the new tank and Stu moved to fill it with the pumped-out diesel while Tom washed out the old tank.

When we were done, Stu went to a freezer with a pair of tongs.

"Ice cream?" I asked.

"Dry ice. I drop it in and the CO_2 will make sure there's no oxygen in the tank. Even if there are fuel vapors, no air means no fuel triangle."

"And no boom," I said. "Makes sense."

It might have looked like a mad scientist scene from a high school film project, but the dry ice seemed to do the trick. Stu fired up the grinder and added showers of sparks to the special effects.

Before long he'd made a nice neat rectangular incision along the bottom of the tank. Tom singed his fingers trying to bend the flap back. Stu grinned and wagged a finger. "Lemme finish opening the soup can before you try to eat."

The panel came free and hit the floor with a loud clang.

Several rows of wrapped cloth that looked like dirty dreadlocks fell to the floor.

Tom had a leather pouch at the ready. He carefully tore one of the packages open.

Glittering thumbnail-sized stones poured into Tom's outstretched hand. He shook out the cloth to make sure he got them all and when he was done, they filled his palm.

Stu gawked. "Damn, son!"

Tom pulled out a jeweler's loupe and peered at the stones, one at a time.

"Please tell me all this crap hasn't been for nothing," I said.

"Oh no, Mate. Not at all," Tom almost whispered. "These are bloody flawless."

"Okay, good." I checked the clock on the wall. A little after midnight. Right on time. "Check the rest and then we get on the horn for the next phase?"

Stu began to put away his equipment. "Gents, it's been interesting. I know better than to ask about where you're off to and why and all. I just ask that you respect my privacy whenever you get where you're going."

"Of course." I couldn't wait to move on and finish this thing. Tom had stressed that the guys had been clear about making sure the next meet was in the middle of the next night.

"Make sure you tell Ryan I said thanks," Stu spun toward the window in the entrance door. "What's this crap?"

Red strobing lights splashed through the glass. My first thought was that the cops were raiding the place. Would I have time to call Bishop? Would it make a difference?

Tom had just stashed the last of the diamonds into the drawstring leather porch. He glanced at me, shook his head and stared up at the rafters.

Before I could think to call anyone, my burner phone for VP trilled.

The red lights and now a whoop of a siren filled the night air. But it only sounded like one vehicle.

"Ah, Christ. It's just an ambulance," Stu said. "Don't these assholes have GPS?" He was out the door before I could stop him.

Tom reacted faster and tossed the stones atop a stack of crates piled higher than his head. He looked ready to bail out a back door, if there was one. I held up a finger for him to wait and answered the call.

"What the hell is going on?" I said.

It was Rollie. "Ambulance rolled up out of nowhere. Cut on the flashers after it drove past once. Must have circled back."

"What is it doing now?"

"I see one person. Wearing a paramedic uniform. Want me to draw a bead?"

I could picture Rollie on the high ground with his rifle.

"Which one?" I asked.

"Not sure."

"Don't fire." I tried to think. "Think they saw you?"

"Probably not," he said. "I saw the guy with you come out, but he's behind the ambulance."

No way this was all a coincidence. But we had to be sure.

"I'll keep the line open," I said. I was carrying a pistol but didn't see the point in waving it around. No sign of Tom. Had he found a back door after all?

I moved toward the side door. Now I could see lettering on the side and some sort of healthcare logo with a green cross. Red light continued to splash over the widows.

VP came on the line. "Rollie is on the gun now. We still only see one guy. Could be Grist. He's got a uniform and cap on, so it's hard to tell."

Now I saw Stu reach the door from the outside. A huge guy had a grip on his shoulders and despite the clean white uniform, the Glock he had in Stu's ear told me he wasn't here to help.

Tom whispered out of the darkness, "Draw him into the room and get him to turn Stu loose. I can get him in the head from behind."

They hadn't seen me yet. I backed away so that Tom would be behind them if they dealt with me. Still it didn't feel right. "Since when were you a shooter?" I whispered back.

"Time for some beginner's luck?" The tension made even Tom's whisper sound higher in pitch.

They'd be inside in a moment. Mauser rammed him into the door and Stu's face against the window was a mask of fear and confusion.

"VP, tell Rollie it's a positive on Mauser at our door, so you have to be looking at Grist." I wondered if I left it at that where he'd take the shot. I didn't dare try for Mauser. I was no gunslinger. I might be able to rush up and get Mauser, but I was equally likely to hit Stu or miss altogether. "And the big guy has a gun on Stu. I can't get him."

Rollie back on the line. "Kid, I can't drop Grist, Mauser would pop the mechanic. This isn't on him. Are you able to slip out the back?"

"Don't think that's an option."

"Then come outside where I can cover you."

"Or they might just blast me." I figured Grist and Mauser had a plan coming in. Slaughtering everyone might cost them the stones, so we'd at least have a chance to make our case. "Remember the phone is on in my pocket," I said. "Make sure you don't say anything, okay?"

"You sure that's the right play?" Rollie said. "They might not be up for chatting."

"No. But if all they want are the rocks, maybe we let them take them."

"No!" Tom hissed from the background.

Damn. I'd hoped he wouldn't have overheard that.

Whatever I might have come up with to change Tom's mind vanished from my brain when the door squeaked open.

Mauser shoved Stu inside. I wouldn't have thought it possible for the red-headed mechanic to look paler, but his face was sweaty alabaster.

"You hide well for such a slab of beef, Kyle." Mauser glanced around and for a nanosecond I thought of trying to draw on him. Nope, might as well shoot myself. "Where's your buddy?" he asked.

I figured he meant Tom, but decided to play obtuse to stall for time. "Ryan's in the wind, hadn't you heard? I got stuck with digging out of this mess. I never wanted to cross up with you and Grist."

"We're a little more than cross." Mauser had a deep voice that made him sound huge even over the phone. "And if you give me another cute answer, I'll put one in this guy's knee."

"Please, no." Stu looked like he might pass out.

"Shut up." Mauser twisted one thumb on Stu's hand and the guy nearly buckled from the pain.

"You don't have to hurt anyone," I said. "That's not why you went to all this trouble."

"Maybe I want to. Ever think of that?" Mauser showed his teeth in more of a snarl than a smile. I'd seen him around enough over the years to recognize him, but never up close. His face bore a C-shaped scar on one cheek and all the skin showed the craggy aftermath of terrible adolescent acne.

"You don't owe us any favors," I said, "but adding bodies isn't going to lower your profile. You two still need to get out of the country. I have my own reasons to keep my mouth shut and not get involved with the cops."

"You looked plenty involved with them when you left the port, didn't you?" He glanced around but his gaze returned to me too fast for me to contemplate doing anything stupid. "Where's Tom?"

I paused and was certain he was going to hurt Stu and then me, but before I could say anything Tom spoke up.

"I've got a gun on you right now, Mauser," he said from the shadows. His voice was steady and strong. I was impressed.

"You better use it while you have the chance, Tommy. Make it count, 'cause now I see you hiding back there."

Mauser was shielded behind Stu, but he shoved the man to his knees and stooped over to rest his chin atop Stu's head. "Ready to play William Tell? Take your shot at the apple. C'mon. Kyle, you can play too, but I won't be aiming at your bum knee, believe that."

My whole body felt like a coiled spring, but unless Tom actually fired, I didn't dare move. I wondered if Rollie still had Grist in the crosshairs, but that was small comfort in here.

"How about nobody shoots?" I said, as much for Rollie as Tom. "Mauser, I'll put my gun on the floor and Tom will come out and do the same."

"You guys are no fun." Mauser keyed a microphone clipped to his shoulder. "Two inside plus the wrench." He listened to a reply and adjusted an earpiece. "Not yet. Won't be long." Another pause. "Understood."

Tom emerged from the corner shadows holding his pistol in two fingers and away from the trigger. That was that. Mauser had us both, but we'd never really stood a chance.

Stu looked like he was melting before our eyes.

"Both pieces on the deck and kick them over to me. Pasty," he said to Stu, "make one move toward them and your brains will cover 'em first."

Stu didn't figure to surprise us with heroics. This had definitely not been part of the negotiations for his fee.

Tom and I did as we were told. I moved extra slow and turned around so Mauser could see me take the gun out from behind my back.

Once he'd taken the weapons, he gestured to the floor. "Take a seat, kiddies. You too." Mauser shoved Stu down. "Three secure," he said into the mic.

Mauser spoke to Tom. "First things first, where are the stones?"

All I could think was, don't say, *"What stones?"*

"If I tell you, are you going to kill us?" Tom said, and I braced for the explosion.

The strobing red ambulance flashers went out.

The door opened a moment later and Grist walked in. "Nope. We won't kill you. We won't even damage your pretty faces."

"Other parts ...," Mauser said.

"For now, we are pressed for time," Grist went on, "so we will remove this gentleman's fingers," he nodded at Stu, "a knuckle at a time. And if you two don't seem to care, well, you each have ten toes, don't you?"

"Did you see they have a floor drain? Very convenient," Mauser said.

Aside from not being willing to be mutilated for a bunch of baubles, I started wondering why they cared about preserving our faces.

"Tell them," Stu said. "I have some cash, you can have it."

Grist turned to Stu. "Did you get them all out?"

"Yes, yes. Tell them," Stu begged us.

"It sounds like you did your part. I wouldn't dream of cheating you out of your hard-earned pay," Grist said. His jaw clenched. "Enough. Tom, let's have them."

Mauser took out a KA-BAR knife and slammed Stu prone to the floor with his other hand. He pinned Stu's right wrist under a thick boot.

Tom's face crumbled. "You bastards. They're in a small pouch on top of those crates."

"No games?" Grist asked.

My mind raced with what Rollie must be thinking. I couldn't be sure if the line remained open with the way the phone jostled in my pocket.

"No. No tricks. Just take them."

Grist scrambled up the crates like a seasoned rock climber despite being at least a decade older than me.

"Yes?" Mauser called up.

A low whistle was all the reply he needed.

Mauser removed his boot from Stu's wrist and allowed him to sit up.

All the while I tried to put myself in Rollie's place. He had no shot with the rifle while we were inside. He couldn't rush the place by himself and I doubted VP even knew how to use a gun. That would be a suicide mission.

Grist climbed down and examined the contents. "My compliments. These are everything I hoped they would be."

"May you never get the chance to enjoy them," Tom said.

I cut in. "No, enjoy them or whatever, but if you tie us up and blindfold us, you're sure to make a clean escape. You don't need to kill us."

Grist looked at Mauser. "So much talk of killing. Who said anything about killing?" Then he took the pouch and pressed it into my hands.

"What?" I said, staring dumbly at it, then up at Grist. "What is this? You don't want the stones?"

"Oh, we want the stones." The two of them were grinning. "Just not yet."

CHAPTER 30

Cold from the cement floor of the garage seeped into my hamstrings and rear end, making a sudden move about impossible. Grist had Mauser place a rectangular piece of plywood to separate me from Tom.

He'd been asking us questions and reading our reactions with the barrier preventing us from signaling each other. He'd been more than clear that Stu would pay the price if he detected deception.

I saw little point in lying and hoped Tom felt the same way. Once Grist gave me back the stones it had been easy to discern the reason. They wanted us to move forward with the deal. Now I understood why they weren't going to damage our faces. It would be hard to imagine Mr. Beautiful feeling comfortable if we were all black and blue.

For now, their greed gave us a moment of grace, but I didn't think they'd care what they did to us after they got what they wanted. Same went for Mr. B and whoever he brought.

Luckily just before they made us sit down for questioning, they forced us to empty our pockets. I managed to thumb off the burner Rollie had been monitoring and they weren't all that surprised that we both carried multiple phones. Presumably they used the same sorts of techniques. They just wanted to know which one was for Bishop, and which one we needed to signal Mr. B's people. The others they apparently just assumed went to some other shady support contacts I had.

For the most part, Tom and I played it straight. We'd both figured out that they weren't aware of Rollie and VP nearby. That was the one thing we kept secret.

Rollie had to have heard enough to know they intended to rob the meet. He and VP already knew where it would take place. After that, I had no idea what to expect.

Would Rollie call Bishop? Other cops? I wondered. At best, the police would take down Grist and Mauser, but also all the rest of us and Mr. B. I could live with prison after playing with fire, and at this stage blaming Ryan for my situation seemed pointless. But I wondered how far a betrayed Mr. B's influence reached. All the way to lockup? Maybe, and not just for me but anyone around me. Rollie and VP?

On the other hand, a wave of cops would most likely trigger a huge shootout with plenty of dead police and others, and no guarantees Grist and Mauser would even get caught.

As I played all the scenarios in my head, I kept coming back to the best one being that Grist and Mauser succeeded but let us all live, with Mr. B blaming them and not us for the rip-off.

And the best part was that Tom and I had no choice but to play along and stall for time hoping when the time came, we'd know the right thing to do. Simple.

* * *

"So," Grist said to me, "they're expecting you and Tom in the truck?"

"That's right."

"Okay, that's what they'll get." Grist looked over at Stu, who had regained some color in his face but hadn't spoken for a while. "What about him?"

"He's in the dark," I said and Tom agreed. "His job was to help with the fuel tank and keep his mouth shut. That's it."

Stu nodded like a bobblehead in an earthquake.

Grist thought for a moment. "In the dark and mouth shut?"

"That's all," Stu managed to stammer.

"It's enough," Grist said. "Now, tell me where you keep the keys to the little backhoe I saw parked around the side."

* * *

ONE HOUR LATER

"You don't have to do this," I said.

The last I'd seen of Stu was Mauser hoisting Stu over his shoulder, no mean feat. They'd wrapped him up in so much duct tape that he looked like a silver mummy from the neck down. His mouth was taped shut, but he could still breathe through his nose.

Grist covered Tom and me with a pistol. "You're absolutely right. Be glad it won't take us long to reach the meet. If we were pressed for time it'd be far simpler to cut his throat and bury him for good."

"Where will you bury us?" I asked.

"If you play ball, you'll live to set him free. He should be fine for a few hours, unless it rains. We put that PVC pipe to good use. If you two try to get in our way, he'll starve before anyone finds him."

"Why should we trust you?" Tom said.

"Tommy boy, you can make this go down smooth and easy if you help, but we can make it happen ugly too, kill everyone and take the stones and the dough. It makes the getaway stickier, that's all. Get it?"

"Yeah," I said for him. In the distance we could hear the backhoe start up again.

"I hope so. The silver surfer in the hole is counting on you. If that doesn't matter, think of your own worthless hides."

Mauser returned a short while later with dirt all over his hands. He grinned at us while he washed up and saw Tom looking at him a little too intently. "What?"

"I was thinking about the proverb about when setting out for revenge, dig two graves," Tom said.

"What revenge? That sap never did anything to us. Now just imagine what we do to those who screw us over." Mauser dried his hands. He glanced over to Grist. "Did he make the call?"

Grist shook his head, picked up one of the burner phones and handed it to Tom. "Care to do the honors?"

I remembered the procedure Tom had briefed me on, all part of Ryan's elaborate safeguards against last-minute double-crosses. I guess he never imagined the two goons with us in the picture.

Tom made the call and spoke briefly with the person on the other end. "He's right here." Tom handed the phone to me.

"This is Kyle Logan. Ryan asked me to help him with this small favor. He said to tell you 'Irish eyes are still smiling.'"

On the other end of the line a heavily-accented voice spoke. Mr. Beautiful. "Okay. I'm sorry he could not be here himself, but he spoke highly of you. You have my missing property?"

"We do. And you have our reward?"

"Of course." He gave me a location a couple of towns away. "We will see you in one hour?" I looked to Tom, who nodded.

"One hour."

* * *

IN THE DELIVERGISTICS TRUCK CAB

Grist sat next to me in the big rig. Behind us, Mauser followed in the ambulance. I'd seen him strap Tom to a gurney in the back and they didn't need to bother further articulating the implied threat. Tom was resourceful and I didn't put it past his capabilities to untie himself, but he wasn't stupid. For now, we still just had to play ball, which for me consisted of "Just drive."

After a brief huddle with Mauser, Grist had known where to go. So far, I'd seen no sign of Rollie and VP. I didn't know if they knew what had happened to Stu or not. I didn't think where Mauser took him had been in their line of sight. Part of me hoped they'd save Stu and stay far from danger, but I had no way of knowing what they were doing.

Grist whistled as the truck rolled through the night. We saw few other cars while we headed southwest, roughly paralleling Laurel Mountain State Park. The moon peeked out between clouds and I hoped it stayed that way so the rain would hold off. I pictured Stu trapped in a shallow grave and those PVC air pipes turning into drowning faucets.

"Kyle, are you going to tell me what really happened to Ryan? This isn't one of his regular deals. Hard to believe he'd miss it." Grist studied my face for a reaction.

"I wish he was here too," I said.

Grist laughed and I realized how it must have sounded.

"No, I mean this never had anything to do with me and—"

"You're 'just holding it for a friend,' is that it?" Grist mocked.

"Ryan wore out his welcome in town before this deal was ready. He has bigger worries than you two." Grist's connections weren't in Fishtown, so my guess was all he had were suspicions but no hard evidence Ryan was gone. In any case I didn't think Ryan would have given Grist and Mauser pause. I wasn't scaring them, that was for sure.

"Does he? Well, bless his heart. As long as you don't, we'll get along just fine."

We rode in silence after that. About every fifteen minutes Grist would check in with Mauser and to my relief all seemed well on the other end. Good, Tom wasn't trying to take on Mauser by himself.

The closer we got, the tighter my chest became. "Are you planning on leaving Tom on that gurney?"

"Do you have any questions that aren't stupid?" Grist consulted a paper map. "I realize your contact knows Tom personally so he has to be part of the exchange."

"How did you find us? You must have seen the cops when we left the port." He wanted a better question, it was worth a shot. "I never saw a tail."

"That's right. You never did. Sucks to be you."

"No argument," I said.

"Pull over at the next turn in for the park entrance. Then follow me," Grist said.

At this time of night, the park would be closed. I also knew we weren't making the deal there. We still had about ten minutes to our destination.

"Bathroom break?" I had a horrible vision of Rollie coming around the corner and right into a trap.

At the turn, the truck's brakes hissed and I saw the ambulance signal to follow. The lot wasn't designed for big rigs, but we had the place to ourselves and there was another exit lane to the road at the other end of the parking lot.

"Shut up and come with me." Grist hopped out of the truck as soon as I stopped.

I followed him to the back of the ambulance. I was relieved both to see Tom alive and off the gurney. He rubbed his wrists.

"Won't be long now," Grist said.

Mauser reached into a storage box in the ambulance and lifted out a windbreaker and then a heavy vest.

"You're out of your mind, mate," Tom said.

"What are you complaining about? You don't have to wear it," Grist said.

"Yeah, you just have to stand next to it." Mauser laughed.

"If that's what I think it is," I said, "you can get another volunteer."

"If you think it's a bomb vest, you have a keen eye for fashion," Grist said. "And when did we say anything about volunteering? You do things exactly as we tell you and you and the shrimp might just live to pull your dopey friend out of the ground."

"Don't forget to accessorize." Mauser took out a baseball cap and I began to understand. The red cap bore the logo for the Philadelphia Phillies, with a white letter "P" embroidered onto a red field. Inside the loop of the letter, I noticed a reflective glint.

He began to plug in some electronics, along with a receiver and earpiece.

"Nothing to worry about, Kyle," Grist said. "I'll see what you see and can tell you what to say."

"And I go boom if you don't like the way I say it."

"Don't be so dramatic. The vest is a bluff for our buddy, so he'll hand over the cash and be a good sport about getting nothing in return."

"So, the bomb is fake?" Tom said.

"Very real. Think of it as an insurance policy."

"And if you have any other thoughts," Mauser said, "I'll be around to keep an eye on you as well." He took out a long case that no doubt held a high-powered scoped rifle.

"Let's not keep our esteemed trading partner waiting," Grist said. "Kindly suit up."

Grist still had the bag of stones. "Are you going to give me a bag of sand to hold up before I have to rip him off?"

"Not at all. We trust you, here." Grist gave me the diamonds and Mauser fitted the bulky device to me. It felt heavy and tight with a wired box of batteries and a phone near my waist. It made it hard to breathe, but that might have been me.

"Listen carefully," Mauser said, with no trace of his mocking tone. "Once I arm it, only he can deactivate it." He pointed to Grist. "He can trigger it long distance, plus it will go off if you try remove it or play amateur bomb squad and mess with the detonator. Finally, you're on a three-hour timer, which should be plenty, unless you get ideas about driving out of range."

"I got it. Behave or else." My voice sounded stronger than I felt.

Mauser held up the cap and an earpiece. "The radio's on the same frequency as mine. He can see you, I'll watch through my scope. If you hear coded talk, it's for me. If you aren't sure and it is plain English, he's talking to you."

"Okay. And if they don't shoot us," I nodded to Tom, "then what?"

Mauser handed Tom the pistol he'd taken off him a while ago. "Tom here has your back. He'll cover the retreat."

"Make it look good, but don't scare them into opening up on you," Grist added.

Tom took the gun. "I don't have to ask if it's loaded, do I?"

Mauser held his arms wide. "Find out."

Tom looked tempted.

"It is if you *believe* it is," Grist said. He turned serious. "Play it straight, both of you. Sell it and follow directions and we won't smoke you and your Mr. Beautiful and his entourage, not to mention Mr. Fixit in Johnstown." Grist checked his watch, a thick diver's style with a jet-black face and luminous numerals. "Ready? Keep it simple and it stays simple."

CHAPTER 31

HIGHLANDS LIMESTONE AND CRUSHED STONE

Now Tom and I shared the cab of the Delivergistics truck. It felt oddly familiar to drive wearing so much bulky gear. It reminded me of wearing a flak jacket and helmet over in the Sand Box, only then I'd been worried about bombs *outside* the truck.

I'm sure Tom had as much to say as I did, but with the helmet-weight baseball cap on my head we weren't going to plan anything out loud for Grist to overhear.

The ambulance followed us down the road and I tried to move just my eyes to the mirrors, wondering if Rollie and VP were out there. I wished I had some way to warn them.

The gravel company had a huge operation in the middle of this sprawling parkland. It was closed at night and clouds played havoc with the light from the full moon, like God was playing with his own dimmer switch. The main entrance appeared to our left, but I didn't need Grist to mutter "Keep going" into my ear to pass it by.

"I know where the damn turn is," I said. "I just hope the old road is able to handle this rig." It looked easier when we planned this out on the map.

Tom and I had studied the area. There was another road leading to the early part of the quarry. Once it had played out, they took the operation to the other side of the street.

There was a yellow metal gate across the drive but I could see the lock was on the ground. Not exactly high security, but who steals leftover crumbs of lime rock? This was probably meant only to discourage gawkers and teenage explorers.

200

It figured. Mr. Beautiful wanted privacy not security. The route on the ground showed it to be a good choice. The long road nestled among thick stands of trees blocking the view from the highway. The flat, narrow road gave way to a series of switchbacks that put my driving skills to the test. The truck was designed for hauling heavy stuff a long way, not for mountain racing. Even so, I was happy to see that the surface was well maintained and had once supported huge rumbling equipment bearing chalky milled stones hewn from the earth.

At the first place to turn off I noticed the ambulance take the dusty secondary we'd just passed. "Stay on this a bit longer," I heard in my earpiece.

Soon after, the moon slipped from behind another cloud and I saw a turnoff to a large, flat area above a pit that looked like a Caterpillar graveyard. Several generations of used trucks and loaders parked side-by-side. I figured there were working counterparts across the highway being kept running with the spare parts from these.

The trees had opened up to reveal a vast, tiered landscape like a huge staircase of stone leading to a muddy pit. A couple crushed stone roads led away from the main quarry. Piles of debris and raw stone bordered the pit like tiny dormant volcanoes.

"Can you still see?" I asked Grist.

"I got you," he said.

"I'm taking the road to the left." I assumed he knew that, but high explosives made me want to be crystal clear. "Any of the others will roll us into the pit."

"I *said* I could see." Grist's voice carried a little edge and made me wonder if he was feeling the nerves. Less confident than he let on? Twitchier?

One glance in the mirror told me there'd be no way to spot the ambulance from down here. I saw walls, and the tops of some of the stone piles. The moon backlit everything and reflected off the light-colored stone.

Got to be getting close. Around one last mini-mountain of rocks and we saw what must have been one of the original mills, complete with ramped conveyors like an abandoned rollercoaster.

At the base of the building sat a van. When it flashed its headlights, I knew we'd arrived. I hit the brakes and left the truck running.

"Okay Tom, let's have the phone." I held out my hand and he slapped a burner into it like I'd been a surgeon requesting a scalpel. I hit the button and put it on speakerphone.

I spotted a glint of gold on a wrist through the windshield of the van and heard, "Yes?"

"Uh, Mr. Beautiful?"

"Mr. Kyle?" I didn't recognize the voice.

"Right. The directions were excellent."

"In position," I heard in my ear, and for an instant confused it with a reply until I recognized it as Mauser's voice. It was an illusion of the high-quality gear that he sounded close. I could almost feel the scope he'd mentioned panning over us. Of course, they didn't need to shoot me to take me out.

"Roger that," Grist said. "Nice and easy, Kyle. Play it his way until I say different."

A new voice came on the line, the same one I spoke to earlier. "Mr. Logan? You are ready for our exchange?"

"Yes sir. My associate who knows you will confirm your identity."

"Step out, please."

* * *

I shut off the truck and climbed slowly out of the cab. That damn vest made movements clumsy and I was trying hard not to shift my body too much for fear of tripping the anti-tamper device.

Tom met me around the front of the truck, where we stood bathed by the headlights of the two vehicles. The van faced us about 25 yards away.

Just as I began to wonder if they were thinking about running us down, the van's engine went quiet and the headlights dimmed slightly as they shifted to straight battery power. The doors opened.

The first guy out was a lanky, Middle Eastern man who held a briefcase in one hand and a pistol in the other.

From the passenger side another figure stepped forward. He was older and heavier, wearing a dark business suit and close-cropped black hair with gray at the temples. He had thick features, a salt-and-pepper mustache and black eyebrows. His dark eyes belied the softness of the rest of his body.

"That's him?" I whispered to Tom.

"Yes," he replied.

"Concur," Grist said in my ear. "That's our boy."

"Good to meet you," I said to the man in the suit. I felt like an idiot, but what were we going to do, just stand there and gawk at each other?

Mr. Beautiful nodded. "You look like the picture Ryan sent. I know Tom already." He stepped forward and shaded his eyes against the truck headlights. He frowned. "You have gained weight?"

"Maybe." I felt desperate to deflect the direction of the conversation away from the added bulk under my jacket. "We didn't go to all this trouble to talk diets. We have your property. May we see the payment?"

"Show me the stones," Mr. Beautiful insisted. His partner stared hard at me and I was keenly aware of the array of weapons trained on me—high, low, and wrapped around me.

I held up the bag and opened it. "Take a few and have a look."

"Aziz," Mr. B said, and his man placed the case on the ground and stepped forward with his empty hand outstretched. He still held the pistol, but it was pointed downward. I put three diamonds in his palm and held back the rest.

Mr. B held his open palm in the headlight and used a jeweler's loupe to examine them. Then he looked up and I saw a slight tug at the corners of his mouth. "I will need to see the rest, of course."

"After I see the case." My heart thumped so hard it felt like it was going to set the damn bomb off all on its own.

Mr. B. nodded to Aziz, who holstered his weapon under a jacket, opened the latches on the black leather briefcase, then set it on the ground. He lifted the lid and I saw it was stuffed with bundles of hundred-dollar bills. He took out a couple and flipped the banded packs so I could see they contained currency all the way through.

"Looks like legal tender to me," Grist whispered in my ear. "Kyle, calmly slide your hand to the pouch inside your sleeve and remove the detonator button. No, in case you are wondering, it doesn't work. Say what I say, and nothing sudden."

I pulled the detonator from its pouch. "That's fine, you can put it back in there," I parroted. My mouth felt dry as cotton. "Are you ready?"

Mr. Beautiful was watching me. He whispered something to Aziz I didn't catch, but his hand went back into his jacket.

I said my line, "Go easy, both of you," and slowly held up the detonator.

"Open the jacket, Kyle. Stay frosty, Scope," Grist said. I assumed the second was for Mauser.

"I'm so sorry." I opened the jacket to reveal the blocks of plastique.

Mr. Beautiful's eyes widened for an instant then turned to slits. He growled something Tom probably understood, but I got the idea. He also gestured for Aziz to leave his gun holstered. "Ryan is a jackal and his friends are sons of dogs."

"That's fair," I said without prompting. "But you've come too far to die over a fraction of your fortune," Grist put in my ear.

"You think to terrify me? You believe this is the first qunbula I have seen?"

That one I knew. The word meant "bomb."

"If you know them," Grist supplied, "then you can see this is genuine."

Mr. Beautiful stared hard into my eyes. "Aziz is not the only one with me. Do you really expect to escape with what is mine? We were not enemies before. Why would you do this?"

"I need the money. More than you." Grist sounded surprised at the resistance. I wondered how well he knew this guy. Mr. Beautiful didn't look intimidated at all.

"Tom, this is how you bargain now? After years to gain my trust?"

Tom stared at his feet.

"He didn't know," I blurted out. "Don't blame him."

"Shut up!" Grist yelled into my ear.

"There is enough blame to go around. But tell me, how do you intend to get out of here? If you wanted to kill me, you would have done so already." The man's gaze never wavered.

"Nobody has to die," I said, Grist the ventriloquist again. "Just give me the case and walk away." I waved with the faux detonator in my hand. I was careful to keep my finger off the button.

Mr. Beautiful looked back and forth between me and Tom. If Grist expected him to wilt, he must be getting upset. The quarry pit was near silent except for a faint insect buzzing in the distance.

"I have seen more jihadi than I'd like wearing such vests, eager for martyrdom. They found death. Only Allah knows if they found anything else." Mr. B had begun to smile. "You have no such fire in your eyes. You are no martyr, just a poor thief, and I can see you fear your own death."

"You got to be shitting me," Grist said. I assumed he didn't want me to relay that.

Mr. Beautiful stepped closer to me. "Do what you must. Let us spend our riches in hell together, shall we?"

"Kyle, you are fucking this up, convince him now!" Grist said. "Scope, ready, aim," he added. Two bursts of static in my ear acknowledged the command.

I held Mr. Beautiful's gaze. "You are making a mistake." I glanced upward and back to him and up again. He followed my lead and looked closer at my hat.

Mr. Beautiful stepped right up to me, reached up and took the cap off my head. Wires traced down the back of my neck and stretched. He pointed the camera at the case and the bag of stones in my hand. He waved to Aziz, who brought the case and set it at our feet.

Mr. B turned the cap around and spoke into it directly. "Coward. You will destroy the reason you came." He held me by the shoulder. "Come out and negotiate, face to face." Mr. B tore the wire out of the cap and threw the cap on the ground, where he stomped the camera with an audible crunch. My earpiece still worked, as Grist about burst my eardrum with cursing.

Grist only stopped when Mauser cut in. "Break. Break. Break."

Grist turned professional instantly. "Go, Scope."

"Just spotted a long gun," Mauser said in a clipped tone. "Don't think he's seen me yet."

"Kyle, tell him I'm coming out," Grist said. "He's a businessman, we'll talk business."

I held the earpiece as much to show Mr. B as to make sure I heard Grist. "They want to talk. Says he's coming." I wondered if Grist was trying to convince me or Mr. B about the next move.

I didn't have to wonder long. The earpiece cracked. "They want to do this the hard way. Long gun first, Scope."

Long gun meaning Rollie? "Don't shoot!" I yelled and waved my arms. "Mauser, no! I'll tear this bomb right off my body. All the loot is near me."

"Scope, new target," I heard Grist say and I knew who the new target was going to be.

I tossed the bag of diamonds to Mr. B, but the drawstring was still loose and the bag opened mid-air and scattered glittering stones in the chalky mud and soil. "Run! They have a sniper!" I shouted and grabbed the briefcase.

Aziz drew his pistol but appeared unsure about what to do next, go with his boss, grab the diamonds, or shoot me. Tom scrambled away and Mr. B ran toward the abandoned building.

I knew I couldn't run fast, but figured I'd stand a better chance if I had a better idea where Mauser was perched. I did a fast-limping zigzag toward the truck. Too slow—my bad knee might as well have been an anchor.

"I got him." I heard Mauser's death sentence in my own ear. I wasn't halfway there when I saw a bright green dot of light dance on one of the stone pile mountains facing me.

"My eye!" Mauser screamed into my ear. "Sonofabitch!"

The road in front of me erupted in a white puff of dust followed a split second later by the crack of a rifle shot. Half my mind thought that the bomb had gone off, but the smarter portion realized Mauser just missed me. Barely.

"Scope, report," Grist called out. "Target status?"

"Somebody fucking lased me," Mauser said.

I heard another shot from a different location. All the rock and stone piles made it hard to be sure where, but I was able to get to some cover from where I'd seen that green light point.

"Taking fire!" Mauser yelled and I saw the muzzle flash from his spot.

Aziz must also have seen it as he knelt down and methodically began to fire his pistol toward where Mauser was hiding. I'd guess it was probably one hundred or more yards away. Not easy for a handgun, but if nothing else it would give the sniper something to worry about.

Aziz and Mauser exchanged a few more shots, but I didn't hear any more from the second location. I wanted to go look, but with the bomb still on me I'd be more of a risk than help if Rollie was hurt, plus I still didn't know where he was.

Mauser's rounds snapped off the ground and hit rocks. Some thunked into the mill building and I hoped Tom was behind better cover than old boards. Aziz knew what he was doing and fired and moved often. The laser that got Mauser's eye must have worked, because a rifle in skilled hands would have made short work of Aziz otherwise.

"Scope? Scope, report," I heard over the radio. No reply and Aziz reloaded during the lull. I could see him and when he looked my way, I put my fingers to my lips then to my ear. He seemed to understand. At least he stopped firing.

"He killed them all," I said. "Why'd you have to do that?"

"Shut up," Grist said. "Scope, check in."

"Did they get him? Maybe they got him, but I think he wasted everyone else," I said.

"What are you talking about?" Grist said.

"Don't hit the trigger," I said. "I have the stuff." I didn't have to try to sound scared.

"Can you see Scope?"

"There might still be another sniper." I hoped that was true, but I couldn't think of why he'd gone so quiet otherwise. If his radio was hit, he could at least fire a shot in the air. "Look, take the stuff and go, but get this thing off me. You won, okay?"

"I know the rig is still on you, I get a signal," Grist said. "Hurry up, and you better not be lying."

"Give me a minute here. I have to run, no place to turn the truck around."

"Screw that. Get on the road, I'm coming to you, meet you halfway up the hill."

Between the weight of the vest, the case full of cash and my damn knee, it was going to be a slog no matter what. I agreed and glanced back to make sure none of the others tried to follow.

Strange how nobody else seemed to want to be close to a guy with high explosives strapped to his body.

I saw Grist's headlights and picked up the pace. My knee was in the sweet spot where it was warmed up enough to give me more movement but hadn't seized up yet. It wasn't a big window, so I tried to make the most of it. I needed to get close to Grist to have a chance.

I still didn't hear anything in my earpiece from Mauser, not even groans or static bursts. From where I lumbered up the hill, he'd have a perfect firing position.

The ambulance approached slowly and through the windshield I saw Grist's face whipping around, trying to spot danger. Mr. B had chosen a good location. Lots of hiding places and the pit seemed to swallow sounds. I wondered if the gunfire would attract the police, but even if the noise escaped the quarry I didn't know if anyone was around to complain.

"I see you, Kyle. Stop there. I'm backing up to you." Grist did a choppy three-point turn and I realized he was plenty worried about rolling the ambulance. I caught my breath while he maneuvered. The backup warning on the ambulance filled the still air with beeps.

Safety first.

I had to remember that Grist's stress was going to make him more volatile. I needed to think of how to exploit his mistakes.

The ambulance shifted into park. I could hear Grist breathing into his microphone.

I heard the double doors on the rear of the ambulance open from both sides. Grist wore his phony paramedic clothes and he held a detonator that looked identical to the one he'd given me. I didn't doubt his was functional. He tore off the wireless rig and my earpiece went dead.

I held up the case and walked toward him.

"That's close enough." He had a pistol holstered in his front waistband.

I agreed. If this vest was half as powerful as I thought, he was well within the blast radius.

He eyed the case. "Open it." I did and a couple bundles fell out.

Grist shifted the detonator to his weak hand and drew the gun. "No tricks." I noticed sweat stains on the blue uniform.

"Sorry," I said. "I'm clumsy, that's all."

"Leave those. Close it and throw the case into the back. Gently." Grist stood aside and trained the pistol on me.

I did as he asked. I figured throwing it at him was just a good way to get shot instead of blown up. But now he had the money I'd been holding "hostage."

"Now the packets."

It was awkward to bend over, but squatting wasn't happening on my knee. I pitched the bundles into the ambulance, where they landed under the gurney. I was running out of time.

"The stones? Where are they?"

I didn't know what else to do. I reached inside my shirt, but instead of pretending to look for a pouch of diamonds that I didn't have, I felt for the straps to take the bomb off of me. The Velcro made an audible tearing sound.

"Don't!" Grist pocketed the detonator and took out another tool that looked like a smartphone covered with a keypad.

I stepped closer and the vest shifted. Now I was holding it against my body. "The diamonds are on the ground back at the mill area. They spilled when Mauser shot up the place. Just leave. There could be some pissed off survivors down there." I curled my fingers under the vest so he could see I was about to remove it right in front of him.

Grist punched a quick sequence on the pad. His forehead was slick with perspiration. "Go ahead, dumbass."

I did. I wasn't trying to be brave. I had a good idea of what he'd just done and I'd either confirm it or this would come to a messy end.

Cool air washed over my stomach and I hoisted the vest over my head and flung it at the open back of the ambulance. It flopped onto the floor at the edge of the open doorway.

"Asshole." Grist raised his pistol and I braced to dive to the side. No way he'd miss, it was only a question of if it would it be lethal. I heard the shot.

Make that shots, and from two directions. I felt nothing but gravel tearing at my bare belly and chest.

I heard Grist swear and more shots, them the slam of the doors. I rolled over and looked and got a face-full of dust and pebbles as the ambulance sprayed gravel and raced up the hill.

While I spit sand and cleared my eyes, I saw Aziz run toward me and slam another magazine into his pistol. He'd followed me.

Aziz continued to fire at the retreating ambulance and then I saw something else. The bomb vest sat on the ground. Grist must have kicked it out before he fled.

I struggled to my feet and ran for the vest. Aziz stopped shooting long enough to realize what I was doing and he threw himself to the ground.

The ambulance was plenty far enough away and I snatched up the vest and swung it like a drunken discus thrower. The vest sailed through the air and over the side of one of the rocky steps cut into the hill of the quarry. I joined Aziz on the ground and looked to see the ambulance slow and stop just before the last turn out of our sight.

An instant later I felt the shock through the ground when the vest went off with a powerful blast. Rocks and dust showered deeper into the pit, but it was far from any of our people. The ambulance disappeared up the road.

"Are you shot?" Aziz asked me.

I checked before answering. Adrenaline can be a funny rush. "Nope, just cuts and scrapes. You?"

"I'm unharmed." Aziz stood with his pistol dangling at his side and the slide locked back on an empty mag. He glared in the direction of the dust trail left by the ambulance.

"Everyone down there all right?"

"No," Aziz said. "Do you know where he is going?"

"Out of the country as fast as he can," I began, then his response clicked. "Wait, someone is hurt? Who?"

"Your friend. In the leg. I think he will live. My boss is tending to him." Aziz continued to stare at the top of the quarry.

"Come on, let's get down there."

Aziz soon passed me. I arrived to find him retrieving some basic first aid gear from their van.

Just inside the mill building Tom lay on a makeshift cot of several crates and unfolded cardboard boxes. A blood-soaked torn pantleg lay on the floor and a leather belt was cinched high on Tom's thigh to act as a tourniquet.

"The smallest target and only one hit. Some luck eh?" Tom looked pale but alert.

Mr. B glanced at me. "I'm glad you are not blown to pieces. Make sure this stays tight." He pointed to the belt. "Aziz." The man returned and I noticed an AK-47 with a folding stock across his back.

Aziz and Mr. B spoke in rapid Arabic and I only caught a word or two.

"Stay here," Mr. B said. "I am going to retrieve my property and Aziz will check on our man. I fear the worst." I noticed a softening to his tone of voice. "Still, thank you for saving our lives," he added.

"Sorry? Your man and Aziz saved ours."

Aziz rushed into the room a moment later. "He's coming back."

Mr. B. drew a pistol and swore in Arabic, where I was on more familiar ground. Something about mothers. He looked at me. "Can you shoot?"

I nodded. I could provide covering fire at least. Mr. B grabbed the pistol out of Aziz's waistband and handed it to me.

"Hang in there, Tom," I said as I checked the chamber for a live round. Then I headed outside.

The moon hid behind some clouds so all we saw were headlights bouncing and weaving down the rocky road. Aziz snapped out the AK-47's stock and shouldered his rifle.

This wasn't the ambulance; the light set was all wrong. Then I heard the loud V-8 rumble. "Don't shoot, it's a friend!"

CHAPTER 32

THE QUARRY

Aziz kept his finger off the trigger but as the Blue Bomber rolled up, he never let his aim waver.

Rollie pulled to a stop and stuck his empty hands out the window.

I looked at Aziz and Mr. B. "He's with me, it's okay." I yelled out, "C'mon out, Rollie."

"You sure?"

"Okay," Aziz said. "Hands in view."

Mr. B finished collecting his diamonds and ignored Rollie until he was satisfied with the count. When he was done, he stepped forward.

"Who are you?"

"I'm Kyle's friend. And I knew Ryan," Rollie said.

Mr. B's head cocked at that. "Knew?"

"It doesn't matter. I'm here for Kyle. You can call me Rollie." He extended his hand.

"Ali," he said, shaking it. "You saved us?"

Ali B? Probably not, it made him sound like a DJ.

"I had help, and with all due respect, we still have a chance to catch Grist."

Aziz jumped like he'd been zapped with a cattle prod. "*Grist?*"

"You know him?" Rollie said.

"We do," Ali said. "He has caused us problems on both sides of the globe."

Aziz was more specific. "He murdered my cousin in Tikrit."

Ali nodded. "One of my couriers, helping Tom with the package." He looked at Rollie. "You saw where he went?"

"Whoever is coming, let's go and I'll fill you in," Rollie said. "Where's Tom?"

"I'll stay with him," Ali said. "What about the other one. Mauser?"

"Your guy got him, but I'm afraid Mauser shot him back before he bled out."

I had plenty of questions, but they could wait until we got moving.

"Aziz?" Ali didn't have to ask twice.

* * *

I jumped into the Blue Bomber still carrying Aziz's pistol. Aziz sat in back and Rollie roared the Bomber up the slopes like he was doing the Pike's Peak road rally.

"What happened?" I said. "If talking won't make you crash. What was that green light? It really messed with Mauser."

"That was all VP." Rollie sawed at the wheel and the old car drifted up the switchbacks. "I'll let her tell you."

Aziz clutched the door handle. I made sure his finger was far from the trigger of that AK.

Rollie whipped the car around a rock pile and skidded to a stop next to where VP sat cross-legged on the ground working a controller and barely looking up from her work.

"Yo," she said to me as she crawled into the back with her gear. She kind of waved to Aziz, then went back to her screen. "Roll out, dude," she said to Rollie. "Hang a right on the main road. I need to land and swap batteries."

"You got him?" Rollie said.

"Had him. He was hauling ass, no way to keep up, but it's thick with trees along here. Not much choice for him. If we hurry it's the only road for a bit." She never looked up from the screen and I couldn't see it from the front seat.

Rollie left rubber on the pavement when we made the turn. The road was dark and quiet, and I saw no sign of police.

"Half a mile up," VP said, "I'm down on the right side of the road."

"What is that?" I asked.

She finally looked up and I could see she was sweating from the concentration. "He drives a car, you drive a truck, and I'm the best damn drone pilot you ever met."

"That's how you tailed us from the truck shop?"

"You know it." She gave a little proud smile. "I'm sorry about your friend. I was as quick as I could be."

"That was your green laser?" Aziz said.

"Rollie was going to try to do a … what did you call it?"

"Counter-sniper." Rollie jammed on the brakes. I saw the drone sitting on the shoulder, otherwise we had the dark unlit road to ourselves. VP jumped out and swapped out a battery pack. As soon as she returned to the car the four rotors buzzed into life and the bricklike body lifted from the shoulder and zipped forward.

We hadn't moved and I realized Rollie was waiting for the drone to scout the road ahead.

"Anyway, I had a better idea," VP said. "We kept the car out of sight once we saw where the ambulance parked. Then I had to change batteries and that goon Mauser gave us the slip. Rollie watched while I scanned the area at a distance. He figured out the best sniping spots and damned if it didn't work."

"We weren't sure when to move because we didn't know what they were doing with you and Tom," Rollie said.

"I saw Mauser shift his aim and we spotted your sniper guy." VP pointed to Aziz. "Then we saw Kyle get all worked up and suddenly Mauser looked like he was going to start blasting you guys instead."

"He was," I said.

"Yeah, well I wish I could carry missiles on my little drone, but I had to make do. I flew as close as I could before I thought he'd see me and when he went all tunnel vision on that scope, I let him have it with the laser."

"You should have heard him," I said. "You saved my life."

"I'm glad he missed. Then your guy shot him, but he kept firing back at him and down at your group. He must have hit your man, he went down, but I saw the rest of you on the ground scatter."

"Tom's hit in the leg," I said. "Could have been much worse."

She and Rollie had seen what happened at the ambulance from a distance, but I filled them in on the details—until I froze. I'd gotten so caught up I'd almost forgotten about Stu. "Did you see what they did with the guy who worked at the truck place?"

"Huh?" Rollie and VP said at the same time.

"They buried him alive." I explained what happened.

"We'll get him out," Rollie said. "First, we nail this piece of garbage." He eased the car forward at VP's okay.

"I think I hit him." Aziz found his voice.

"Are you sure?" I asked.

"No, but it spoiled his aim when I began to shoot," he said.

"It sure did," I said. "I thought I was a dead man."

VP interrupted. "Got a bunch of turnouts here, but nobody parked."

"I hit the ambulance a number of times," Aziz said.

"Grist knows we can describe the vehicle," I said. "Bullet holes will only look worse. He's going to ditch it first chance he gets."

"Whoa," VP yelled. "I got him."

"Where is he?" Rollie asked.

"Just the ambulance. It's in a little empty parking lot on the right side. Careful, the driver's side door is open."

Rollie goosed the gas pedal.

"There's a hiking trailhead," VP said.

"Can you follow it?" Rollie asked.

"Better not. It looks really narrow, I think I'd just wreck it on a tree and tip him off."

"Just let me out," Aziz said.

I wanted to warn him about how dangerous Grist was, but of course he already knew that. He also didn't look like he was in any mood to listen.

Rollie killed his headlights and pulled over before the turn into the parking lot. We were still the only ones on the road this late. I figured we had a couple hours of darkness left. Grist could be long gone by then if we didn't catch him.

Rollie got out of the car and I saw he had his old .45 with him. He pointed to Aziz and me. "You two take point and approach the back doors. I'll cover the driver's side in case he's still in there. Make sure you know where everyone is before you fire, I'm too old to get fragged."

"Fragged?" Aziz had followed Rollie's directions until that last. He'd had some training.

"He just means be careful," I said.

"VP, can you loiter with that thing and watch the trail in case he comes back this way?"

"Yeah, I'm still okay on juice. If I see him, I'll go nuts with the laser and blow the horn."

Rollie nodded. "Let's check that meat wagon."

The moon was in and out of the clouds but we gave our eyes a minute to adjust. We approached the lot and saw the ambulance parked at an angle at the other end, maybe fifty feet away. The dome light was still on from the open driver's door and as we got closer, I thought I could make out some dark smears on the interior door panel.

I tried to be as quiet as possible hating the crunch of gravel under my feet. Aziz moved like a cat and Rollie, despite his age, regressed into the marine sniper he'd been decades ago, moving forward in a crouch, stopping to listen every few feet. I strained to pick up any sound from inside the ambulance, but no luck. Other than my big feet, all I could hear was the faint whirr of VP's drone. The electric operation may have devoured batteries, but damn was it quiet.

Rollie had shifted to hand signals and Aziz seemed to follow them just fine. He held his AK like a soldier and kept his finger off the trigger.

When we got close to the back doors the dome light worked to our advantage. We could see inside the windows and Grist would have to be crouched down, but even so, we'd be ready if he burst out.

Rollie had melted into some of the roadside bushes and had a perfect vantage on the driver's side. If Grist bailed from the passenger side Aziz could hit him from the right.

It was hard to tell from where I stood if the ambulance had been parked or crashed. I got to the back door and Aziz stood off at an angle, weapon raised. I yanked hard on the handle and hauled the door wide open and scrambled to the side bracing for a burst (or bursts) of gunfire.

"Clear," Aziz said.

Rollie moved to the front and echoed Aziz. "Looks you did hit him earlier, young man."

Blood smears and spatter decorated the back floor and streaked toward the driver's seat. A couple empty bandage boxes sat on the passenger seat.

I noticed the case I gave him was missing. "He took the money."

"Blood trail," Aziz called out, and shone a shrouded light toward the ground and we all saw intermittent droplets leading toward the trailhead.

"Wait here," Rollie said. "Let me get my rifle. We don't know what he's packing."

I nodded and Rollie jogged back to the car.

"*You* wait," Aziz said. "I can follow a blood trail." He padded to the trailhead and squatted. He touched the ground and licked his fingers.

"Don't," I hissed.

He grinned and dashed into the woods.

I had a split second to decide. I jogged after Aziz. I knew Rollie would be pissed, but I trusted him more than Aziz not to shoot me by accident. If I was close to Aziz, at least he'd know where I was.

* * *

The instant I left the parking lot I questioned my decision. Dark went to near inky blackness in the trees. I had to crouch to avoid losing the trail, and the trees and brush intruded across the path and scratched my face. I strained my ears. I heard a shuffling sound and followed it around a bend in the trail. Where the hell did Aziz go? No sign of the flashlight. He'd either turned it off or was concealing the beam well.

I was about to go back toward the trailhead when I damn near ran into Aziz, who whipped around and pressed the rifle barrel into my chest.

"Stupid!" he said in a fierce whisper. "Look." He pointed and by now my eyes had adjusted enough to make out faint distinction on the trail and sure enough I saw the money case and more dime-sized black droplets that had to be blood.

But no body.

Aziz reached for the case and the hair on the back of my neck stood up. I snatched his arm back with so much force he tipped over onto his butt.

He cursed in Arabic, but quietly, and I leaned toward his ear and said, "Boom?"

Blood trails and jungle warfare weren't my strong suits, but I was very familiar with booby traps and IEDs.

Now I saw the whites of his eyes for a moment and knew he got my meaning. He patted my arm in gratitude.

"He's got to be close," I said.

Then we heard crackling branches and a loud grunt followed by a thump like a sack of grain smacking the ground.

CHAPTER 33

IN THE WOODS NEAR THE TRAILHEAD

It was hard to pinpoint exactly where the sound had come from, but I was sure it was closer to the trailhead rather than deeper into the woods.

"Rollie," I whispered and started back along the path we'd come. Aziz heard the same thing and being faster, took the lead.

I ignored the swelling in my leg and forced myself to keep up. When we were close to the entrance, I nearly ran into Aziz for a second time.

Aziz stepped over a prone body and I saw it was Rollie. Aziz had his rifle up and swept it left and right looking for Grist. I knelt by Rollie and gulped in relief when my fingers found a pulse in his neck. His breathing was shallow and I felt a knot on his head just behind one ear. His rifle lay under a bush.

Before I could think what to do next, I heard a crackle of branches and a pair of coughing sounds.

Aziz cried out and dropped his rifle without firing a shot. He fell to his knees while clutching his belly. I raised my pistol and tried to stand when a sharp blow struck my wrist and the gun dropped out of my hands. I saw a dark figure in front of me and swung with my left, but the shadow ducked and I felt another blow on my good knee that caused me to sink to the ground in agony.

"Stay right there," Grist's voice came from the specter. He wasn't dressed like a paramedic anymore. He was in all black with a balaclava covering his face. The moon emerged from behind the clouds and I could see a little better. I also realized how close we were to the entrance where the trail opened up.

Grist held an automatic pistol with an enormous suppressor on the end. The big can was aimed right at my face. "You got nine lives or something?" He glanced over his shoulder.

Aziz groaned and I saw blood, way too much blood, washing over his fingers.

Grist saw the same thing I did. "I have saline and some other gear that might pull him through until you get him to a hospital."

"What do you want now?" I asked.

"What I came for. You had to get cute, didn't you? Your friend here." He nudged Rollie with his boot. "That's no hunting rifle. He's more than just a nosy landlord, isn't he? Is he the one who blinded Mauser with that laser?"

I thought of VP out there. How I could somehow tell her to get away, call Bishop. Hell, any cops. "Yeah, I think so."

Grist patted Rollie down and took the pistol. "Where'd he put it? I'd love to end his sniping days with it."

"I don't know," I said.

"Here's the deal, Kyle. We're going back to the quarry before it gets light. You are going to find those diamonds and I'm going to leave."

"Or?"

"You might not care about this mutt, but the old guy, that's another story."

"Okay, I'll show you," I said. "Can we try to help Aziz?"

"Why not?" Grist smiled. "One last thing."

"What?"

"Tell VP to join the party."

I felt like I'd swallowed a bucket of ice. "Who?"

"Never play poker, Kyle. I overheard the old man say something."

"You may have misheard. We're it."

"While we wait for this one to bleed out, maybe I'd understand better with someone else's ears." He held the pistol and with his other hand pocketed his collapsible baton and drew a cruel-looking double-edged knife.

"Don't."

"I learned this over in the Sand Box. Mauser showed me. One-handed, the key is quick hands and a really sharp blade." Grist pressed the flat of the blade against Rollie's head just above his ear. "Watch, now," he said.

I heard a buzz getting louder.

"I'll tell you," I said. "I hardly know him, but VP is—"

Grist heard the sound too and he sprang to his feet like a cat and turned toward this new threat.

The buzz rose in pitch and all I saw was a quick shadow dart from the sky. The impact with Grist's face sounded like a raw egg hitting pavement.

Grist fell backward, tripping over Rollie and landing on Aziz. I saw the knife drop from his hand, but he retained his grip of the pistol.

Like a boxer about to get a standing eight count Grist struggled to try to regain his feet. At first, he seemed to be tangled up with Aziz then I realized they were fighting. Aziz grappled with him and Grist still seemed dazed, concentrating on breaking free.

I looked around felt around under the bushes until I found Rollie's rifle. I had no I idea if it had a round chambered. I made sure I wasn't too close to them and aimed it at Grist. I couldn't get a shot, not yet. He needed to get clear from Aziz.

Grist pushed Aziz in the chest and I heard that coughing sound again when he shot him point blank. Aziz fell back but had Grist's knife in his fist. Grist managed to stand and he made a horrible gargling sound as he reached for his throat. Blood on his chest that I thought had come from Aziz now poured from his neck.

Grist turned toward me, but he seemed to look right through my body. The muzzle of the pistol wavered in my direction, then the gun dropped to the ground as Grist sagged to his knees, pawing at his neck, and then he pitched face first into the dirt.

I kept the gun on him, waiting for him to pop up with another gun or blade, but he didn't move. Then I looked at Aziz, who'd lost consciousness again. I went to his side. "Aziz, stay with me."

He didn't respond and I felt for a pulse. Nothing.

"No, No, No!" I rolled him over and tried chest compressions and mouth-to-mouth. It didn't help, but I tried again anyway, keeping an eye on Grist.

"Is that everyone?"

I whipped around to see VP in her hoodie, crouched and holding a can of pepper spray. She saw my look and said, "Don't know how to shoot." She stepped closer. "Oh crap, I'm gonna puke."

"Later, I need help with Rollie."

That seemed to shake her out of her revulsion. She scampered up the trail and between us we managed to get Rollie to the back of the ambulance. I searched the cabinets inside the ambulance and was surprised to find some of the supplies Grist had promised. I took some smelling salts out of a first aid kit.

I wasn't sure if they were a good idea or not. Before I could decide, I heard Rollie groan. I made sure he didn't try to roll over and off the gurney, but knew he had to stay on his side. If he woke up on his back and vomited, he might choke.

"Hey, buddy. How you feeling? It's Kyle. You're safe."

His eyelids fluttered and opened. He started to look around. "Ah my skull."

"Stay still. You got clipped in the back of the head."

"Hospital?"

"Grist's ambulance."

"Is he …?"

"Yeah."

VP called over. "Welcome back. The good guys won."

Had they? Somehow it felt more like the "less bad" guys won. That said, I was pretty damn glad to be alive.

"VP, see if you can find an ice pack and more bandages," I said. Grist had done a decent job wrapping up his wounded arm and considering the trap he'd prepared he hadn't been as injured as he let on.

VP rummaged through the rest of the cabinets. "Clothes, whoa, that looks like explosives, bandages." She tossed those to me. "Instant ice pack, and damn, there's your walking-around money."

"What's that?"

"I think I found all the cash that was in that case," she said.

I cracked the instant ice pack and shook it to speed up the cold reaction. Rollie was breathing steadily and I hoped it'd be nothing more than a concussion or just a bad headache. I looked over and saw the stacks of cash.

It all made sense. "He wanted to lead us into the woods and find the money case. It had to be a trap. After it sprung, he'd come back to the ambulance. We found the case up the path and I just got the sense something wasn't right."

"He would have killed everyone, right?"

"After he got what he wanted," I said. "You saved us."

"No, I just had to stop him he was going to …" She glanced over to Rollie, who was still kind of out of it.

Her breath hitched and I opened my arms and pulled her in for a hug. "It's okay."

She hugged me back and rallied. "I had no idea if it would even work," she said.

"Sucker punch from the gods."

"I like that." She gave me her crooked smile. "Dude?"

"Yeah?"

"You owe me for a new drone."

* * *

THE TRAILHEAD

I left VP with Rollie. He needed a doctor but didn't seem in imminent danger. The most important thing was to make sure he stayed put and definitely did not try to drive.

I scrambled up the path and first retrieved the weapons and remains of VP's drone. I dropped them into the trunk of Rollie's car.

It would be light soon. The clouds had rolled in heavier and it looked like it might rain. I thought again of Stu.

We still had two bodies here and as far as I knew two more back at the quarry, not to mention a deadly surprise for anyone stumbling onto the scene.

Back at the ambulance I could hear Rollie trying to be difficult.

"Man," VP said, "if you move, your brain will fall out or something." She was trying to keep it light, but there was no mistaking the concern in her voice.

"I've had worse hangovers."

I poked my head in. "Rollie, we've got this. VP, did you come across any of my phones? I can't remember Ali's number."

"Who?"

"Mr. B."

"Oh. Yeah, there's a bunch of them. Are some of these yours?" She pulled open the cabinet that also contained a brick of C4 plastique.

Thankfully they'd used a different brand of phone and I gathered mine from among them. I'd scratched identifiers into each so I could remember who was who.

I found the one for Ali and dialed, praying it wasn't sitting in Aziz's pocket.

Someone picked up but did not speak. Of course, it could have been anyone calling, especially Grist. Then again, it could have been anyone answering.

I broke the silence. "Hello?"

"That's all you have to say?" Ali said.

"Are you guys okay?"

"I'd prefer a private discussion. Are you nearby? And how was the … party?"

"Wilder than I ever expected. We have a couple who will need a ride. I'm sorry to say they are asleep. A stranger and a friend."

Apparently familiar with careful communications, Ali seemed to understand what I meant.

"Where are you?"

I told him and he hung up.

"Ali and Tom should be here in about ten minutes," I said.

Rollie was sitting up holding the ice pack to his head. I saw an aspirin bottle at his side and a bottle of water. "VP told me what she did and what's still out there. We need to get the stiffs and this shot-up vehicle out of here, preferably while it's dark."

"Your brain's functioning," I said, "but your bedside manner needs work. Aziz saved my life as much as VP."

"Fair hit," Rollie said.

"And we're screwed if someone notices the bullet holes in the back." I looked in some of the medical kits. "Yeah, this'll have to do."

VP and I spent the next few minutes patching the ambulance's wounds with white medical tape. It would look like the world's worst stripe job in broad daylight, but in the half-light of morning we might get by until we could relocate it.

CHAPTER 34

The approaching van flashed its headlights at us before turning into the lot. We appreciated it. We weren't expecting possible attackers, but were very concerned about police or park rangers, not to mention innocent bystanders who might become suspicious.

I heard a rumble of thunder in the distance.

Ali got out of the van. Up close I could see Tom inside so I stepped up to check on him. "How are you doing?"

"Brilliant." Tom flashed a sleepy grin. "Ali's got a proper party in that kit of his. I really must get shot more often."

"Morphine," Ali said. "He's stable but will need more attention."

I pictured chatty Tom, who wasn't even supposed to be in the country, going to an emergency room. If we could help it, maybe there was another way. "I know someone discreet," I said. "I'll have to wake him up."

Ali shook his head. "Not necessary. I have help on the way. They will remove that murdering swine and care for Maloof's remains."

"Maloof?"

"My rifleman. He didn't make it. Aziz?" Ali looked around. "Did you mean Aziz in your call?"

"I'm sorry. He was very brave." I explained what happened on the trail.

"My people will be here in a few minutes. I've already told them to expect work in two locations."

I wondered about trusting so many strangers, but then again, it wasn't like I knew Ali, either. He was alone at the moment and could have left Tom and disappeared with the diamonds.

Thunder rolled closer and I felt a couple drops.

Ali nodded. "Rain is good, it will clean off the quarry stones and keep away hikers."

That reminded me. "I found the money."

"It is yours. You earned it, despite your being forced to betray our deal."

"I hope you understand we had no choice."

"It's done. And despite losing two good men, men with families, if I told them they would be able to avenge our losses at the hands of those butchers, they would have gladly traded their lives."

"Before your men go on the trail, I have to make it safe." I told him about the booby-trapped case.

Ali shook his head. "If you trigger the device, it will make noise. We are too close to the road and I think some homes."

"We'll have to risk it. No way I leave something out there for a hiker to find. I don't know how to disarm bombs, though. I spent too much time trying to avoid them."

"I do. My business requires many skills. Show me."

"This way," I said.

* * *

Ali paused to say a silent prayer over Aziz and then spat on Grist's corpse. When he was done, I took him up the trail to the case, still sitting in plain sight on the trail.

Ali took out a penlight and examined all sides of the case without touching it. He then took out a long knife with a thin blade and probed around the edges that touched the ground.

I wanted to move away, but considering all that had happened it seemed wrong, so dumb or not, I stayed close to the bomb. "Can I help?"

"Shh."

I could do that.

Ali stopped sliding the blade and withdrew the knife. He then used it to dig in front.

"Take the light." He held it up and I repositioned so he could see what he was doing.

"Lower."

Ali was on his stomach and I understood what he was trying to do. He must have found some sort of switch, and now he was slowly digging underneath to try to expose it without triggering the device.

After a couple minutes of slow removal of the soil he wiped off the blade and turned it flat.

Rain began to patter down faster. A fat, cold drop hit the back of my neck and I concentrated on keeping the light steady.

Ali slid the blade along the underside and used one hand to hold the flat side against the bottom of the case while the other pressed on top of the case. Now he lifted the case and I felt a cold chill wash through my body.

My testicles climbed about to my belly, as if that might protect them.

Nowhere to run, nowhere to hide, boys.

Aziz lifted the case and I heard something shift inside.

He must have heard it too and I think I saw him flinch. He exhaled. "He must have been in a hurry. It's a simple pressure switch."

"Now what?"

"Hold this." Aziz had balanced the case so it rested in his palm like he was a waiter about to carry a tray of drinks. He used his left hand to take the penlight and place it in his mouth. "Feel the switch under here with your finger," he spoke around the small light. "Keep the pressure on it."

I let him guide my hand and did feel the rounded spring-loaded switch. I pressed, hard enough to make sure my hand couldn't start trembling.

"Hold it steady," he said. "I am going to open the case."

As bad as this idea sounded, I didn't have any better. At least if it went off neither of us would feel a thing. I hoped.

Aziz snapped the chrome catches, which popped open loud enough to send a zing of adrenaline through my body.

"In sha Allah," he whispered and raised the lid.

Both of us exhaled when we realized we still could breathe. "Don't move," Ali said.

Inside I saw a battery and some wires attached to a detonator that was stuck into a fat wad of clay-looking C-4. It looked simple, but that too could be a sucker's bet.

Ali pulled the detonator and grabbed the explosive and threw it deep into the woods. I knew the stuff was stable and safe if left on its own. He cut the wires to the blasting cap and the trap was defused.

* * *

When Ali and I stepped out of the woods and into the clearing we saw another van and a half-dozen men all looking like they were Middle Eastern. Rollie and VP stood together and it was clear one or more of the men was covering them, even though I didn't actually see a weapon.

"Your guys?" I said. "You want to tell them to back off a bit? It's been a long night."

"Of course." Ali spoke to them in Arabic way too fast for me to follow, but I thought I caught the word friend. The men around Rollie and VP relaxed a fraction.

One of the men carried a white sheet and another took out black body bags. A pair went to the entrance, presumably to watch out for unwanted visitors.

The rain was doing a good job of preventing hikers. I walked over to Rollie.

"How's the head?"

"Hurts but it's still on my shoulders," Rollie said. "You okay?"

I told him about the booby trap. "But we're not done. We need to get out of here and back to the truck garage. If it's raining like this at his place, he might be in trouble."

"Trouble?" VP said. "I'd be out of my mind if I was trapped like that."

"I didn't get a lot of say in the matter." My words came out harder than I meant. "Sorry."

"It's cool."

"So, what are we waiting for?" Rollie said.

I didn't like how much attention we were still getting from the guys not working on the bodies on the trail. "We need to leave on good terms," I said. "By good terms, we have to be seen as part of the solution and not a loose end ourselves."

"He wouldn't ...," VP began.

"We've had some nice bonding time—bullets, bombs, blood and all—but I just met the man."

"What about Tom?" Rollie said.

"I hear you. Sit tight, let me talk to Ali."

I found Ali directing the removal of the bodies. Two men carried Aziz with utmost care and I saw the body wrapped in the crisp white cloth. A third, a big guy, dragged Grist out by the foot end of the body bag.

One of the men stood between me and Ali, who hadn't noticed my approach. The guy didn't say anything, but his body language spoke volumes. I tapped my limited Arabic vocabulary and said the word for "Boss."

Ali turned at the sound of my voice and turned the guard aside with a brief flick if his hand.

"Yes, Kyle?"

"Ali, we have a friend to rescue." I explained Stu's situation. "But I can't leave until I'm sure we have an understanding."

"What do you mean?"

"I have to get the truck at the quarry. If you have people attending your man Maloof and Mauser's bodies, I need you to let them know we are coming and not to mistake us for some sort of threat."

"Of course." He looked at me. "There was more?"

I didn't want to insult the man, but neither did I need another threat over my head. "Yes, well, I just want to make sure you're clear that I was forced to wear that bomb and everything. I hope we are ... square. Do you know the term?"

Ali nodded. "Kyle, Ryan spoke highly of you," he said. "I don't say that lightly and neither did he."

"Of course."

"Despite the way the deal was tainted in the end, you delivered my property. You have your payment."

"What about Tom?"

Ali shook his head. "I have someone waiting for him now. He has a most private practice. Tom will be fine."

"Tell him his share will be safe and waiting for him. Can you ask him to contact me as soon as he's able?"

"If you have his share, I could hardly stop him, could I?"

We shared a brief laugh, then turned serious. "The ambulance?" I said.

"By the end of today, the vehicle and the dogs that drove it will be mere memory. Perhaps not even that." Ali mimed locking his mouth and throwing away the key.

"So, we are done?"

"This business is concluded. If you have any new affairs to discuss in the future, if Ryan is unavailable to ask for himself of course, Tom will know how to reach me."

"Believe me, this was a one-time thing," I blurted out and wondered why I felt the need to say it at all.

"Go and get your truck." Ali looked at his men and they melted away from us like we weren't there.

CHAPTER 35

THE QUARRY

The rain drummed on the roof of the Blue Bomber. That sound combined with the engine roar still couldn't drown out Rollie's non-stop bitching at me because I'd insisted on driving.

"Fine, Rollie," I said as we neared the quarry. "You drive. But VP, you have to ride with him and make sure he doesn't slip into a coma or something."

"Coma, my ass," Rollie groused.

If not for the rain it might have been light outside already. I'd driven down the switchbacks and noticed at the top the fresh tire tracks, but no sign of Ali's people, or police. By the time I reached the truck, I saw that our original tire marks were blurring.

"Get to the repair shop as quick as you can," I said. "Look for fresh dig marks in the back area and white PVC pipe sticking up. I'll go as fast as I can without crashing, but no sense holding you back."

"You just want to get out of digging," Rollie said as VP jumped into the front seat.

* * *

Down near the pit and the old mill, I had room to turn the truck around. I wondered if I should check inside the mill for evidence left behind of the makeshift emergency room, but Ali had as much or more to lose than I did. Besides, we'd more than pushed our luck already.

I knew the stone and dirt roads were designed for heavy equipment and that the engineers had surely allowed for the chance of inclement weather. Even so I had little trouble imagining straying too close to the edge in the heavy truck and the saturated sides going avalanche on me.

The sides held. At least the raw fear worked better than coffee to keep me focused.

The truck's wipers beat time like a metronome as I drove in the early morning gloom. The hour-long trip felt like a year. I never saw Rollie, so I had to assume he and VP were already there and I prayed that Gallagher's Truck Service didn't have any customers scheduled early that day.

When I pulled in to Gallagher's I saw the Blue Bomber parked around the side of the metal building. I shut down the truck, leaving it blocking the entrance so that even if a customer arrived, we'd hear the honking before anyone could see what we were doing.

I'd hoped to find the three of them inside working on a pot of coffee. Fat chance.

I lumbered out of the truck and worked some of the stiffness from my leg. The rain poured down and I didn't bother trying to go around the puddles. All I could think of was Grist's warning about it not raining.

I shivered and not because I was already soaked to the skin, but at the thought of Stu drowning in a muddy grave.

"Hello?" I called out. Still better not to use names. No answer. I tried again, but the rain was too loud. It roared off the metal roof of the building like an endless drumroll.

I hobbled to the back and spotted the little backhoe. Not far past it was a little dirt road for access to the rest of Stu's land. Mostly I saw trees, so I headed for those. It had to be somewhere the backhoe could reach, they'd worked fast.

"Over here!" I saw VP emerge from little more than a wide path. Her hoodie was down and her hair plastered against her face.

I limped as fast as could to her. "Is he still alive?"

"Yes, hurry." She took my hand and tried to pull me along faster.

Inside a stand of trees, I saw Rollie covered in mud. He worked a shovel at the edge of a small trench that would turn into a moat soon. Rollie looked more like he was bailing than shoveling.

Rollie paused to put his ear to one of the pipes that stuck out of the ground. He shouted into it. "Hang in there. More help is here." He saw me and waved me over.

The rain seemed to sense my arrival and redoubled its efforts.

"Can you hear him?" I took the shovel and hit the spot he'd been working.

"I can't hear shit in this storm, but I think so," he said.

"If he's talking, then he's breathing," I shouted. The shovel might as well have been a spoon for all the good it was doing. "Christ, we need a pump, not a shovel." I remembered that Stu had just such equipment in his shop.

Impossible. We'd never get that heavy equipment out here and certainly not in time. Something hand-operated? Then what? The rain didn't look like it was going to let up anytime. This guy needed out, now.

"The backhoe!" I shouted. "They used it put him in."

"I thought of that, but the closest thing I ever drove like that was a forklift and it's been years."

"VP, can you check if the keys are in it? If they're not, look in the office."

She'd been talking into the pipe and trying to keep water out of it, though the way the stuff must be coming in from the sides that was probably a waste of time. "On it," she ran back to the machine.

Rollie stood where he could see her while I continued to dig. All I did was slip down the sides. I tried to scrape some of the earth covering the wooden tomb and water and mud rushed to fill the gap. By the time I made enough progress to lift up the boards he'd probably drown.

Rollie shot me a thumbs down.

Screw this. I dropped the shovel and ran as fast as I could to the backhoe. VP must've been searching the office for the keys. Rollie joined me, panting. "She can look," I said, "but Grist and Mauser may have chucked them in the woods. Got a knife?" I found the ignition slot.

Rollie handed over his rugged K-BAR.

"Hot-wire, good call." Rollie said. I worked the blade in the ignition housing until I could pry it from the dashboard. I cut the wires and began to play with the copper strands to get the thing running. "We have to get enough dirt off the wood box they made to pry up the boards and get him out before the water rushes in."

Rollie nodded. "That could work." VP came back, shaking her head. Rollie spoke to her. "Forget the keys, let's find a couple pry bars," he said. "Meet you there."

I made a spark and zapped my fingers for my trouble, but after a couple hits the small engine coughed to life. I had a lot of experience with large versions, but during downtimes in the Sand Box there'd been a few of the baby excavators to play with as well.

I familiarized myself with the controls and did a couple quick test scrapes in the ground to get the feel. It wouldn't help the poor guy to just claw him in half.

Satisfied, I put it in gear and rumbled toward the dig site. VP and Rollie were right behind me. They carried long crow-bars and the way they held them made me think of soldiers following a tank into battle.

At the site I positioned the excavator at what we figured was the foot of the box, away from the pipe where they could hear him. "Ready? As soon as I expose the edges, yank up those boards."

They nodded and I gunned the engine. The controller felt slick in my soggy hands, but it wasn't difficult to use.

My first pass with the excavator bucket barely made a groove in the soupy mud on top. I went a little deeper and a clap of thunder reminded me that I was sitting on a motorized lightning rod. The idea of getting fried at this point made me want to laugh and I realized the long night and lack of sleep was making me punchy. I refocused my attention to the controller.

Deeper this time, and water rushed to fill the void.

Steady, steady. I scooped again and again, spinning the excavator and dumping the bucket of slop.

"I hit something," I yelled over the engine and storm. "Get ready, he could be underwater now."

Another hit and this time we all could hear the scrape. Before the muddy water flowed over the section, I got a glimpse of the structure. It was made of logs, like someone decided to make a tomb instead of a cabin.

The metal teeth of the bucket caught on a knot in one of the pieces of wood. The entire log shifted and the water poured like a river straight into the exposed space.

I heard one gargled scream, then silence. I bore down and used the bucket like a big metal-clawed hand to drag another log back.

"Stop, I see him!" VP yelled. I moved the bucket out of the way and jumped off the machine. All three of us leaped into the space and up to our waists in cold, muddy water.

We bent and searched with our hands.

"Got him," Rollie shouted and I reached down and got an arm around the slick, taped-up midsection of Stu's body.

"Pull!"

The other logs were shifting back into place. He didn't have time for us to get them out of the way. We yanked and tugged. Stu's head appeared above the water line and he spewed brown water and coughed. Then he screamed.

The logs were closing in and squeezing his body. I immediately let go and lay on top of the logs where I could use my legs to press against their pincer effect. Rollie and VP each took an elbow and pulled.

The tight wrapping of the duct tape, so hard to grip, finally worked in our favor and he slid up and out.

They staggered back up the muddy sides of the trench and collapsed in a row with Stu in the middle. I stopped fighting the logs and let them come together, being careful to make sure my legs stayed free. It wasn't easy, the logs shifted easily as the trench filled up with water. Rollie sat up and gave me a hand and I managed to get up the side and onto flat ground.

VP rolled Stu onto his side and he continued to cough. Silver duct tape stuck to his cheek, but he'd chewed through the sticky gag to clear his mouth.

Stu's eyes darted around and his teeth chattered with cold. His whole body shivered.

"Stu, can you hear me?" I asked.

His head moved as much as it could and his eyes bugged out like I'd materialized in front of him. "Wha? Who?"

"He's in shock, let's get him inside," Rollie said. "I'm liable to cut him, the way he's shaking."

"There should be some shears we can use. We can get some hot liquids going too."

"It's okay, buddy. I'm going to carry you and we'll get you out of this. You're going to be okay."

I picked him up and he tried to struggle. He wasn't a small guy and his wriggling was a hell of a lot harder to control than some barbell. I settled for a modified fireman's carry over my shoulders.

He made some gibberish noises in protest, but I was able to move toward the building. This close to my face, there was no escaping the fact that he smelled like a guy who'd been buried alive and left for dead.

Rollie and VP were able to get the door open and Rollie snapped on the lights. We were all soaking wet, but Stu came first. I was more familiar with the layout and pointed out the kitchen area and Stu's office, where he had a cot and some blankets. I got the heat cranked up and, most important, we found some tin snips that worked fine to cut the guy loose.

The duct tape cocoon wasn't designed for sanitary comfort. "This is going to be a little messy," I warned VP.

"I'll take KP duty," she said.

"He's got coffee and maybe some soup or something back there," I said.

Rollie went to get the shower going. Stu had a little home away from home in the shop and we were glad to see some clean clothes as well.

"How did I get here?" Stu was still way confused, but I guess it was a good sign that he recognized where he was.

"I'll tell you in a minute. Try to hold still, let me get this off of you."

That message got through. I started at his feet, working the shears at a steady pace. I heard the water start running for the shower and then Rollie returned with some towels. Once I uncovered Stu's legs, Rollie checked his feet.

"Ice cold." He began to rub them, trying to stimulate circulation. He poked the sole of the foot.

"Ow," Stu said and his foot twitched.

"Good sign," Rollie said. "Bastards had him bound up like a python."

I kept snipping and when I got his arms free, they just flopped to his sides. He did start to take deep breaths and that seemed like a good thing, at least as long as he didn't hyperventilate.

Some of the tape had stuck so much to his clothes that I just went ahead and clipped those off too. I didn't think he was going to want them back after this anyway.

"Get him down to his skivvies," Rollie said. "As soon as he comes around a little, we can go with the shower. A tub would be best but we'll make do."

We put a blanket over him. VP stepped out with a couple steaming mugs. "How's he doing? I made this hacker strength. You've been warned."

"Ow, my arms," Stu said, but he was rubbing them, which meant he was moving them.

"Stu, do you know where you are?" I asked.

He was like a sleeper snatched out of deep REM mode. "My shop. I remember you, but who the hell are they?"

"Friends. We can do introductions later. Think you can hold a cup of coffee?"

"Gimme." Stu took the mug from VP and gulped it down. I was glad it didn't burn him. He looked at VP. "Who told you how I like my coffee?"

* * *

Once Rollie had helped him into the shower Stu began to recover, at least physically. He emerged wearing clean blue jeans and a thick cotton work shirt.

He looked human, but his eyes had that post-battle shell-shocked look I'd seen too often in the Sand Box. No doubt Rollie knew it better than I. His manner with him was gentle and calm.

We took turns using the shower ourselves and Stu didn't seem to mind our borrowing some clean clothes. VP looked comical inside Stu's outsize wardrobe. Stu even cracked a smile, a good sign.

"Take a seat," Rollie said, "and let's see about getting you something to eat. Are you hungry?"

"I'm not sure. I feel shaky. Tell me again who you people are?"

"We were watching out for Tom and Kyle while you guys worked on the truck," Rollie said.

"Why didn't you stop them?" Stu pointed at me. "And you never told me about those maniacs. I would have never have helped if I'd known those freaks were out there."

He made a fair point. "We thought we might have scared them away earlier." It sounded lame to my own ears.

VP spoke up. "We were watching, but we had no idea they had that ambulance and they moved inside so fast, even if we'd wanted to stop one, the other might have killed everyone."

Her anguish came through and I thought Rollie would have gone to his rifle if he'd been confident of getting them both.

"We had nothing but crap choices," I added. It was true, but I doubted it helped.

"Why'd you leave me there? You could have called someone. I thought I was going to die in that dark." Stu wiped away tears that welled up in his eyes.

"I swear we didn't see what they did with you. We thought they—" VP stopped herself.

"Killed me?" Stu said. "They damn near did."

"Me too." I told him about the bombs, strapped to me and hidden on the path.

Rollie gave me a look, but I don't think his heart was in it. Maybe it wasn't a good idea to share too much detail about what we'd been doing, but I felt like we owed it to Stu to understand we hadn't simply used him and thrown him away.

The information soaked in and Stu sat in silence while he processed what we told him.

"So, they are really gone?" Stu spoke in a slow deliberate tone.

"Both," Rollie said. "I'm not proud to say I wish I'd been the one who'd got them, but unfortunately, they got the ones that did."

VP nodded. "I saw it. Wish I hadn't, but those were the scariest dudes I ever ran into."

"Will there be more of them?" Stu said.

"No," I said. "They followed Tom all the way from Iraq. They thought they could pull off one more big rip-off and keep running from all the crimes they'd done overseas."

Stu thought about that for a minute. It seemed like his mind was working, but only in first gear. "Okay. I'm hungry."

Chapter 36

We all raided Stu's refrigerator and I checked in with Cliff at Delivergistics, letting him know there'd been a glitch with the truck, but it would be delivered later today.

A glitch. More like a wrecking ball through too many lives, but there it was. I even asked him if everything was okay.

VP asked to see me outside.

"What's up?"

"I know we've had some distractions, you know, with people trying to kill us and all. But ever since those thugs showed up here last night, I've been wracking my brain about how they did it."

"Yeah." I felt the same. "How *did* Grist and Mauser manage to avoid our police escort and then you and Rollie watching out for them?"

"Some of the time we used that drone to see where you guys were headed," VP said, "so our car could stay out of sight. But I don't think that's how they were following you."

"If they'd been using a drone, wouldn't it have been stored in the ambulance when they weren't using it?" I said. "I didn't see anything like that in their gear."

"Exactly. I didn't get a chance to search the vehicle all over, but drones with range are not that small."

"Okay so what is your theory?" I asked.

"It has to be a tracker."

Of course. "Damn. They were all over the truck before we scared them off at the Delivergistics lot."

"Maybe they didn't want to steal the truck after all."

"I guess we'll never know, but it's a hell of a backup plan," I said. "But why are you worried about it now?" My brain was tired as well.

"Because the tracker is still on the truck somewhere, and guess who has all the stuff left in the ambulance? Bombs, guns and spy gear, right?"

"I think we can trust Ali, but who the hell knows?" I said. "I barely met him, and sure as hell don't know the people in his organization."

"You see my point?" she said. "All it takes is one person to get the idea for an easy payday and Ali might never even know."

* * *

The search didn't take that long. I limited it to places they could have reached that night they broke into the lot. After that I ruled out aluminum, thinking it was most likely magnetic.

Sure enough, I found the small metal box stuck just behind the wheel well on the driver's side.

"Smash it," VP said.

"No, if anything is up, they'd come to the last place it gave a reading. I have to get this truck going anyway. I'll make sure the tracker vanishes along the way. I like the idea of them searching a sewer." I grinned.

"Yeah. That's better."

* * *

Back inside, Stu looked much more alert, even wary. He had a mug of soup in his hand and peered at Rollie over the top of it.

"How you doing, Stu?" I spoke softly, but he still nearly jumped out of his skin.

"Great, never better." He spoke fast. "Well, a little better maybe. Thanks for coming back to save me."

"Stu, I'm sorry about what happened and wish I'd figured out a way to prevent it."

"No, no, no. I understand. You couldn't know there were crazy people following you." He stared at the floor.

"We never thought it was going to put you or any of us in danger."

Neither of us sounded very convincing. He was scared shitless, and I felt guilty as hell.

"No, I get it," he said. "And don't you worry. I'm okay and I won't breathe a word, promise."

I reached into my back pocket and his eyes grew wide. I put up my free hand up in a palms-out gesture. "It's okay, I just wanted to give you this, to say sorry and to cover the clothes and all."

I extended my hand so he could see I wasn't planning to hurt him. "Please take it." I held out a packet of cash, another ten thousand to go with his original payment.

"You don't have to do that," but his gaze did go to the money and after a moment he accepted it.

"If you need anything, anything at all," I said.

"I'm good, really. Just tired. I might sleep for two days is all."

"I understand. I'll check in with you tomorrow, all right?"

"If it's all the same to you, I'd prefer you lose my number."

* * *

We stood by the Blue Bomber. VP still wore Stu's clothes and I'm sure was more than ready to get home and sleep in her own bed. "That was awkward," she said. "Not that I can blame him."

"Better than tragic." I rubbed my eyes. "At least we got to rescue him," I added.

"You going to be okay for that delivery?" Rollie said. "I can follow you."

"You two saved my life, more than enough for a full day's work," I said. "You have the rest of the payment?"

He nodded.

"Better to secure that and get some rest yourselves. Rollie, you should get checked for a concussion." Why did I bother?

"Don't start. It wasn't that bad. I only see one of you, okay?"

I gave up. "All right. I'll get a company car to take back. If I hit the wall, I'll stop somewhere to get some z's."

* * *

The trip to Pittsburgh was a mere hour and a half. I did divert to a truck stop where I got more food and caffeine. I chucked the transmitter into a dumpster and took the truck through the giant car wash.

I wished I could wash off the prior night as easily.

At the Delivergistics depot in Pittsburgh I noticed a police car waiting. For a fleeting, overtired instant I thought I was about to be busted. Of course, the officer was there courtesy of Cliff, in case Grist or Mauser would appear.

"What was the problem?" the manager, a guy I didn't know, looked over the paperwork.

"Spark plug wires, no big deal. I just needed to wait for the guy to bring them, then I decided to head out the next day."

The guy's mind was already onto other tasks. "No worries. The way things are going we'll probably end up selling the thing. I heard the guys who started the whole shitshow were poking around in Philly?"

"That's what they said. I had an escort driving out and everything. Overkill, I'm sure, but it was nice to feel important."

"Well, good luck heading home. Keep your fingers crossed maybe we'll see you again."

"You never know. I was over there and the Iraqi locals want blood. Their government seems willing to oblige."

"So I hear. They'll get it, and the company too, maybe."

"What are you gonna do?" I reached for the keys to the company car.

"Hope for the best and dust off my resume. If worse comes to worst, I'll find something around here. Grist and Mauser won't work again anywhere, that's for sure."

"I bet you're right."

CHAPTER 37

FISHTOWN

I'd arrived home by dinnertime. My body was on autopilot and I left a note by the coffee machine for Rollie to let him know I was upstairs. I checked on him to see that he was already asleep but breathing fine, so I guess he was okay.

I hit the bed and was out before my body could bounce.

* * *

I dreamed that I was trapped in a hole like Stu had been and, when I woke up, panicked for a moment when I couldn't move my arm. I'd slept so long and hard that my arm was asleep as well. The pins and needles drove off the remnants of the dream. There had been other dreams, too. It was that kind of night. Ryan was in some of them. He'd show up from time to time like he was going to give me advice or warn me of something, but I always woke up before I'd learn anything.

I stretched and marveled at the cracks and pops of my body. I still felt tired, but I thought I'd develop bedsores if I slept any longer. I could hear Rollie moving around in the kitchen and smell the coffee. I cleaned up and when I felt human again, I headed downstairs.

Rollie looked like himself, not counting the gauze bandage he wore behind his ear where he'd been hit.

"Morning," I said. "How are you doing?"

He glanced at the clock on the wall. "It is still morning, isn't it? Just. I haven't slept that long since, maybe ever." He handed me a full mug.

It smelled like heaven. "I'm okay. Swelling is down on my goose egg. A little headache, but nothing some aspirin can't handle."

"Mind if I check your eyes?"

He leaned forward and his pupils looked okay.

"A hard head but a soft heart," he said.

"Sorry you got dragged into another fine mess." I glanced over at the array of burner phones. Some of the message lights were blinking.

"My arm's not sore from twisting. It's nice to get out to the country and sample the fresh air." He grinned.

"Well, in all the commotion I don't think I thanked you properly."

"You're breathing. I am too, and I wasn't much more than a spotter on this op. Thank VP. Interesting kid. Got a lot on the ball."

"That reminds me," I said. "She'll need her cut. Definitely earned it. You too."

Rollie waved it off. "I don't want your money. Or Ryan's or Ali's or whoever's. I'm getting the hang of this poverty thing. Gimme gas money and we're good."

"How about a prepaid gas card for fifty-grand?"

He laughed. "All the shit we got through, that'd be a hell of a way to get nailed for laundering money."

Jokes aside, it raised an important question. "What *are* we going to do with it all? That's a lot of coffee cans buried in the back yard."

"I hadn't thought about it," he said. "I'll bet Tom has some ideas. We'll see him soon enough. Ryan didn't have anything in his diary?"

"I'm not sure. Some of them were only listed with respect to how they could help with this operation."

"Poker winnings?" Rollie suggested.

"Great idea. I'll doublecheck the list for a good tax attorney." I failed to keep a straight face.

Rollie clapped me on the shoulder. "Now you're thinking like a diabolical mastermind."

* * *

I sorted through the burner phones and checked the messages. Sandy wanted to know how I was. I assumed as in, was I still alive? Bishop had returned the late call I made before I went to sleep asking to hear about my trip over coffee when I got a chance. I'd kept my message vanilla and cryptic, just that I'd delivered the truck and thanks for his help. Some rough potholes out in the country, but everyone he knew was okay.

I didn't know Aziz, or the rifleman Maloof, who I couldn't have picked out of a lineup since I never saw his face. Ali told me he'd been a dedicated family man who did whatever he was asked to serve Ali's business. I couldn't get Aziz's face out of my mind. Both those men had also saved us, and paid the price for their efforts. But, like Rollie, they'd acted for their own reasons as much as out of loyalty or for a payday. I can't imagine what I'd feel if I went up against someone who'd murdered my cousin and defiled his corpse by filling the decapitated head with marbles.

I didn't feel anything for Grist or Mauser. Destined to be forever missing but never missed, they wouldn't see their day in court. I suspected Delivergistics, and in effect everyone who worked for them, would get stuck with the rest of their bill.

At a personal level I wasn't sure how I felt about that, either.

* * *

I reached Sandy on the phone I'd given her. I still didn't know where she had gone, but I could tell right away by the sound of her voice that I'd be seeing her again.

"You're back?" she asked. "Is that the right term?"

I laughed. "I'm not sure of all the terminology, but yes I am very glad to be back and as far as I know, you're in the clear. I don't think you need to worry about a certain chiropractor."

"What did you do to him? He called me a couple days ago and said my lease was torn up, and to stay as long as I like but to lose his number."

"One of his people accidentally ran into the guys waiting for me." I gave her the quick version of what happened. "I guess it's not all bad if he thinks it was me. As long as you know it wasn't."

"And what about those other ones?"

"I'll tell you more later, but it's over." I hoped she really wouldn't want to know, but I'd tell her as much as I could if she asked. "You wanted help rebuilding your client list?"

"Yeah, maybe." She sounded happy to change the subject. "But I found a new location that just came available."

"Where?" My heart dropped, fearing she'd say Indiana or something.

"Over in Olde City. It's a little small and needs some work, but it's a great deal if we put in some sweat equity." I could hear the smile in her voice.

"Check you out." Relief washed over me. "If you need cheap labor ..."

"I was hoping you'd say that," she said. "Hold that thought for when I get back to town in a week."

* * *

Oliver hadn't tried to mess with Rollie's place again. Rollie had searched all over, looking for signs the house had been breached.

The idea of someone poking around the place brought to mind the huge amount of cash we now had squirreled away. Including Tom's share, we had nearly a million bucks on hand. Few people knew it existed, but that was little comfort. My first thought was to sneak it into the bank and put it in the safe deposit box Ryan had left me, but it wouldn't all fit and that would initiate a paper trail.

We'd just have sit tight for a while until we could figure something out.

* * *

I knew at some point in the near future Rollie and I needed to get all his stuff out of our hideout at the photography studio. I also knew I'd rather do about anything else rather than lug Rollie's steamer trunks full of ammo and hardware, so instead of dealing with it I arranged to meet Bishop in person.

It felt good to drive my own truck again without fear of getting run off the road by mercenaries.

He asked to meet at a small nearby arboretum. I saw his car at one corner of the lot. We had that part of the parking lot to ourselves. I leaned against the tailgate and let the afternoon sun warm my face.

"All's well that ends well?" Bishop said.

"It ends, and yeah, we made the trade. But the reason we didn't call backup wasn't because it was a piece of cake."

"They found you?"

I filled him in on how Grist and Mauser had caught us and tried to rob the deal.

"Damn. You know I wasn't too far from Johnstown, kind of loitering in case you called. If you'd reached me from the quarry, I couldn't have done much other than send in the local cavalry, but they would've been by the book." Bishop's way of saying cops not in his informal network.

"We weren't exactly at liberty to chat." I told him how the bomb was rigged on my body.

I tried to be a little vague when describing how it went down when the shooting started. Trust or not, I didn't want to directly implicate friends.

"A laser blinded Mauser 'somehow'?" he asked.

"Right out of the sky. Turns out they are terrible for your eyes, especially if you are looking through a scope. Crazy kids screwing around, I guess,"

Bishop gave a little nod indicating that he figured that must mean VP.

"Unfortunately," I said, "Mauser could see a little and he started blasting. So I'm told. There could have been self-defensive return fire."

At this I knew he'd assume I meant Rollie. I shook my head. "Rollie was busy. Mauser seems to have gotten into a gunfight where both sides lost. We all came home, but the other guy's team wound up down a couple players. Mauser will not be jumping any cops again. *Never* again."

"And Grist?"

"Grist had car trouble." I described the crashed ambulance. "Our makeshift posse couldn't agree on the best way to chase him and that cost one man real bad, and let Grist get the drop on Rollie." I mimed the hit to the head. "He had me dead to rights," I said. "And he was going to make me cooperate at Rollie's expense." I could see by his expression that Bishop understood.

I could have simply told him we won and they lost, all the way, and he didn't need to know more and he could get his payment and that was it. However, I was learning that in this weird favor economy, trust was an important part of the collateral. Bishop needed to know what and who he was dealing with.

"You got him?"

"Those damn kids playing around with drones, those things are dangerous. Knocked him flat and the other guy he thought was gone had enough left to return the favor. I tried to help him afterwards but ..." I shook my head.

"I heard nothing on the radio."

"They picked a good spot for a meet and then felt strongly it was a good idea to be like the hikers and leave no trace."

"A drone? That's impressive. I'll have to buy him a drink sometime." It felt odd that Ali and his people knew VP was female but Bishop didn't, but that still had to be her call.

"Maybe we can make that happen sometime," I said. "Now, about your gratuity."

"Get settled first. We have time." He walked back to his car. "I hope the little guy feels better soon. He's good for traveling?" I assume Bishop meant immigration.

"He's very resourceful."

CHAPTER 38

I was starting to get concerned about Tom when he hadn't called, but he finally checked in on one of the burners.

"Where you been? Are you okay?"

"Training for the marathon, mate, what do you think?"

"How's the sore leg?"

"They say I'm very lucky." He chuckled. "I always felt that way when they missed. Shows what I know, eh?"

"So, it looks good otherwise?"

"It looks rather horrid, but the med people seem pleased."

"And you're satisfied with your care? I could offer you something private if you like." I hated tiptoeing around topics on these dopey phones, but it would have to do until we could meet up face to face.

"All good, mate. I trust you have my things secure?"

"We do. We're out of the studio and back home. Sorry you missed all the heavy lifting. Your paycheck is here as well."

"Brilliant."

"How's Mr. B?"

"All's fine on that score. He wishes things had gone smoother of course, but he understood the competition."

At least we knew that he didn't hold any grudges. That was good to know. "When do you think you'll be up for travel?"

"No worries. Just a couple more days, if Rollie doesn't mind me crashing there for a bit."

"He said he's already working on a list of chores." I'd already discussed the idea with Rollie. He didn't mind and other than the fact that Tom had sneaked into the country and presumably would be sneaking out, with his share of the cash, he wasn't in any other trouble.

"I'd love to help, but my paperwork says I'm on holiday." It was good to hear him in high spirits.

* * *

FISHTOWN: IN FRONT OF CREAM OF THE CUP

Now that I was more or less back on solid ground I'd started driving and walking the neighborhood. I kept going past Beet's place and the coffee shop. Sooner or later I needed to resolve his situation, but I wanted to speak to him before confronting Milosh and whatever goons he had hanging around.

I felt like we'd been out of pocket for ages, but of course to the rest of the world it had actually only been a few days. When I pulled up to the coffee shop, one look at the hunched figure wearing the sandwich board told me that for Beet it might have felt even longer.

"Beet? Is that you?"

The guy turned around in little shuffling steps, the advertisement rotated to face me. He wore a neck brace, and his left arm was in a sling. I couldn't see the old bruises on his face for the rash of fresh ones. He had a bandage above one eyebrow. "Kyle. I thought you weren't coming back." He wore a Cream of the Cup T-shirt.

My heart sank in my chest. When it came back it would be on a wave of fury, but I had to tamp it down to speak with him. "Of course. I came back as soon as I could. What did they do to you?"

"Don't be mad at me. I did what you said." He looked frightened.

"Huh?" It was getting difficult to think straight.

"They wanted me to do other jobs. Easy ones, like deliveries. Secret packages and stuff, but I always said no."

"Because I said you shouldn't?" I already knew the answer.

"They said I shouldn't listen to you and it would only get me in trouble." He eyed the ground. "Then I started having more accidents."

Simple thoughts had to push through a red haze clouding my mind. "So, they beat you?"

"They said I was a slow learner and so were you." Tears squeezed out of his swollen eyes.

"Get in my truck, okay? You don't have to work for them anymore."

"I have to pay my debt," he said. "Dad always said a man pays his debts."

I nodded. "You more than paid them. I'll take care of this." I helped him out of the sandwich board and threw it on the ground.

I started toward the storefront. It felt like a magnet pulled me and if I didn't walk, I'd fly right through the glass. Beet's voice stopped me.

"Kyle? You're going to work for them. We're going to work together?" I actually heard a note of optimism in his voice.

"Is that what you think?"

He nodded, sort of, the neck brace forced him to rock in the seat. "They said you would come to your senses or I was going to keep having accidents."

Something clicked inside my skull. I'd never felt anything like it before. All of a sudden, the solution hit me and I couldn't get away from the shop fast enough. Even as I was sure a certain someone was inside laughing at me while I stood there. I climbed into the truck and left rubber pulling back into traffic.

"Beet, listen carefully. Did you see what was in those packages they wanted you to deliver?"

"They said it was coffee, but I think they put something inside."

"What was it?"

"I didn't look, but it was wrapped up tight in a package."

"Did they have it in the store?"

"Nope. They had me meet them at a corner by a van."

"A van? Where?"

"It didn't hurt to go listen, but you told me, no packages, so I said nope." He paused. "That *did* hurt."

"I'm sorry, buddy."

"When they punished me, they said to tell you what I saw, just like I did. They said anytime you wanted to take my place to get in touch."

"Anything else?"

"Yup. They told me to say, 'Tell the cops to come by the place anytime. Coffee is half price for law enforcement.' Do you know what that means?"

It meant they were never going to quit and they dared me to try to get them busted. Most of all, it meant that a 'no' from me wouldn't be over *my* dead body.

"Hard to say, but thanks for telling me."

I dropped Beet over at Rollie's and let him know that I'd be back for him, but to keep an eye out for our Kosovar friends.

"And I was just starting to get bored," Rollie said while Beet tucked into some ice cream in the kitchen. "Where are you going?"

"To eat some crow."

CHAPTER 39

I walked to the door wearing a light windbreaker. The blackboard easel sported bright pastel-colored chalk letters that spelled out, "Closed for Private Event."

One of the servers stood by the door and, when he walked me inside, pointed to a decorated archway that I realized was a disguised metal detector. I stepped through and when I didn't beep, he pointed to the rear of the shop.

"Thanks. I know the way." I walked past all the empty tables.

Milosh sat at his table grinning like the Cheshire cat. The Tank sat at the next table over where he could see me and the front door at the same time.

This back table sat near the small kitchen and hidden from the front part of the shop.

"Welcome, Kyle. I'm so glad to have heard back from you."

"You're a persistent man."

"Relentless," he said. "Can I offer you a drink? Coffee? Something stronger?"

"Let's get started, shall we?"

"Right to business. Very good. You wish for me to release Beet from his obligation?"

"No." I took out an envelope. "I want you to accept fair payment for his loan and then he has no obligation to you. Nor will you hire him to work for you in any capacity."

"Are you going to define 'capacity'? I am just an immigrant, after all." He smirked.

"Save the act for the customers."

He shrugged. "As you wish. Now then, are you prepared to move forward?"

"I am." I felt coated in filth.

"Let's outline the terms. You'll find I can be reasonable."

"Fine. I will work, using the network and contacts from my colleague and what I have developed myself, to solve problems and help deals get done. In essence, I will be available to work outside the system in ways that provide discretion and support outside normal expertise."

"That's not very specific," he said.

"What do you want, a legal agreement? Let's try again. I can provide things, goods, services and information not available elsewhere, for a fee," I said. "And in the interest of clarity, I will not support violent activities, provide or broker weapons, or work with recreational drugs. I'll be happy to give the underserved community access to funds, paperwork or other services, not to mention apply leverage to facilitate bureaucratic logjams." VP had helped me come up with some of the verbiage.

"Logjams? Loans? We already do that. You have some large group of customers outside our territory? You have some permissions I am not aware of?" The confusion spread across Milosh's face.

"Permissions? Yes, you could say that. I was planning on doing the loans right here in Fishtown."

"I don't need help with that. This is bullshit."

"You're right, you don't need help with that work." I took out another envelope and placed it on the table.

"What is that?"

"That, Milosh, is your franchise fee. Pick it up, take it with you, and close up shop. Go back to Kosovo, go anywhere but here. I'm buying you out."

Milosh laughed, but his eyes darted toward Tank. "You have balls, more than brains, but you have enough of those to know who will work for who."

"Correct. I won't work for you, and I'm not here alone." I put my fingers in mouth and blew a shrill whistle.

Tank reached inside his jacket. I heard the front door jingle and the metal detector shriek, pause and shriek, again and again.

Behind us, heavy feet stomped in the kitchen and down the back hall.

Milosh said something to Tank in what was probably Albanian. I think it meant something along the lines of, "Don't get us killed."

The handful of staffers working the front were ushered into the back by some freckled heavyset guys, all with dark or red hair. The guy leading the group in the back was almost as large as Tank and he had black hair to go with his black eyes. A bone-white scar crossed his forehead and his nose canted to one side.

I didn't recognize most of the men. This last guy I knew by reputation and his notation in Ryan's codebook. He was known on the street as Cullen the Killer.

"How we doing?" he asked me.

"I'm not sure. Milosh, how are we doing?"

"Just like that?" he asked. "I take your money and disappear?"

"For you," I said, "it's exactly that simple. For me, a little more complicated. But that's my problem. The idea is that you take the money and go so you can avoid the disappear part."

One of the red-headed goons found that funny.

I continued. "You had to keep pushing. Couldn't leave Beet alone. Or me. Well, you got me in the game, after all. Just not with you, Milosh. I made a deal with the Irish."

"You lie."

Cullen came forward. "You know who I am?"

Three Irish guys stood behind Tank. First time I ever saw him look nervous.

"I do," Milosh said.

"Good." Cullen nodded at me. "He's with us. That means you don't say yes or no to him. You take his money and say goodbye, or deal with my people. Right here and now."

Milosh wasn't stupid. "We accept the deal." He picked up the envelope. "Perhaps we can do business again in the future." He looked at me with pure malice.

"Live long and prosper." I gave him the finger.

* * *

In five minutes, we'd all filed out of the place. I looked back and saw one red-headed guy lock the door and hang a "closed" sign. The rest of the "lads" cleared out and I was alone with Cullen.

"Thanks for the whiskey," Cullen said to me.

"I hope the boys enjoy it." I'd given him the bottle of rare whiskey that I received in gratitude for the cancer meds for that guy Ross's sister. Apparently, she was already feeling better. Sounded fast, but what did I know? It felt nice to try and do a little good.

"I'm sure they will."

I took a small package from my pocket. "This is for you. Thanks for getting my back."

Cullen took it and tore it open, then looked shocked at the plastic-encased baseball card. "Yastrzemski? This real?"

"It better be, or I'll give you his name."

His eyes narrowed.

"I'm kidding. It's real." Mental note: do not joke around the tiger cage.

"How'd you know?"

"I'm in the knowing business," I said. "Hey, the boys aren't keeping me around 'cause I scare anybody."

He was lost in his new card like a little kid. Well, a kid who was six-five and killed people for a living.

"I'm supposed to wait until you go," Cullen said.

"Okay, I'm out of here," I said and got into the truck.

"See you around." He waved.

God, I hoped not.

* * *

I drove back to Rollie's feeling kind of sick to my stomach. Also confused. Also good, because when I saw Beet he would be a free guy. Milosh was pissed, of course, but his fear of the crew in the coffee shop wasn't feigned.

Hell, they scared me, and I realized that was exactly what the O'Briens intended.

There was a police car double-parked in front of Rollie's, holding an open spot for me. I pulled in and got out of the truck.

Bishop sat in the driver's seat. "Get in."

"Front seat or back?"

"Funny guy." He pointed to the seat next to him.

I hadn't been kidding.

"We going somewhere?"

"Just talking. I've been where you are. It's going to be okay."

"How do you mean?" I said.

"I was watching how you handled yourself," he said. "You have the toughest guy in Fishtown eating out of your hand."

"That's what you saw, huh?" I paused. "I'm surprised they didn't make you."

"Oh, they know who I am. I guess that's nothing to be proud of, but that was my point. You probably will never see most of those guys again. I don't deal with them and neither will you."

"You sure about that?"

"Is that what you want? All in for the family and like that?"

"No!"

"Newsflash, they know that. Look," he said, "they've got a lot of dirt on me. I have no illusions about that. But I fill a niche for them from time to time. I decide if it isn't okay. I'm not looking to hurt anyone, never have."

"Neither am I," I said.

"You have connections that can be useful. They have plenty of heavies, as you saw for yourself. And our connection to them can help us, get it? Doc Crock isn't around to work for us."

I had to admit he had a point.

"I can't help but feel like I sold my soul," I said.

"Do I look like a priest? You're a favor broker, live with it," Bishop finished.

I got out of the car and went inside to see Rollie.

* * *

"How'd it go?" Rollie knew what I'd been doing. "You're here, so it couldn't have been too bad."

I took the beer he offered. "Where's Beet?"

"In back. I told him to pick some weeds for me. He seemed happy to have something to do."

"Busy as a one-armed weed-puller?"

"Something like that."

I let the pause hang in the air.

"Rollie, what did I just do?"

"You did what you had to. And, no small thing, I think you probably saved that guy's life." He pointed out the kitchen window.

"I guess that's true."

"You ran off that scumbag at the coffee shop, didn't you?"

"By working with other scumbags."

"So?"

"I never saw so many Irish wise guys in one place," I said. "Talk about coming out of the woodwork."

"Yeah, they can do that. But you solved the problem. Milosh was going to push you until you gave in. Personally, I don't need the house tossed again and if he'd come after me, I'm too old to fight with him. I'd be up for murder or in the morgue."

"I wish I could say you were wrong."

"It's not perfect, but you found a way to scare him off without bloodshed. Bishop would tell you the cops couldn't prevent it. They'd just be there when Beet or I or you got a toe tag."

"And now I'm mixed up with them."

"Think of it as they're mixed up with you." Rollie finished his beer. "Ryan wasn't a saint, but that doesn't mean he didn't do some good. You've seen that for yourself, already been part of it. You color outside the lines, but I know you're a good person."

"It gets messy, though," I said.

"Kid, the older I get, sometimes I think the only difference between messy and clean is who got caught." He rinsed the empty beer bottles and placed them in a recycling crate. "Trust your instincts. Ryan left you with a toolbox. It's up to you how you use it, not him, and not the Irish Mob."

"You're a hell of a career counselor, Rollie." I clinked my fresh beer against his.

This next was going to be hard.

"And if I'm going to replace Ryan," I said, "it's probably a good idea for me to move out of here. I figure his old house is as good a place for me as any. I'd hate to drag you down if I screw up."

Rollie nodded. "I appreciate that, but you need me, I'm just a phone call away. Except no collections. I'm too old to be a leg-breaker."

"I'm sure I can use all the help I can get. Think Tom will want to stick around?"

"When he gets here, I'll bring him by Ryan's place for you."

"VP told me if I didn't work with her, she was going to dox me into oblivion."

"Is that bad?"

I laughed. "I'm not sure. Guess I better not find out."

Beet came inside. One arm was filthy, but he'd kept his cast arm pristine. "Hi Kyle! Did you talk to Milosh for me?"

"Yup. You're all set. No more coffee shop."

Beet beamed. "Thanks! I thought he'd never let me quit."

"I guess I'm in the helping business now. Hey Beet, wait here. I got something for you."

I went up to my room, which was about to revert to a spare bedroom in Rollie's house. I found the package and brought it downstairs.

"What is it?" Beet said.

I opened the bag for him since he only had one arm to use.

"A new Spock shirt!" He worked at wiggling his slinged arm free, then gave up and grinned at me. "A little help?"

The End

ACKNOWLEDGEMENTS

I would like to thank my wife whose first draft reading challenged me to raise my game and helped make for a much better story.

I want to recognize the outstanding cast of editors, David Downing of Maxwellian Editorial Services and proofreader Michael Dunne. Finally, thank you to E-Book Launch for the great cover art and formatting work!

Note from the Author:

Thanks so much for reading. If you enjoyed this book, I'd greatly appreciate a review on Amazon or Goodreads. They can go a long way to help reach new readers.

If you have a question or comment you can reach me directly at gregsmithbooks@yahoo.com.

You can follow upcoming releases and author doings at my Facebook page here:

https://www.facebook.com/J-Gregory-Smith-Author-297074464674/

You can also find my author page from Amazon here:

https://www.amazon.com/J.-Gregory-Smith/e/B002VW9IIU/ref=dp_byline_cont_ebooks_1

www.ingramcontent.com/pod-product-compliance
Lightning Source LLC
Chambersburg PA
CBHW031709170626
46808CB00005B/1674